ON A DARKLING PLAIN

A LOST VILLAGES MYSTERY

MAGGIE WHEELER

GSPH

GENERAL STORE PUBLISHING HOUSE
499 O'Brien Road, Box 415
Renfrew, Ontario, Canada K7V 4A6
Telephone 1.613.432.7697 or 1.800.465.6072
www.gsph.com

ISBN 978-1-897508-20-6

Cover, design, and layout: Magdalene Carson / New Leaf Publication Design
Printed by Custom Printers of Renfrew Ltd., Renfrew, Ontario
Printed and bound in Canada

Library and Archives Canada Cataloguing in Publication
Wheeler, Maggie A., 1960-
    On a darkling plain : a lost villages mystery / Maggie Wheeler.
ISBN 978-1-897508-20-6
    I. Title.
PS8595.H3852O6 2009   C813'.6   C2008-906121-7

Cover photography provided by Pat Patterson; used by permission.

While the background of this novel is based on actual history, the characters and plot lines are products of the author's imagination and are in no way intended to resemble real events or people, either living or dead. M.W.

"Rockets" lyrics by Marc Jordan, c/o Cafe Productions.

Also by Maggie Wheeler:
A Violent End
The Brother of Sleep
All Mortall Things

DEDICATION

To the men and women of all nations
who built our beautiful province of Ontario
with their hopes, their dreams, and their lives.

To those who still dare to love and dare to dream
on this darkling plain.

To Farran. As Captain James T. Kirk once said
to Spock and McCoy, "It was fun!"

And most of all, to the three life companions
God has blessed me with — my wonderful daughters
Anna, Evan, and Lindsay. You continue to grow
like willows near the great river, being my source of
inspiration and amazing me by the people you are.
I love you "to the moon and back" — and I always will.

SPOILER ALERT

Do not read this novel unless you have previously read *A Violent End*, *The Brother of Sleep*, and *All Mortall Things* — the first three novels in the Lost Villages mystery series. Many facts and secrets revealed in those novels are discussed openly in this one and would ruin the surprise revelations of the first three.

And for those of you who recognize where most of the chapter titles come from, take note that I matched them on the basis of what would be most appropriate. However, there are no clues based on the content of the original material written under those titles. I was just having fun again, writing the second draft during the month of July 2009 — forty years since Armstrong and Aldrin created the original moonwalk, paving the way for our future in space, real or imagined.

Maggie Wheeler

TABLE OF CONTENTS

CONTRIBUTORS

First and foremost, a sincere thanks to my readers for their patience while this last novel was written!

Thank you to the following people for their time and their memories:

- Ruth Fetterly, formerly of Old Iroquois.
- Enid Casselman, Sheila Cornell and Shirley Patterson, all formerly of Old Iroquois.
- Pat Patterson, New Jersey, formerly of the Hartshorne Brothers House Moving Company.
- Ross Walker, formerly of Iroquois Constructors Construction Company, Iroquois, Ontario.
- Ginger White, formerly of Waddington, New York.
- Murray Richer, curator, Carman House Museum, Iroquois.
- Dalton and Nancy Foster, Wilson Hill Island, New York.

Thanks to Pat Lawson for the notes and newspaper clipping of Old Iroquois that clearly showed me what a pretty village it had been.

Thank you to my publisher, Tim Gordon, and to my editor, Susan Code McDougall, for taking this journey with me.

Also a special thank you to Canadian singer-songwriter Marc Jordan for the use of his song "Rockets" to open Part Four.

Last, but not least . . .

I must acknowledge the contribution of Bagel the Beagle, my housemate, family member, foot warmer, and the best listener I know. She sat with me, slept near me, and snored around me as my constant companion through the writing of the book. Without her valuable support, this novel might never have been completed.

AUTHOR'S NOTE

This has got to be the quietest place on earth.

I am sitting in the Pioneer Memorial on the grounds of Upper Canada Village, Morrisburg, Ontario. Each time I have begun a novel in the Farran Mackenzie series, I have come here to begin. To do what I really do, underneath the writing. I listen.

Here I walk and read the old tombstones moved from the village cemeteries during the Seaway construction half a century ago—so many young women dying, probably in childbirth; so many children taken by accident, or by a disease we no longer fear. One family recorded here lost two young daughters in two days. This is a grief I pray never to know.

Here is the stone for Mary Hoople, the woman who saved her community from starvation at the age of seventeen. Her stone sits beside that of her husband, Henry Hoople, yet it does not bear her name, as the top was lost. I wrote of her amazing life in the third Seaway novel, *All Mortall Things*. When this book is done, I remind myself, I will fulfill my promise to her to have the tombstone clearly marked.

So many are here, in this quiet place. And I am still listening. To the voices of history and legacy. To the stories of our pioneers who lived lives of determination, hardship, and sacrifice. To the sound of a new nation being born.

When I first sat here in 1999, stumbling my way into my first novel, *A Violent End*, I didn't realize I was starting a journey that would take almost a decade to complete. I just thought I wanted to write a story that would encompass the great St. Lawrence River, the St. Lawrence Seaway and Power megaproject, the six villages and three hamlets on the Canadian side that refused to die, and the birth of my neurotic alter-ego Farran Mackenzie.

It was an important beginning in my life.

Today, I'm here to begin the last novel in Farran's story. I'm here to say goodbye.

Once, when I was doing a workshop on *A Violent End* at the University of Ottawa, a student asked me if it would be difficult to end the series and let the characters go. It will. I will be saying goodbye to those who have become family to me. Personally, I feel I've done quite enough of that in my adult life. But there it is.

I will miss Farran most of all. We have been partners and sidekicks during this amazing time. I've helped her discover her father as a person while unmasking his killer. Together we faced a sad truth from her own past as she helped a stranger deal with one of his own. And together we watched as Inspector Jerry Strauss came face to face with skeletons from his own closet, in his own inimitable way.

Farran also stood by me as I grew into a novelist, became a public speaker, and developed into a Lost Villages ambassador throughout Eastern Ontario and Upper New York State. She was there when my marriage ended and I struggled as a newly single mom with three intelligent and vivacious daughters. And she will be there when I graduate with my master's degree, moving into my new career.

In *A Violent End,* we acknowledged loss and the need to grieve it. With *The Brother of Sleep*, we faced the rage that can follow, shutting our living down. *All Mortall Things* took us down the path of granting who we've been, so we can build the new self with the best from the ashes of the old. Now, we're going to take the final step together: integration of the new self fully into life.

This time I will also add a new layer to the history—the American side of the Seaway. Our American cousins lost much less land and only one hamlet to the construction; however, their story is unique in its own right and could give birth to a series of its own. I hope to do their part of this history a little better justice in the pages of this book.

Jerry Strauss will be given his share of personal space, again, to offer his perspective as we go along. I guess the important issue here is, who is going to have the last word? I hope you enjoy the answer to that question.

So, dear readers and friends (and both, as so many of you have become), it's time to follow Farran once more as she goes back in history to the Old Front.

And it is time to begin to say goodbye.

Maggie Wheeler
Misselthwaite Cottage, Ingleside
July 2009

AUTHOR'S TIME OUT—ONE MORE TIME

In the previous novel in this series, *All Mortall Things*, I did a "timeout" with the reader to explain a growing disparity between story time line and real time. Here we have a similar challenge: This novel begins about one month after *All Mortall Things* ends, making it technically the summer of 2006. However, Celebration 50, the week of events honouring the 50th anniversary of the inundation of the village lands in July of 1958 took place in the early summer of 2008.

Once again, I am asking the reader to bear with me as I mould and twist time for our purposes. As I said in the timeout from *All Mortall Things*, I'm asking for a continued "willing temporary suspension of disbelief" as we make our way through our last tale wrapped around the Old Front.

Maggie Wheeler

FOREWORD

Mr. Jim Brownell, MPP
Stormont, Dundas and South Glengarry

As member of provincial parliament for the riding of Stormont, Dundas and South Glengarry, and the immediate past-president of the Lost Villages Historical Society, I am honoured to have been invited by Maggie Wheeler to write the foreword to *On a Darkling Plain*. As it was when Maggie asked me to write the foreword to her first murder mystery, *A Violent End*, it is a privilege to salute an author who has brought respect and integrity to her craft.

It was a little over ten years ago that Maggie Wheeler first entered my life. She appeared at my classroom door at Longue Sault Public School, at the end of a long school day, to discuss with me the idea of a murder mystery based in the Lost Villages, and to pick my brain on ideas and facts for its content. Never did I expect then (and I'm sure Maggie didn't either) that a ten-year passion for writing would one day lead to this fourth volume in the Farran Mackenzie saga.

Through four volumes of mystery and intrigue, woven together with words that spell MURDER, Maggie has taken captivated readers on a roller coaster of suspense and drama. She has skilfully woven fact with fiction, and has brought attention to one of Canada's greatest historical and engineering achievements: the Hydro and Seaway development of the St. Lawrence River in the 1950s.

When Maggie Wheeler brought us Farran Mackenzie, OPP Inspector Jerry Strauss, and other characters ten years ago, the citizens of the Seaway Valley were remembering and celebrating the loss and rebirth of communities through the events of Celebration 40. They were remembering the loss of picturesque and vibrant little towns along the St. Lawrence River, from the hamlet of Maple Grove in the east to the town of Iroquois in the west. They were remembering the physical loss of communities and neighbours, but they were remembering, too, the benefits brought to inhabitants by the creation of new towns.

With Maggie Wheeler's first three mystery novels, and with the wonderful celebrations in 2008 and 2009—Celebration 50 and Beacon 50 respectively—we have come to acknowledge and appreciate the emotional and social side to the Hydro and Seaway stories, the sense of loss, rebirth, and accomplishment.

As a young ten-year-old lad at the time of the inundation on July 1, 1958, I remember the sense of loss and sadness by the townsfolk of the Lost Villages. While our family farm was not directly affected by the inundation, I truly felt the loss of community, especially when I witnessed the fires that consumed churches, schools, and private residences — buildings that could not be relocated to higher grounds. Forever etched in my mind will be my dad's sense of loss when we trampled through the burned-out ruins of St. Andrew's United Church at Moulinette, or mine when sitting in a classroom at Mille Roches Public School watching the wrecker's ball turn the massive stone walls of the Provincial Paper Mill into rubble. These were the physical treasures we lost, but it is the emotional and human side of the story that has made the 50th anniversary experiences so meaningful and rewarding for all of us. Maggie Wheeler's creative words have helped us on that journey, too.

With the 50th anniversary events behind us, Maggie's latest novel, *On a Darkling Plain*, will be a wonderful legacy for all of us who were there to witness the "big story." For those who were not there in the 1950s, but who still have enjoyed the first three novels, her latest novel will bring the adventures of Farran Mackenzie to a close — and what a close it is! As already said, Maggie Wheeler has woven great tales of mystery and intrigue into the lives of her novel's fictional characters. These characters have become household names to all who have enjoyed her novels, allowing us to understand the drama of the "Lost Villages" of The Front and to appreciate the new villages that many of us call home today.

Having had the opportunity to read this final manuscript in the series, I can say that Maggie Wheeler has left no stone unturned in successfully concluding the adventures of Farran Mackenzie. In her four books, Maggie has moved the entire length of the Seaway, from the Moses-Saunders Powerhouse site at Maple Grove, to the control dam and Seaway locks at Iroquois. With *On a Darkling Plain,* Maggie brings us across the St. Lawrence River to Massena, too. Just as we were introduced to Mildred Keeps at Sterling House in *All Mortall Things*, and we now look around the corner as we step into the Nightingale House Bed and Breakfast in Ingleside, we will think differently as we cross over the threshold of the Carman House Museum in Iroquois. Read on, dear reader, for I shall not give it away here, but I guarantee you will never have the same experience as before when visiting the museum and Iroquois Point vicinity in the future.

In writing these few words, I am mindful of my enthusiastic phone call to Maggie after reading the manuscript (albeit minus the last chapter). I told Maggie how I could not put the manuscript down. With a heavy schedule of government work and appointments, little time exists for absolute pleasure reading, but with *On a Darkling Plain* in hand, things were different. There I was, up at 3:00 a.m. on the Sunday of Thanksgiving weekend, reading. By 5:00 a.m., I could have screamed to a quiet house, "I need that last chapter!" I know, however, the wait will be worth it.

Maggie, you and Farran Mackenzie have built up a loyal following, with people from far and wide captivated by your every word and action. We thank you for allowing us to get caught up in the mystery, intrigue, fact, and fiction that have made your novels so popular. The success of your writing is obvious through the multiple editions that have resulted, but the real success has come through the support of loyal readers. I join with your many, many loyal fans who have had the opportunity over the past ten years to enjoy and appreciate this outstanding literature.

Maggie, in my classroom the slogan was "Go for the Gold!" From *A Violent End* to *On a Darkling Plain*, you have gone for the gold with every word you have written. The ten-year rollercoaster ride of mystery and intrigue has been most pleasurable!

To Maggie's loyal fans, when you spot that FARRAN licence plate, it's Maggie behind the wheel. I hope she's out on another writing adventure, so give her "two thumbs up." Well done, Maggie!

PART ONE

Ah, love, let us be true
To one another! For the world, which seems
To lie before us like a land of dreams,
So various, so beautiful, so new,
Hath really neither joy, nor love, nor light,
Nor certitude, nor peace, nor help for pain;
And we are here as on a darkling plain
Swept with confused alarms of struggle and
flight,
Where ignorant armies clash by night.

—Matthew Arnold
"Dover Beach"

ONE

THE CITY ON THE EDGE OF FOREVER

Iroquois, Upper Canada
November 12, 1813

The cold wind whipped into the man's face. He could hear the hoof beats on the old highway and knew he was almost out of time. The smell of smoke from the burning farmhouse a mile away reached his nostrils. Frantically, he threw another shovelful of earth on the chest in the ground. If they found him with it, and found Fenton where he'd left him, it was a lynching for sure.

It was real money, the most he'd ever seen in his life. If Forsyth's men were still in the area, they'd be all over it in a minute, the ruthless looters they were.

The shovel bit the earth again. The image of Crysler's field covered in American dead rose in his mind. Good thing he ran when he did. And he wasn't the only one, he told the twinge of guilt hovering in his chest. Two more loads of earth followed quickly. If he didn't finish in time, he'd be one of the dead just the same.

The ground was covered with ashes and the shovel thrown in the bushes. The man mounted the shivering horse tied to a nearby tree and made his way out of the clearing. In the distance, he could see green coats on horseback. Were they the Glen infantry or Forsyth's regiment?

Minutes later, the sound of gunfire echoed across Iroquois Point.

Iroquois, Ontario
September 2, 1957

The wind whipped at the man's face as he shovelled in the dirt. With all the construction for the Seaway and the international lock, there were no trees to block the elements around the Old Point any more.

Or block eyes.

He could hear the trucks working in the distance to keep moving forward on the project. It was nighttime but the work went on twenty-four hours a day, as it had for over three years now. Bulldozing, building, moving houses, pouring concrete—even in the dead of winter. Relentless progress and lots of money to be made.

But this was better than any money you could make on a crew. This was pay dirt. He would love to show everyone that he had been no fool to look for Fenton's fool's gold. But he had a good reason not to—and it was under the earth where the trucks were even now filling in the land and covering his secret.

It had to be here. He'd paid the ultimate price for the chest, and he intended to cash in on his investment.

The shovel hit something solid. He threw it down and began to dig with his hands. He couldn't risk a flashlight with the workers just down the way, so he had to feel his way to the object. It felt like a wooden box.

Running his fingers around the edge, the man located a latch. He took the shovel to the old metal and it gave way. Eagerly, he pulled up on what seemed to be the lid and—despite the danger—flashed his light down on the contents.

A minute later, over the sounds of the machines, came a human cry from the Old Point.

The woman stopped in her tracks and strained to hear above the wind. Was that a cry?

Sam. She had to warn him. Potts' words earlier that evening came to her mind.

"I ain't splittin' what I find with that kid from New Jersey. It's for you and me, alone."

Sam. She pointed her flashlight down the old highway—the only reliable marker left in Old Iroquois—and ran in the direction of the Point.

The man sat with a coffee on the porch of the rooming house. It was one of the few buildings left in Old Iroquois, soon to be demolished when the crews left the village site. The wind brought the sounds of the machines that still worked around the clock to finish the eradication of Old Iroquois.

Sam.

It shouldn't have ended this way. But no man is immune to the poison of easy money.

His hand tightened around the mug.

No one.

New Iroquois
Late Spring

The man had watched the group for several weeks now, at the river's edge. He'd even gone with a group of nosy parkers to hear what was going on.

Environmental stuff. Always the environment. If the word had been even remotely a consideration fifty years ago, the Seaway would never have happened. Now it was the hot topic—as was the environmental debt the Seaway had created.

But the yellow tape had disturbed him. What business was it of the OPP if the environmental people were there?

A flash of memory. A windy night so long ago.

He rubbed his beard thoughtfully. No. Not possible. It had been just another disappearance of an itinerant worker in a sea of people with nothing to connect them but the jobs.

Nothing . . . right?

The woman stirred her tea and opened the morning paper. Almost time to head to the Hartford for another shift. Her spoon stopped in mid-stir, headline in black before her.

Remains Found in Iroquois by Environmental Team
OPP suspect foul play

The picture showed an officer standing by the water's edge on the old No. 2, surrounded by yellow tape.

Remains. That meant old, from the old days.

The face of a young man with a laughing grin flittered across her mind.

Sam.

She carefully closed the paper and left the table, tea untouched.

Detective Sergeant Jordan Wiley stood by the river, looking around at where Old Iroquois used to be. He combed his fingers through his fair hair and put his cap back on to spite the sun. The grid search was almost finished, and the water level people would be back tomorrow. Despite the brilliant day and the crime scene team, he felt the loneliness of the area. He'd seen pictures of the old main street in the pre-Seaway days and still struggled to imagine such life in such an empty place—empty, except for the pleasure boaters who now used the old canal.

He suddenly thought of another day in a lonely place with a grid search. The bird sanctuary and the ghosts of Aultsville. The remains of one Hal Leonard, father to Farran Mackenzie.

And all that the discovery of the body had set in motion . . .

His cell phone rang and he answered it to hear the voice of his superior, Inspector Jerry Strauss. Wiley was only forty, and not even born when the Seaway went through. On the other hand, as a boy, Inspector Strauss had watched his entire village disappear. This was probably another Lost Village death, and the inspector always took a special interest in those. Almost like a personal offence for a mark on the local history.

"Wiley," came the words, "just thought you'd like to know we located the brother. Still living in New Jersey. Not an easy phone call, as you can imagine."

No. Not easy at all. Never was, no matter what the time frame.

"He's flying up tomorrow to make a positive ID. I'll let you know when he arrives."

"Thank you, sir." Wiley disconnected and turned from the shore.

You lying bastard . . .

"What?" he responded.

But the searchers were oblivious in their work, and Old Iroquois had no reply.

TWO

ALL OUR YESTERDAYS

Gatwick Airport
London, England, 1982

The young woman sat in her assigned seat, heart thumping. She didn't hear the stewardess ask if she wanted the backpack put up in the overhead storage. Somehow it was decided she did, and the luggage was stored above her. The seat beside her was empty, except for her purse.

The other passengers continued to file in, dealing with seats and luggage. Lost in thought, the woman looked out the window, hand coming to rest on the small bump in her abdomen. For the child, she reminded herself. For us.

The bump gave a small movement and she smiled. Tucking some long blonde hair behind her ear, she looked down at her stomach.

What kind of mother would that make me?

Her heart began to bang in her chest, and she felt nausea threaten. This had nothing to do with morning sickness. This had to do with . . .

"No!" The woman got up hastily, grabbed her purse and made her way to the airplane door—no small feat for a pregnant woman against the last of the passengers going the other way.

"Ma'am, where are you going?" the stewardess called after her. "We're taking off in just a few minutes."

The woman didn't answer. She reached the door and headed down the ramp to the waiting area, past the clerk at the desk, into the crowd, disappearing into the coffee shop. She sat for some time shaking and undecided, talking quietly to herself. Finally, the young woman rose, left the tables, and walked over to the wall of pay phones. Looking through what was left of the phone book's pages, she found the number at the front, dropped a coin into the slot, and dialled.

"Scotland Yard," came the voice.

"I think he's going to kill her," she whispered.

Forty-five minutes later, Flight 39—with 115 passengers and crew—dissolved into a fireball over the waters of the Atlantic.

London, England
Autumn, Present Day

The man sauntered into the squad room, eternal coffee in hand. He glanced up at the TV news, then picked up some of the paperwork that was also eternal. He sighed and looked at the top sheet.

". . . the other woman injured by the bomb blast," the TV murmured on, "was Dr. Farran Mackenzie, a family friend that Perry-Standish had been secretly staying with during the threats on her life . . ."

He suddenly wasn't reading. Farran Mackenzie. *Farran Mackenzie?*

". . . is now in critical condition in hospital, under police watch. OPP say only that the investigation, now tied to a previous car bombing, continues."

He snapped around in time to catch a glimpse of reporters chasing a large, imposing officer who was grimly ignoring them as he climbed the stairs of a police station.

But before that had been a photograph. Only for a second, but a second long enough.

Farran Mackenzie. He'd know that face anywhere, despite the change of years he'd thought she'd escaped.

He stood for some moments absolutely still, oblivious to the noise of the squad room around him.

"Farran," he whispered. "Why are you still alive?"

The woman snapped off the television. Very unexpected news from CNN this morning. Should have stayed with the BBC. With shaking hands, she poured a shot of light brown liquid into a glass.

Farran Mackenzie. That woman. Unmistakable. After all these years. But why?

"Farran," she whispered, "does he know you're still alive?"

The man stood looking with unseeing eyes out his study window, a folder in hand. The report was one he had been waiting for, but it seemed unimportant to the bombshell he'd just witnessed on the television.

Bombshell. Car bombing. Bomb on Flight 39.

"So," he said slowly, absorbing the shock of his own words, "you are still alive."

Victoria, British Columbia
Winter

The two women sat in silence. The television was now off, but they could both still see the images of Alison Perry, Farran Mackenzie, and the burnt car under a tarp with the police barricade around the house.

Finally, one put her hand on the other's shoulder.

"What are you going to do?" she asked gently.

"I don't know," the other admitted. "But I have to do something. Farran Mackenzie is still alive."

"Are you sure?" The brunette looked at the laptop with scepticism, then with genuine concern at her friend in the hospital bed.

"Yes," said the blonde firmly. "I've done a thorough check. It's her."

"Look," said the brunette, sitting down on the bed to face her friend. "You've had a lot to deal with since your parents . . . since the accident. I know how much you want to find her, but maybe right now isn't the time. Maybe . . ."

"It's her." The blonde snapped the laptop shut. "I dug the clip up from CNN. And it looks like I just about lost her again. Anything new?" she added, turning to the redhead who stood quietly in the corner.

"No," came the grim answer. "Nothing new on the accident report. They still don't know why your brakes failed."

Trouble . . .

The blonde ignored the whisper of her heart and the worry on the faces of her friends.

Mom—no, not ever that. That belonged to . . .

The black hole inside yawned open, threatening to swallow her again. She fought back and fought the tears. *God, I miss you both. So much . . .*

But maybe . . . maybe . . .

Mother.

The word set off a storm of emotion long denied and she began to lose the battle.

Trouble . . .

Her mother was in trouble.

Mother.

The young woman covered her face with her hands.

Mother of God . . .

Office of Inspector Jerry Strauss
SD&G OPP Detachment
Long Sault, Ontario
Spring

The woman put her mouth to the ear of the man sleeping in the office chair.

"I love you, Jerry Strauss," she whispered.

"Are you ever going to tell him when he's awake?"

Farran Mackenzie jumped at the sound of the voice and straightened up to look into the twinkling eyes of Lynn Holmes, standing in the doorway, leaning on the frame with her arms crossed.

Mackenzie flushed and fussed with the coat she had laid over Jerry's sleeping form.

"Say what?" she countered uselessly to her friend.

Lynn grinned.

"It's okay, Fan. Your secret is safe with me. For now. And," she added, "for what my opinion's worth in this, the feeling is mutual. Now," she came over to Jerry's desk, "we need to talk."

"We should get him home," Farran said dubiously, looking at Jerry's somewhat sprawled position. "We can't let him sleep in this chair all day."

"That can wait a minute," Lynn insisted, coming around the desk to take the woman's arm. "I have some news for you. You've led me a merry chase these past few days, and I've been wanting to tell you something. It's important."

Lynn steered Farran to a nearby chair and sat her down.

Farran looked at her for a clue as to the gravity of the news.

"What is it, Lynn? Bad news or good news?"

She sighed and crossed her arms again.

"To be honest, I'd say both. The good news is that, after all these months, I think we've found her."

Farran was very still. "Who?" she asked quietly.

"Your daughter," Lynn said simply. "Haley. I think we've found Haley."

"And the bad news?" came the reply.

"The bad news is that your instincts last year were right. If my information is correct, she's in trouble. In fact," Lynn's mouth became a grim line, "I'd say we found her just in time."

PART TWO

"You can spend your whole life with someone
and not know her."

—Farran Mackenzie, *A Violent End*

THREE

WHAT ARE LITTLE GIRLS MADE OF?

I have two cigars.

Not real ones, as I don't smoke. They are imaginary, psychological tools I use to navigate the adult world that just won't leave me alone.

I don't quite know when they arrived in my life — probably sometime after I ran into Inspector Jerry Strauss. One belongs to Winston Churchill, the other to Groucho Marx, and they reside in my back pockets ready for use, one or the other, or both, depending on the gravity/insanity/comic value of any situation I find myself in.

On this particular day, I had one in each corner of my mouth as I faced Carolyn, waiting for her mother to model the final dress choices. Carolyn Berkley and I had finally forged a friendship over the past year, after starting off rather badly several years ago when I sort of led her mother to drive her car into the St. Lawrence River. In my defence, I must add that I was in pursuit of my father's killer. However, Ruth Hoffman Tremblay almost died, and I am amazed that Carolyn found the capacity to forgive me for that. I haven't been able to do the same.

"Well, what do you think?"

The voice, the gesture, the breathless excitement belonged to a teenager. Ruth Hoffman, a slim and stylish woman in her late sixties, walked into the living room, turning around to show the ivory silk dress, as though the last fifty years hadn't happened. I was suddenly back in that same room several years ago when I first met her — my late mother's former best friend. Since then, car in the river notwithstanding, she had become my best friend, too. I loved her dearly.

And now Ruth was getting married again.

"Maybe it should be longer." Carolyn, a younger version of Ruth except for the jeans and long, dark hair, walked around her mother. "A few more inches below the knee."

I chewed on Groucho's cigar. "I don't think so," I offered. "At the knee is fine. You've still got great legs, Ruth. If mine looked like that in my sixties—hell, if they looked that good right now—I'd be showing them off."

The two women turned to me, daughter with a look, mother with a smile.

"Hey, I really like that one." The voice came from the kitchen, where Lynn Holmes stood holding a manila envelope.

"So do I," said Ruth, brushing a hand down over the skirt. "Well, at least *that's* done. We still have so much to do. Maybe I should have waited until after Celebration 50 to get married."

"We're fine on both accounts," Carolyn said brusquely. "It's only May. We have three weeks before the wedding, and Celebration 50 doesn't start until the end of June."

I privately took a deep breath and let it out. Celebration 50 was the name for the fiftieth anniversary of the inundation, the flooding of the great headpond in the St. Lawrence Seaway and Power Project that marked the end of four years of construction—and the end of the villages both Lynn and Ruth had called home, along with 6,500 other souls.

It would also be the fiftieth anniversary of my father's murder at the age of eighteen, taken from his young wife and unborn child. The old rage flickered down in my stomach. Some hot coals never go out.

And, I guess, let's do the math. This summer would also mark the approach of the Big 5-0 in the life of Farran Mackenzie. Fifty. Me! Hell, where had the time gone?

Celebration 50, fifty years since my father's murder, sliding into home plate of the half-century personal milestone. Ah, yes, I smiled grimly inside, toying with the Churchill cigar this time. Another summer of light emotional entertainment.

"Can you stay for lunch, Lynn?" Ruth asked, heading back to her bedroom. "I'm making something to eat as soon as I change."

"I'll take a rain check, Ruth, but thanks," said Lynn. Then she turned to look at me. "I'm just blowing through on my way to Cornwall, but I wanted to stop and give Farran this."

"This" was the manila envelope. She held it out to me, and I could see two lines of writing on it.

"What is it?" I asked. Curiously, my arms stayed at my side. It wasn't easy. Being a coward does take a lot of energy.

Lynn continued to hold out the envelope. She also continued to look in my eyes.

"It's what you've needed to know for the last twenty-six years," she said quietly.

I took another deep breath and reached out for the envelope. On the front were two lines in Lynn's hand — two names actually.

Stephanie Amelia Harrison
Haley Leslie Mackenzie

The first meant nothing to me.

The second meant everything.

It was the name of my daughter, the baby I had given up at birth.

In the company of those who loved me, I crushed the paper to my chest and tried to breathe.

So much for a summer of light emotional entertainment . . .

You lying bastard . . .

"Alison?" I mumbled.

My eyes opened to take in the St. Lawrence River — early morning with the river mist promising a hot spring day. I hesitated for a second as to where I was. Perhaps *when* I was would have been more accurate. After I had given Dave's gold watch and all it might have said to the river last year, a winter of silence had settled in. But lately, Alison had returned to me — on my mind, in my heart, and in my dreams, as though she had something yet to tell me from that horrific summer.

Not sure if I had heard or dreamt the voice, I sat up and whispered again, "Alison?"

No reply. Probably a good thing. No clue as to what I what I would have done if there had been. Throwing off the covers, I got up and padded out to the kitchen where the table was strewn with papers from the plans to winterize this little cottage I had rented on my first arrival and now called my own. Home? No clue there, either. Yet.

On top of the papers lay the brown envelope Lynn had given me yesterday, unopened. Next to it sat a brandy snifter, the continuation of the one Ruth had offered me yesterday when my knees stopped working after reading the name *Haley Leslie Mackenzie*. It seems my friends have learned to keep brandy in stock for the crises that tend to roll through my life on a fairly regular basis. Not one to acknowledge the obvious statements that made about me, I passed on a refill for breakfast and opted for food, my other life companion.

The envelope stayed shut and in plain view.

I was doing dishes when the doorbell rang.

"Professor Mackenzie?" The young woman standing there looked like she belonged on a campus somewhere. Birkenstocks, backpack, IPod, long brown hair in a single braid, and no makeup.

"Yes?"

"I'm Jenn Farley. I'm doing a masters on some of the effects of the Seaway. I spoke to the Lost Villages Society last night."

"Oh . . . yes. I had intended to go but . . . something came up. Please come in." She hesitantly entered the hallway and then the living room at my gesture. I thought of myself in my MA days and a thousand other girls in that same costume that had paraded through my classrooms over the years. Funny how some things never seem to change.

"I don't mean to barge in, and I won't keep you, but I was hoping I could catch you before you left for the day." Jenn looked around the living room. "I'm using your latest book as part of my research. Could we make a date at your convenience for an interview?"

"What's the research about?"

"Memory. How people use memory in the face of the eradication of artefact, preserving and commemorating their losses."

"Sounds very interesting," I agreed.

A memory was stirring in me, trying to surface. One that hurt. I shut it down.

"When would you have an opening for me? I'm supposed to go to Montreal later this week, but how about sometime early next?"

Had I ever been that organized?

"Sure. How about just after lunch on Monday? I don't think I have anything scheduled." I thought of my so-called office with the swirl of papers.

She handed me a card and smiled. "That's wonderful. I so appreciate it, Dr. Mackenzie."

I smiled back, hiding a sudden, disturbing feeling of incredible emptiness.

"I see someone coming in your driveway," Jenn added, looking over my shoulder at the front window. "I'll get out of your way."

It was Lynn, her sandy curls wild all over her head as usual. At moments like this, it was easy to catch a glimpse of the young scamp who had grown up with my mother in Farran's Point. Now she was turning sixty, and had a long and successful career in the media that was due in part to those natural nosy skills she'd honed in the Lost Village.

Lynn stood at the door with a look on her face that meant business. She came in and looked into mine.

"You haven't read the file, yet," she pronounced grimly. "I can see it in your face."

"I . . . I'm working up to it," I said lamely as she headed for the kitchen.

"I know you are," Lynn stopped in the doorway to look back at me, suddenly so much like someone we both would never forget . . .

"It isn't your place to say what?" I opened the door slowly and stood in the doorframe. "What do you mean by 'wickedness'?"

Meredith stood for a moment, framed by the large patio door across the cottage. Behind her, the setting sun had turned the river to milk. I can see her yet in my mind's eye, struggling between dropping a bomb with flourish and stepping back from going too far. I try to use that picture now to wipe out the other, ugly memory.

Good upbringing won the fight.

"Your family didn't fall on hard times—they were torn apart. Wickedness, it was. The rest you won't hear from me." She pushed past me and was gone.

Wickedness. Oh, Meredith.

". . . pretending this is going to be easy for you. I can't imagine what you're feeling right now." Lynn paused. "Fan?"

I took a deep breath and let it out.

"Sorry. It was just the way you came in . . . and stood . . . You reminded me . . . made me think of Meredith."

We looked at each other for a long moment, having one of those wordless conversations close friends can have about things that need to stay unspoken.

Lynn nodded, grim again.

"Coffee, Mackenzie. Then we get to work."

Many times in adult life, the surreal sets in and disembodies you from the present moment. I say adult life, because as children, we instinctively understand and don't argue with the mind's ability to move outside itself when necessary; therefore, disembodiment doesn't happen. I sat at my kitchen table with the morning sun coming in, listening to Lynn's voice and watching myself, as though from a distance, do something I had thought about for a quarter century.

I found the daughter I had given up so long ago.

I remember the sight of the papers and the photo on my table, the feel of Lynn putting the photo in my hand, the sound of her voice carefully saying, "Haley."

I looked at the little girl: dress, braids, smile. Finally, the eyes.

"She has your eyes, Fan." Lynn smiled and put her hand on mine.

"It's okay, Mom. It's Fan. I'm here. Everything is okay."

Her eyes seemed to clear for a moment and she touched my face.

"Fan." It was almost a whisper. "Father's . . . eyes."

The little girl continued to stare right into me from the picture.

You look like your father . . . I wonder Gordon didn't see it.

Meredith . . . This time I said nothing. First Alison, now Meredith. I closed my eyes. What was this—old home week for ghosts and memories in honour of Celebration 50?

"It's the most recent picture I could find, and trust me, I searched," Lynn explained. "After the kidnapping, her parents put a blackout on any more publicity around their daughter and no media camera ever saw her face again. Being who they were, the Harrisons could pull that off."

I shook my head. "Okay, start again. I've been taking only part of this in."

Lynn squeezed my hand and got up to refill her mug. Mine was untouched.

"Haley Leslie Mackenzie was adopted at birth by Frank and Amelia Harrison, of the Harrison media empire. She was christened Stephanie Amelia and raised in luxury in Victoria, B.C. She has no siblings." Lynn sat down and looked at me. "At the age of eight, around the time of that photograph, Stephanie was kidnapped and held for ransom. It lasted for three weeks. The Harrisons paid a million dollars for her release and got her back unharmed. The kidnappers were never caught. As I said, that's the last time Stephanie's face was seen by the public. Even the paparazzi don't go near her. Word is, if you did, you'd never work again on this continent, and in many ways the media have closed ranks around the girl to protect one of their own." Lynn grinned. "We can be human sometimes, you know."

"Yes, I know." Several times since I had met Lynn Holmes, she had bent the rules or delayed taking action to help me out—despite her editorial position with the *Ottawa Citizen.* "What is she doing now?"

"From what I can gather, she's involved with the family empire and has directed both work and charitable donations into many environmental projects. Nothing about being married or having any children, not that I could dig up anyway. As you can imagine, I have to walk very carefully with this one. Fortunately, Stephanie's recent misfortunes have made it a little easier."

"Misfortunes?" My hands tightened around my cold mug.

"You may remember from the news that Frank and Amelia Harrison died about six months ago in a plane crash in the mountains. She's now sole owner of their part of the business. Stephanie is a very rich woman."

"Then maybe this isn't the right time to make contact," I said, hazarding a quick glance at the photograph again. "She's grieving and dealing with a lot of stuff professionally."

"She's also in trouble." Lynn looked straight at me.

Trouble . . .

Dark.

Light.

Grey sound.

She was both mine and the girl from Farran's Point.

"Mom?" *I whispered.*

Mist and distance, back again.

No, Fan. Go back. Not now . . .

My arms reached out vainly to hold her one more time and I cried.

Someone else. A man.

Haley . . .

I started to sob. "Mom, please."

Haley . . . Find her . . .
Tears filled my throat. "Come back," I pleaded.
I couldn't see her face now.
Trouble . . .

"Trouble," I repeated. "Yes."

Lynn sat forward and leaned on the table, arms crossed. "Fan," she said, eyes locked on mine, "You said last year when we first started this that we had to find Haley because she was in trouble. That you just had a feeling. I didn't press you at the time, but now I have to ask you again how you knew that? If you have something—anything—we can use here, you need to tell me."

I picked up the photograph and looked into those eyes again before meeting Lynn's. If my little girl was in trouble, then I had to put everything on the table. I took a deep breath, let it out, and looked up.

"When Alison died . . . when I died for a minute . . . my mother told me. She told me I had to go back, to find Haley. She was in trouble."

When you think about it, there aren't a lot of people in this world you can say something like that to. Fortunately, I had at least one in my life. Lynn just thought about it for a minute and then nodded.

"The Leslie I remember was no drama queen. If she said trouble, she meant trouble with a capital 'T'. Life-threatening. And I think she's right. The media business has been crazy in this country for some time, with buyouts and takeovers and market grabs. There was a hostile takeover of the Harrison empire being tried at the time of the parents' accident. The plane crash was ruled suspicious, but no charges were laid. And the investigation was enough to shut down the takeover, at least for now. But," Lynn added grimly, "there are rumours floating around that there's been an attempt on Stephanie's life. Another suspicious accident. But I haven't been able to pin it all down yet. I will, though."

"So that's why you told me before that we had probably found her just in time."

"Yes. I think Leslie's right, and we need to find her."

"If we can. She's probably more out of reach now than ever. And honestly," I sighed, "what could I ever do to help with this?"

"Be her mother," Lynn shot back. "Fill a gap that's been there forever, however you can. But as for finding her, trust me. We will. In this world, there is no place to hide. There's always a way to find someone if you really, really need to."

I said nothing. Inwardly, I acquiesced on Lynn's prediction about finding Haley. However, on being able to be of any use to her, let alone her wanting me at all, I was unconvinced.

I looked at the photograph again, tried to imagine what she looked like now, who she was, what she was feeling . . . what she might say to me if/when we met. Better yet, what the hell would I say to her?

Trouble.

You lying bastard . . .

My stomach lurched for a moment.

For this one, at least, I had no cigar.

FOUR

TOMORROW IS YESTERDAY

The man was elderly—the report said early eighties—but grief had etched at least another decade on his face in the last forty-eight hours. He was slim but built, with a full head of white hair. Hands of a labourer, Jerry Strauss noted with his sharp grey eyes as he listened to Wiley fill in the bad details for the visitor. Workman of some sort, he added to himself, but the stance spoke of military background somewhere.

"Mr. Wallace," Detective Sergeant Wiley's tone was apologetic, "the remains were found by a research team from Toronto doing tests on water erosion in the St. Lawrence River. The body had been buried near the river, and, over time, the fluctuating water levels eroded the soil, bringing the remains to light." Wiley cleared his throat. "Unfortunately, the river had already taken some away. However, we have the skull, which will allow us to do a dental records check if you think this could be your brother Sam."

Strauss, a tall James Garner type just turned sixty, wordlessly handed Wiley a manila envelope. Wiley took it and pulled out its contents.

"Mr. Wallace," he continued, "do you recognize this?"

Carl Wallace raised his eyes from the floor, then slowly put out his hand. He cradled the pocket watch cupped in both hands as though it would shatter. Then he closed them over it and looked up.

"It's Sam's," he said simply. "I give it to him when we come up here fifty years ago to work the Seaway. Couldn't wear one on your wrist. Too dangerous with the machines." The hands tightened. "Was it an accident? Did he fall? Sam liked his drink. I tried to watch him with that . . ."

Wiley looked at Strauss and back to Wallace.

"No, sir," he replied quietly. "This is a homicide investigation."

A look Jerry couldn't label passed over the man's face. Couldn't, but would work on that.

"Homicide? Murder?"

"That skull also tells us your brother died from a gunshot wound to the head." Strauss spoke for the first time, his grey eyes still locked on the old man's face. "Can you remember anyone who might have wanted to kill him?"

Wallace was silent for a moment, the officers waiting for him to take it in. Finally, he shook his head.

"You're talking a busy time, a long time ago."

"I grew up in Aultsville," Jerry shot back, "one of the villages destroyed by the expropriation. It's yesterday to me."

Wallace did not respond.

"Mr. Wallace," broached Wiley, "you said you and your brother came up to work on the Seaway Project. Just came up on your own looking for work?"

The old man ran a hand through his hair and sat back. He shook his head.

"Nope. Came up on Bill Hartshorne's crew to move the houses. Seven of us, and the Hartshornes. From Moorestown, New Jersey. I was already on Bill's crew, and I asked him to take Sam on so he could come with me. Both our parents were dead by then, and Sam was a stretch younger than me. I wanted to keep an eye on him. They said we'd be gone a while with this one."

"Had you been working for the Hartshornes for long, Mr. Wallace?" Jerry eased the man into the past.

"Since the war," came the reply. "I come out of the service in '46, and there wasn't a job to be had anywheres. So I went to work for Bill. He had the house-moving business himself at first. His younger brother, Clarence, had taken the dairy farm from their father, and Bill the house-moving. The dairy farm started sinking after a while and they could only save one, so Clarence sold the farm and the brothers became partners with the house-moving."

"They obviously did well," Jerry continued, keeping the conversation general. He shot a look at Wiley, which was returned.

Wallace nodded. "They was in the business at the right time. Building going on everywheres. Expressways. New Jersey Turnpike, South State Parkway, Long Island, Pennsylvania . . . we done them all. Then it started costing more to move a house than tear it down. Areas were built up. Overhead wires and trees to deal with." He cleared his throat. "But I worked for them for fifteen years, 'cept when I went to Korea."

"You served in Korea, sir?" Wiley pulled up a chair.

"Three years."

"Can we offer you a coffee, Mr. Wallace?" Jerry changed tack again.

The old man opened his hands to look at his brother's watch, then closed them again. "Yes, sir," he said simply. "Black, please."

Jerry stood alone with his back to the office door, looking out the window at Longue Sault Public. The school was quiet for the moment, classes going on inside. Longue Sault—the old French fur trader name for the great rapids in the St. Lawrence River that had precipitated the Seaway and Power Project half a century ago and ultimately been eradicated by the construction. The village bore the Anglicized version: Long Sault. The metal letters on the school were the last physical remnant of the original name. Jerry wondered if any of the current students knew why the spelling was different.

A busy time, the man had said. *A long time ago.*

Eric jumped off the truck when they arrived. Men had already started two bucket brigades, but the fire was moving quickly in the wind. Piles of lumber blazed all over the yard, and the office was beyond saving. The heat was almost unbearable.

"Hal!" Eric called. His son left the line and came over, his face and hands dark with smoke and ash. "We've got help comin'. Get two guys and take the engine over to Murphy's well to fill the tank. Thank God, Hydro's not too fussy about closin' wells. Where's Bill? Is he here, yet?"

"I haven't seen him, Dad." Hal shook his head, then wiped his eyes with a streaked handkerchief. "There was no answer when I knocked earlier." He started toward the fire truck, then stopped. "Dad, there's Em and Jerry."

Eric looked around, and headed in their direction.

"Emme, where's Bill? I need him to direct the men on the other side."

She looked confused for a moment. "What do you mean, Eric? He's here."

"We can't find him. When did he find out about the fire? Maybe he went to the new town for help."

"No," Emme shook her head, pulling her son close. "The truck is at the house. No one told him about the fire. He's been here all evening, working on the books."

They looked over at the office. At the same moment, the men nearby gave a shout and moved back as the roof caved in.

"He's working on the books," she repeated tonelessly. Jerry broke free of her hold and started to run.

"Poppa! Poppa!" he screamed.

Hal made a dive for him before he got too close and they hit the dirt together. Jerry struggled, but Hal held firm.

"We don't know he's in there, Jerr. We don't know," the young man yelled over the noise, trying to keep his voice calm. "He might have gone to get help." The boy became still and they sat together in the light of the inferno.

Gordon went over to them. "Don't worry," he said. "We'll find him."

"Yesterday," Jerry had replied.

Despite his words, Carl Wallace had had little difficulty providing background to his arrival with the Hartshorne crew.

"We come up late in '55. There was awful high unemployment in Canada then so we had to become 'supervisors' and take on some Canadian workers. Joined the union as an operating engineer," Wallace smiled briefly. "Became a Teamster when I ran a truck. Neither was really legal, so that was stretching the rules.

"Brought the machines up by train. Unloaded in Iroquois and put both together right there by the old inspection station. That's where we started moving," he added. "Iroquois. Whole town had to move right away 'cause they was putting the control dam there. Rest of the towns was partial. We stayed for about three-and-a-half years. Moved a house about every two days."

Jerry remembered the huge machines with tires taller than a man backing up to the houses and surrounding them. Then they would be gone. As a boy, he'd watched many of the houses lumbering down the road out of Aultsville or Farran's Point toward New Town No. 1, now Ingleside. Unlike so many others, he'd never tired of watching the amazing process.

"What job did your brother Sam do?"

"A bit of anything and everything." The old man rubbed his chin for a moment. "He was new to the crew . . . and the work. Sam did whatever odd job had to be done. We had to be 'supervisors,' like I said, so Sam had a group that would go wherever extra hands were needed for the day. Sent him all over the place. I might work with him once a week, depending on what was going on."

"Who did he chum around with during his off hours, Mr. Wallace?" Jerry asked quietly. "Stick to his own crew? New friends? Any local girl he was sweet on?"

Carl had been shaking his head, until the mention of a girl. Then a dark shadow passed over his face. He looked down at the watch without speaking.

Wiley glanced at Strauss, who signalled silence and began to tap a pencil end-over-end on his desk. The early afternoon sun warmed the room, lighting the present and the past. Finally, Wallace looked up at the officers.

"There was one guy, but he wasn't a friend to Sam in my books. Bad influence. Liked drink, liked gambling, liked girls. Didn't care much for hard work. Potts, his name was. Ricky Potts. I tried to keep Sam away from him, but Potts was on his crew when he first showed up. And he was from home, so to speak. American, from New York State. Came over to get some work."

Strauss's pencil became still. "There would have been lots of work on the American side, in Massena and the area. Why would Potts have to come here?"

Wallace shrugged. "Can't say for sure. Never got to know the man real good. Sam said something once about Potts having a wife back home he was trying to get away from. He was trouble. Maybe there were other people he had to get away from, too," the man said ominously. "I know he owed Sam some money before Sam left . . . uh, was . . . was killed."

"You said Potts liked girls," Wiley ventured. "Any local girls he spent time with? With Sam?"

"They'd go to the dances . . ." Carl's voice trailed off. Strauss studied him, waiting for the man to return from wherever, *whenever* he'd gone.

"Vivienne . . ." It was almost a whisper. "Haven't thought about her in fifty years. She was trouble, too. Maybe that's why Potts liked her. Two of a kind, you know." Carl's voice grew hard. "She played people, including my brother. She'd get guys into fights over her just for entertainment. Guess she was bored. I told Sam to stay away from her, but he'd fallen for her pretty hard. First big crush, I think."

Wallace looked at Strauss. "They all disappeared around the same time. Potts, Sam, and that woman. I always thought she was the reason he left."

"I guess I'm thinking now that maybe she's the reason he died."

Strauss pulled into the gravel driveway outside the little cottage and killed the engine. He remembered the first time he'd come here, after they had had an almost pleasant lunch together, to tell Farran the bad news about Alice Hoffman. He'd waited until she returned and then met her in the driveway.

"I don't mind the meetings, Mackenzie . . . I just wish they weren't always about death."

Farran had leaned on her car for support.

"Death? Another death?"

"It's Alice. The call was waiting for me when I got back to the office. Alice Hoffman died this afternoon..."

He had still been wondering then about Farran Mackenzie, who she was behind those green eyes, what dangerous motives she was working with along with all the other emotional baggage that followed her on wheels everywhere she went. He hadn't yet ruled her out where Meredith's murder had been concerned. She was there, had been there to see Meredith by her own admission, and was on the scene when Meredith had died.

And when Alison had died, right in this driveway.

The sight of Farran's car in flames, doors and windows blown away, fire trucks, ambulance, and a victim being strapped onto a gurney had greeted him when he'd arrived in a squad car minutes after the 911 call had come through. Then the days at the hospital waiting for her to come back to him—and forgive him for letting it happen at all.

"Are you coming in, or do I bring the coffee out to the car?"

The voice at his shoulder made him jump. Farran stood beside the car, arms crossed, blonde hair in a swirl around her face. T-shirt and jeans, no makeup—beautiful. Without a second thought, Jerry got out of the car, took Farran in his arms and kissed her till he felt like stopping.

Thankfully, she kissed him back and didn't pull away in surprise. She did, however, give him a close look when she was able.

"Okay, Inspector. What's up? Not that I'm complaining, mind you."

"Anything and everything," Jerry echoed Carl Wallace. "I have something for you. And I'll take my coffee in the house."

When they reached the kitchen, Strauss saw the two cups on the table amid the mess of papers. He noted the photograph.

"Am I interrupting something?"

Farran shook her head and pulled out two more mugs.

"Lynn was here this morning," she replied. "We went over what we have about Haley."

"May I?" He indicated the picture. Getting an all-clear, Strauss took a good look at the little girl. "She looks like you. How old is this?"

"Close to twenty years ago. It's one of the last pictures you can find of her." Farran filled him in on the background. "So now I don't want to sail in just after she's lost her parents, but she may be in trouble."

"In those circles," Strauss began, "that would definitely be . . ."

"I know. I know." She cut him off. "A matter for the police. I get that. Trust me, I'm not going to run into this with my usual herd-of-elephants style. But I can't just sit by, either."

"Let me help." Strauss looked at her standing there. "Let me dig around first and get the lay of the land — "

"No!"

The sharp reply startled them both.

"I mean . . ." Farran handed him his coffee. Her hand trembled slightly, but he said nothing. "I mean, thank you, and I'll take you up on that offer soon. But Lynn is still using her contacts to bypass the fortress walls. I need to see what's there first . . . I . . . I need to absorb all this."

She added something under her breath, but Strauss didn't catch it. He also didn't push it.

"Okay. Let's sit outside. It's a nice day." He tried to lead her to the patio door. "And you can look at this." He held out a brown envelope.

But Farran wasn't listening—at least not to him. She turned her head slightly as though trying to hear something.

"Farran?"

A look crossed her face and then she shook her head. "Sorry. You were saying . . .?"

Strauss held out the envelope again. "Let's sit outside and you can take a look at this."

Farran shot a glance at the brown envelope on the table with its scattered contents and then gingerly put out a hand to take the other. "What is it?"

Jerry allowed himself a slow smile as he passed it over. "Nothing as upsetting as *that*," he said, nodding toward the papers on the table. "Just another sleeping murder to wake up."

FIVE

OLD IROQUOIS

Some men come to call and bring you roses. Mine brings me bodies. I wonder what that says about me, let alone my relationship with Inspector Jerry Strauss.

I stood, a few days later, where Old Iroquois used to be with a man who had helped make its death a reality.

When you speak of the Lost Villages of the St. Lawrence Seaway, Iroquois—like Morrisburg—is not included. Like Morrisburg, it was affected by the construction, but still remains on the map. Unlike Morrisburg, which lost only its canal and first two streets, Iroquois stood mostly where the control dam and international lock had to go and was moved in its entirety one mile north of the original location. In doing so, the village lost many historic buildings and was redesigned to reflect contemporary tastes. It also lost its riverfront access and social connection. Old Iroquois vanished, and what the older locals still refer to after half a century as "New Iroquois" took its place.

We stood in a field that lies between the end of the houses and the new riverfront, where traces of the old village remain: the original lock, the decaying foundation of the swing bridge, the original roads vanishing into the river, and the old lockmaster's house sitting empty on the hill between us and the international Seaway lock.

At the end of the old No. 2 highway pavement in front of us, the yellow ribbon still marked the search area where Sam Wallace's remains had been found. His brother looked away.

"So goddamn quiet here," said Carl. "It was so busy. Everybody running around doing everything. A village that turned into almost a city overnight with all the machines and workers." The man shook his head. "I remember they had a slogan up on a billboard. Said, 'We have to go but watch us grow.' What happened?"

"A lot of the economic promises of the Seaway never happened," I said quietly, feeling more than a little like the Ghost of Christmas Past giving Scrooge his tour. "Did you ever come back before now?"

"Nope." The answer was curt. "No reason to. Sam had taken off for who knows where with that woman, I thought. I went home to New Jersey and went into construction. Thought Sam would come home someday. Never did." Carl turned to look at me. "It's been fifty years. And everything is gone. Someone killed my brother a long time ago. What can we do now?"

I took a deep breath and let it out. With my academic background in history and my experiences over the last few years, I have become a cross between a social archaeologist and a ghost whisperer. For those who are interested, this was not in my daybook. But like the man says, life is what happens to you when you're busy making other plans.

And in the midst of life, we are in death.

"Not everything is gone," I replied. "And I'm not just talking about physical remnants. What happened here was a very human thing. And it will be in the people involved that we'll find the truth. Personalities. Memories. There must be people still here that remember. Then we'll pin down who was where and when."

Carl looked unconvinced. Then he shrugged. "The inspector says you're good at this sort of thing. Calls it 'listening to the past.' He doesn't strike me as a quack."

I smiled to myself. "'Quack,'" I said dryly, "is probably the last word I would ever apply to Jerry Strauss. So, Carl," I added, "tell me about your Iroquois."

AMERICAN RIVER PROJECT WORKERS WALK OFF JOBS
Wage Strike Halts Seaway Work in US
WILL DISCUSS WATERFRONT FOR IROQUOIS

IROQUOIS (Special) — Ross Strike, Hydro's vice-chairman, will meet Iroquois property owners on March 22 to discuss future plans for the new Iroquois waterfront, a problem which to date has not been thoroughly aired.

15-ROOM HOUSE MOVED TO NEW IROQUOIS LOCALE
CONTRACT LET FOR CALDWELL LINEN MILL

IROQUOIS (Special) — H.J. Caldwell, president
of Caldwell Linen Mills Limited, announce today
that a contract has been awarded to Pentagon Construction Company of Montreal for the construction of their new plant in New Iroquois.

Spring 1956
Cornwall Standard Freeholder

"Okay, back away now." Carl Wallace waved his hand at the small crowd of onlookers in front of the Hartshorne house-moving machine that was set to roll out on the road with the newly raised house on its lift. Another day, another house. And they were setting them all over the place, wherever Hydro said to go. Didn't seem to make any sense or pattern, but they must know what they're doing.

He waved again, and the people moved reluctantly away from the machine. The great lift slowly pulled away from the house's former foundation, its tires dwarfing the men who stood beside it.

"She's up." A younger man who resembled Carl came up to him. "I'm heading for lunch before the place is full."

A cloud passed over Carl's face, but he only nodded. "I'll be along later, Sam."

He knew his brother's hurry wasn't about food so much as it was about who was serving it. The woman was trouble, but he couldn't do much about it. Sam was his kid brother, but still an adult. Carl figured he would have to learn the hard way. The way he had before Korea.

The diner was packed by the time Carl made it in. He spotted Sam sitting at the counter, making a joke with the blonde waitress in the tight dress. The others were just making eyes. Carl knew there had been fights among the Canadians about Vivienne. But his brother seemed blinded by her face—and it was the prettiest face around, under the makeup and hard eyes. For a moment, Carl wondered why she hadn't grabbed some poor slob in marriage by now. Many of the local girls had used the opportunities the Seaway had given them. But not Vivienne. And it certainly wasn't because of a lack of them.

"Hey, Viv, what about my coffee?" someone complained.

"Hold your horses," came the reply. "You all can come in at once, but I can't serve you at once." The woman moved to give a refill, but the job was taken by a younger girl with her hair in braids who got a glare from Vivienne for her trouble. Maybe the fight would be behind the counter today.

"The usual, Carl?" The girl with braids came up to stand beside the seat he'd managed to find at a crowded table.

"Please, Shelley." Carl took off his hat. "But no tomatoes. They been bothering me lately."

Shelley shook her head and smiled. "Not tom-ah-toes, Carl. To-may-toes. You Americans sure talk funny sometimes . . ." Her voice trailed off as another man sat down.

"Rollie will have the same," said Carl. "And no 'tomaytoes,' either. They bother him, too." The other man nodded. Shelley looked wordlessly at Rollie for a moment and then headed for the kitchen. They watched her leave, and Rollie looked at Carl.

"How long have I been here?" he asked. "And it's still like she never seen a coloured man before." Rollie was one of a few blacks working on the crews.

"She hadn't," Carl said simply. "See any Negro families around here? You're still a . . . a novelty, I guess. Like a lot of other things." Shelley silently brought two Cokes and set the glass bottles on the table. The noise rose at the counter, and they all looked over. Vivienne was holding court like a dancer in a saloon. In some ways, this little family diner felt like a saloon, filled every day with strangers who had come here for work with good wages, like miners looking for gold. And like the Gold Rush, it wouldn't last. Not only would this frontier empty out when the work was done, it would vanish forever under the waters of the St. Lawrence.

"When we got here, it was a quiet little village. Pretty, too." Carl still stood looking toward the hill—and away from the yellow tape. "But we come from New Jersey, the cities. Coming here was like stepping back in time about fifty years."

"How so?" I asked, already knowing the answer.

"No city water for a lot. Iroquois had it—Morrisburg, too, I think—but the other villages didn't. Hydro had to put in pipes, so they could sit on the lines in the new towns.

"Iceboxes in the kitchens," he continued. "Woodstoves inside the houses for heat. Hydro had to build outside chimneys for a lot of the houses and switch them to furnaces." He was quiet a moment. "But they weren't backward. Just old-fashioned, like their homes. Honest. Decent. Trusted government. They just wasn't ready for that kind of change."

Who the hell would be? I thought, then said aloud, "What happened to Vivienne and your brother?"

Carl didn't answer for a minute, his back to me, his face toward the old Iroquois Point out of sight behind the hill.

"The usual," he said, finally. "They dated, they fought, they broke up. Then they'd start over again. I don't know how many times she spun him around. I thought he'd finally just get tired of the bullshit, but he didn't. Don't know why. Guess she had a real hold on him somehow. And there were always other guys mixed in," he added. "Fights with them over her. But it was never serious. Just macho crap. Too many men too far from home."

Carl took a deep breath and let it out. I stayed silent, feeling something coming.

"And then . . ."

"Yes?"

"And then Potts showed up. And everything changed."

NEW CIVIC, SHOPPING CENTRES ARE SIGNS
OF NEW WAY OF LIFE
IROQUOIS CONTROL DAM CONCRETE POURING ENDS
IROQUOIS' BIRTHDAY ENDS WITH FANFARE

IROQUOIS (Special) — A mighty birthday celebration is over and it is estimated that, within the four days it was held, a record-smashing number of people came to Iroquois to help celebrate her centennial.

Summer 1957
Cornwall Standard Freeholder

"What do you mean, you quit?"

The brothers stood facing off in the small bedroom they shared in the rooming house. Sam raised his chin defiantly.

"I said, I quit. Hartshorne, not the project. Bill's almost done here, anyway. I'm working on the Point, now, with the big dozers."

"Iroquois Construction?"

"No, with the yardscrapers digging out the shoreline."

"Dangerous work, Sam," Carl said quietly. "And the pay isn't much better than what we get with Bill."

"It isn't the pay . . ."

"Potts put you up to this, didn't he?"

"No!" The denial was a little too quick in coming, and Sam flushed. "I can think for myself, Carl. I know you don't believe that, but . . ."

"Oh, I know you can think for yourself," Carl snapped back. "You just don't think right."

"Not right, according to you." Sam picked up a duffle bag that was lying on his bed.

"Where are you going?"

"I'm taking a room with Rick. We . . . we have some things to do. Things that . . . that will make . . ."

"Things like gambling, drinking, and that woman. What would Dad and Ma say, if they were alive?"

"That's not fair."

"Fair?" Carl sat down on the bed. "Are you in trouble? I mean real trouble? Do you owe that Potts money or something?"

Sam hoisted the duffle bag on his shoulder and looked down at his brother.

"You always think the worst of me, Carl. But I'm gonna show you. Show everybody. Real soon. Have everything taken care of. You watch and see."

Sam walked out of the room, leaving Carl sitting alone on the bed.

"I never spoke with him again. That was summer of '57. He worked with the scraper crew on the Point and hung around with the Canadian guys that were 'dozing the earth around from the Point to wherever they could find room. I would see him in the distance from time to time, and he might wave, but I didn't track him down. Felt he'd left, so he needed to track *me* down. Too proud . . ." Carl fell silent and didn't turn around.

"What do you think he meant by having 'everything taken care of soon'?"

At that, the man turned to face me.

"Can't say for sure. Never asked. Didn't want to know. Heard that weasel Potts cranking my brother up one night when they were in their cups about lost gold." Wallace shook his head. "Then Sam and Vivienne disappeared. All these years, I thought they'd run off together. Potts left around the same time, I think. I didn't really keep track of him." Carl finally looked over at the yellow tape. "And now it's all wrong. Sam's been here all the time. Someone shot him and buried him in the new shoreline. Why?"

My ears had pricked up at the mention of lost gold, but that could wait. I recognized the sense of emotional overload and burgeoning grief in this elderly man. Carl Wallace had suddenly been faced with all his yesterdays and needed space to absorb the shock. We stood in silence for some time, as though waiting for an answer to his question. For the time being, however, for that day at least, the past had nothing to say.

SIX

NEW IROQUOIS

CENTENNIAL OF CONFEDERATION
CARMAN HOUSE MUSEUM
ERECTED BY THE VILLAGE OF IROQUOIS IN
PERMANENT COMMEMORATION OF THE CENTENNIAL
OF CONFEDERATION IN CANADA IN 1967.
CONSTRUCTION WAS MADE POSSIBLE THROUGH THE
COOPERATION OFTHE PROVINCE OF ONTARIO AND
THE GOVERNMENT OF CANADA.

I really didn't know where else to start.

I read the plaque that stood in front of the small stone house that faced in temporal defiance toward the riverfront that had changed so much half a century ago. An empty field lay to the south and east where Iroquois' main street had once been, and a lone white car drove slowly by on Carman Road on its way to the international lock. It was a sunny day, but I could feel the shadows of the past all around me.

Since the days of the Iroquois nation, these lands were the centre of human activity. The Iroquois used the Old Point in particular for encampments, crossing the river at the narrow point in the water, and trading with the British after the fall of New France. The end of the American Revolutionary War brought many United Empire Loyalists up the St. Lawrence to settle in then Matilda Township.

By 1817, the township had its first post office in the village of Iroquois, named so for its first inhabitants. The completion of the Galop Canal system in 1845, and the arrival of the Grand Trunk Railway in 1854, brought prosperity and expansion to the village, which grew with many fine homes, productive farms, a distinctive town hall, and large, stone public and high schools. It was a beautiful village by the river, with a small harbour at its front next to the river canal. Population at the time of the Seaway was just over 1,000, and official predictions were of a post-Seaway growth to 10,000. The slogan in 1954 was, "We have to go—but watch us grow!"

As with many optimistic projections, the expectations for a larger Iroquois were never realized. "The best town by a dam site" was given a state-of-the-art shopping mall, new streets, street lights, new schools, and a community centre all designed with the projected growth in mind. The Seaway took away the traditional river economy, and Highway 401 the road commerce just a few years later. Population at the time of the last census was around 1,200—little changed from the days of the project. Although Iroquois is still on the map, the older generation says the new town never quite matched the old, and refers to Old Iroquois as "the seventh lost village."

"One of only four houses that were untouched by the Seaway," said the woman in period dress. "And, of course, the oldest house in the village."

The sense of déjà vu suddenly hit. The tour guide had the same salt-and-pepper hair, had the same manner, and was about the same age as Meredith, Lynn's cousin, who had died such a horrible death after I started digging around about my father's murder. I was momentarily back to that day we had met in Crysler Hall at Upper Canada Village. It had turned out to be the first of many encounters of people shocked and uneasy about my existence.

"How old is this place?" I looked around the front room and its exhibits. To my right was a drawing room and through the door ahead a dining room with a kitchen peeking out behind that. The walls were painted a yellow-beige, the trims dark; the windows were deep and high. The heat had no grip here, and the house, although small, seemed spacious and bright.

"Our best guess is around 1815, just a few years after the war. The property was originally the Fenton homestead, granted to Ira Fenton from George III, as was the Carmans' farm right beside. When Fenton died in 1813, he had no family to claim the land, so the Carmans purchased the homestead and built this house on it."

Fenton. I remembered Carl's words from that morning when I had eventually quizzed him about Potts' story of lost gold.

"A fairy tale about some lost gold in Iroquois during the War of 1812. Some ancestor of Potts passed the story down in the family,

and the weasel was fool enough to believe it—or at least say he did. He called it fool's gold. Fenton's fool's gold."

"What can you tell me about Ira Fenton?" I asked.

"Not much. He was UEL, like the Carmans. Ran a small general store and a lumber mill."

I thought of my grandfather, Eric Leonard, doing that same thing in Aultsville until the fire took it away.

"Did he do well during the war with his lumber mill?"

"Fenton? Well, he did get a contract to build a British fort on his property at Iroquois Point, but the fort was never completed. Fenton died around the time of the Battle of Crysler's Farm, and that was the end of the campaign on the St. Lawrence by the American forces. The fort—what was built of it—was dismantled and left to ruins, I guess."

By now we had drifted through the dining room and into the kitchen. The house was Georgian cottage style, indicative of middle class, my guide told me. The kitchen boasted a traditional large open hearth and an untraditional but not unique beehive oven for baking bread.

"I have an odd question for you, Mrs. . . . ."

"Parmeter," she supplied cheerfully. "Fire away. I'll do my best."

"Well," I eased into it, "this morning I heard a story about some gold that was lost around here at the time of the 1812 conflict."

I expected glazed eyes perhaps, or at least a raised eyebrow. I got a smile.

"Fenton's fool's gold! Well . . . I haven't heard that spoken of in years. Who told you that old legend?"

"An old man," I said honestly. "Do you know the story?"

"What child didn't?" She smiled again. "It's a colourful story, and more than one Iroquois child spent summer days searching for the lost chest of Fenton's fool's gold—at least before the Seaway."

"So it was fool's gold?" I echoed. "Not real?"

"Oh, it was real enough, according to the story." Parmeter walked me back to the front door. "Fenton was to be paid $3,000 to build the fort. He worked on it over the better part of a year. Payment was supposed to be over time, but the strains of the war made things fall behind. Fenton wouldn't take paper money, trusting only coin, as so many did back then. He insisted on 3,000 Spanish coins, meaning Spanish silver dollars. But that's not what he got."

We stopped at the door. I put a $10 bill in the donation bowl and waited for the punch line. A good story, in the hands of a good storyteller, always has a punch line.

"According to the legend as my mother told it," Mrs. Parmeter continued, "two chests of Spanish silver dollars were delivered just prior to the American forces' landing on the Canadian side of the St. Lawrence. No one knows why—maybe the army couldn't come up with enough silver coin—but Fenton found a surprise when the soldiers were gone. Only the surface was silver. The layers underneath were Spanish gold doubloons."

I opened my mouth and then closed it, fighting images of Orlando Bloom in *Pirates of the Caribbean*. I had to admit, fighting thoughts of Orlando Bloom was a first for me.

"How was the gold lost?" I managed finally.

"No one knows. Fenton was murdered the day after the battle on Crysler's field. No one was ever hung for the crime. They found his body in the ashes of his house. It had been set on fire, possibly to cover the murder. The house burnt to the ground, taking all the outbuildings with it.

"The chests of Spanish gold doubloons," she finished with a flourish, "were never found."

"Spanish gold doubloons."

"What?" Ruth asked as she opened her front door.

"Just muttering to myself," I muttered, entering the hallway.

"You missed the presentation last night," Ruth chided. She gestured toward the kitchen. "Coffee?"

I followed her there with a suitably hang-dog posture. "I forgot. I went with Jerry to speak to someone about the Iroquois murder and fell asleep when I finally got home." I fought the urge to look into the living room to see if Alice Hoffman, Ruth's late mother, might still be in her chair by the window. I mean alive, of course, not some kind of weird Norman Bates thing going on. Alice had died suddenly several years ago and her presence was still tangible in the house—or maybe it was just me. I'd never broached the subject to Ruth, and certainly not to Carolyn.

"Refresh my memory," I continued. "What's this all about?"

"Memory," came the reply. "How the Seaway and loss of the villages was commemorated fifty years ago and how we look at it today." Ruth put a cup of coffee on the table in front of me and set a paper beside it.

It was a thesis proposal, about seven pages long, addressing the "land expropriation and consequent relocation of people as a result of the St. Lawrence Seaway and Power Project of the 1950s." Unlike my recent publication about the cultural impact of the project, this study was focused specifically on how the affected communities preserved their memories and commemorated their losses, "incumbent upon a study of how these memories are reconciled within the framework of social change and modernization that characterized North America following World War II."

There was no name. "Who presented this?" I asked, flipping through to read the resources to be used. Ah, yes, there was my book.

"It's a group coming from UBC. The whole group wasn't there last night at our Lost Villages meeting, just the one woman. Her name was Farley. Jenn Farley. Real academic."

"That sounds negative. Should I be insulted?"

"No," Ruth laughed. "She's just very quiet and serious."

"Research is serious work, trust me. Not a lot of giggles for the most part." I looked through the proposal again. "She wanted interviews?"

"Oh, yes. That's all we seem to do. With the fiftieth coming up, it seems like everyone has suddenly remembered the Seaway."

"And it was pretty much forgotten for so many years."

Ruth sat down with her own cup. "She also wants to talk to you. Farley said your work was fundamental in the research, being so current and having a lot of overlap with their focus. Wondered if anyone could put her in touch with you." Ruth gave me a schoolteacher look—pretty good, coming from a retired secretary. "Seems they've written a couple of letters this spring, but no response. Did you get them?"

"Not that I remember," I said honestly. I was fighting another image—this time, the wild mass of papers and mail on my desk. Not as pretty as Bloom Boy. "But she already tracked me down. Dropped in early this morning to set up an interview."

"That's odd. I promised her I would give you her card. I didn't give her your address." Ruth set it down in front of me. "The cell phone number is on the back.

"Paul is coming home for the wedding," she added, giving me a sideways glance.

I felt for Ruth on many grounds. She had been my mother's best friend and then lost her suddenly in high school, spent decades believing that Leslie was dead (only to find she died just months before I popped up in the Seaway Valley with an agenda), loved me, too (and I was part of the reason for the car in the river, remember), had her long-lost son unmasked in the presence of friends (also me), and knew that Paul had feelings for me, while I had feelings for Jerry—whom Ruth also cared about (did I lose you yet?). And now Paul was coming back from the East Coast for the big day, with weddings traditionally being contagious.

"It will be good to see him," I said noncommittally, confining my sideways glance to my coffee.

The summer Paul Vaughn and I had done a tango with past secrets had ended with Alison's death. Although Paul's issues had had nothing to do with our digging into Alison's father's murder, the memories were irrevocably linked and so was the pain. This, I think, Ruth also understood.

"How are things going with the search for Haley?" Ruth gamely changed the subject. "I asked Lynn, but she said to talk to you. She's not sure how you're handling it."

"That makes two of us," I sighed. It was my turn to hand over some paperwork, the envelope with Haley's childhood photograph. I brought Ruth up to speed as she looked at my little girl.

When I was done, Ruth gently touched the face in the photo with her hand.

"She definitely looks like you, Fan," she said, "but there's also something . . . something there of your mother. Something in the expression that reminds me of Leslie."

"I hope she's like Mom inside, and not like me." The words came out unbidden, and Ruth looked up at me pensively.

"Why would you say that, Fan?" She reached over to cover my hand with hers. "You told me that you gave your daughter up for adoption for a lot of reasons. I've never asked, but I want you to know that there is nothing you can't tell me. I'll love you anyway."

Not trusting my voice, I kept my eyes on the table and put my hand over hers, giving it a squeeze.

"I know, Ruth," I whispered. "It's so weird. I'm going through the motions, and I understand what Lynn is doing, but it doesn't seem real. I'm trying to not think about what I will say to Haley, if she'll talk to me. I'm scared. Scared it may be too late to ever have a relationship. And she's in trouble . . ." I faltered to a stop.

"You said that last year."

You know how I said you don't have too many people in your life that you can casually tell about messages from your dead mother? Well, I have two. I told Ruth exactly what I had told Lynn earlier that morning; as with Lynn, Ruth didn't bat an eye.

"Then don't worry right now about how to get a relationship going," came the pragmatic reply. "If Leslie said Haley's in trouble, believe it. Find your little girl and help her. Maybe that's why you've finally found her after looking so long. It's time, and she needs you.

"And she does need you, Farran Mackenzie." Ruth gave my hand a return squeeze. "If you don't want to take my word for it, talk to Paul. Ask him how he felt about my finding him. She may not know what to do with you at first, but she does need you. You are her mother."

Mother. What a loaded word. I knew what it meant for me as a daughter, and how much I still missed my mother. But me as mother to someone? That would take time to settle in, if it ever did. I didn't feel I had a right to the label.

The old, nameless fear swept through me.

You lying bastard . . .

I jumped at the sound, and Ruth glanced around the kitchen. "What?"

"I have to go," I said, jumping to my feet.

Ruth gave me the fish eye, but said nothing as she rose to walk me out.

"Is the 'committee' meeting still on for tomorrow?" I now gamely changed the subject over my shoulder. "Wedding's coming up pretty fast."

"Don't remind me."

"Hey," I turned to face her in the doorway. After what I'd said to

Ruth in that very doorway my first summer here, I was still amazed that I had ever gotten to return. "No jitters, I hope. Ernie is a great guy."

"No," Ruth gave me a hug. "No jitters. Just feeling the pinch of time. I know I'm a lucky woman. As you could be," she finished with a directness Alice would have been proud of.

I flushed and turned to make my escape. A white car across the road that had been idling its motor slowly moved away, its driver hidden behind tinted windows.

Trouble . . .

"I don't mean to trouble you, Dr. Mackenzie."

I recognized the voice on the phone from the museum the day before.

"Mrs. Parmeter. No trouble. What can I do for you?"

"I'm glad to say it's what I can do for you. I promised I would try to dig up some names from the Seaway days for you, and one just arrived here at Carman House. Jeremy Pollan lives in Iroquois. He's retired and comes when he can to help maintain the house."

"He lived in Old Iroquois?"

"No, not technically, which is why I didn't think of him when you were here, Dr. Mackenzie. Jeremy wasn't born here. He came to work on the Seaway with the Americans and stayed. Took a job with the lock after the construction finished and worked there until retirement. He may know something or someone that could be helpful. But you'd better hurry," she added in a whisper. "He's a bit of a hermit. He comes and works and doesn't say much. If you want to ask any questions, you need to get him now, while he's in a social mood."

Jeremy Pollan was not in a social mood.

"Anything you can remember about those days would be helpful, Mr. Pollan."

"Too long ago," came the gruff reply.

I was usually very good at interviews, with all my years of practice in research. This time, I had my work cut out for me. Pollan was in his seventies, but seemed quite spry, with grey hair and a full beard. He clearly wasn't a talker, didn't like strangers, and was safely out of reach at the top of a ladder while he painted some of the facia around the house.

I stepped back to dodge some drops of white paint.

"I understand you came to Iroquois with the Seaway construction."

"Yep."

"Did you work with the house-moving?"

"Nope."

"Did you work on the new lock on the Point?"

"Yep."

Did I mention I am Scottish on my mother's side? Temper, temper, Farran.

"Sam Wallace worked on the Point in 1957," I fired back. "He was murdered and buried just south of here. Did you know him, Mr. Pollan?"

The paint brush stopped in mid-stroke. Then it was laid down, as Pollan turned to look at me for the first time.

"Murdered?"

"Yep." (Couldn't help myself.)

"He came back?"

"Nope." This was rather fun. But I wasn't there for fun. "He was murdered in 1957 and buried with the landfill that was being put all around the shoreline from the lock construction." Nasty, but I wanted to keep Pollan off his balance as long as I could. Something told me the window of opportunity on that wouldn't be open too long.

Pollan came slowly down the ladder and picked up a rag to wipe his hands. He said nothing for a minute, seeming to gather himself after hearing the news.

"He was just a kid," came at last.

"How well did you know him?"

"Not well. As well as you get to know anyone in something like that. Busy, busy time. Just follow orders and don't try to figure out where they're going with the plans. Guys would come and go. Some would get hurt and have to leave. A few died. No safety supervisors in those days. So that's why the police were there." He fell silent again, probably exhausted from the prolonged conversation. Finally, he added, "Nice kid, as I remember. Liked his drink, though. Are you sure it wasn't an accident?"

"No. He was shot." Something occurred to me. "Mr. Pollan, did a lot of guys have guns on them?'

He grunted. "Could have. Most of us had served in the war, or in Korea. Laws were different back then. A fella didn't always turn in his gun, or any souvenirs he might have had."

"Did you have one?" It popped out before I could bite my tongue. Too much time spent with a certain police officer.

"Nope." He glared at me, then turned back to the ladder.

Shit. Before his boot made the first rung, I fired again.

"What about Rick Potts? Did he have a gun?"

Pollan froze. His face turned red and he turned on me.

"Potts? Rick Potts? If he didn't, he should have." He started up the ladder.

"Why?" I asked his back.

"Half the men on the site wanted to kill him," Pollan said without turning to face me. "Going after all the women and borrowing money from everybody. Owed me, too. Disappeared and never paid up."

"How much did he owe you?"

"What difference does that make? If you're trying to pin a murder on me, officer . . ." He picked up the brush. I backed out of range again.

"I'm not a police officer," I explained to his boots. "I'm asking around for a . . . for . . . for Carl Wallace. He's here and he wants to know what happened to his brother."

Pollan stared into his paint can. I wasn't sure he heard me.

"Should've been Potts out there," he muttered, and began to paint.

I knew the conversation was over. I walked around to the front of Carman House and looked over to where the yellow tape still fluttered.

Should've been Potts out there.

From what I'd heard so far, I was inclined to agree with the man.

But it hadn't been Potts. It had been Sam Wallace.

Why?

SEVEN

THAT WHICH SURVIVES

"I have nothing to say." Jerry waved his hands in self defence. "I'm just a guy. I know nothing about weddings." Out of the corner of his eye, he saw Farran cover a smile with her hand.

"Well, you're helpful," Lynn shot at him.

"I'm not a wedding planner. I'm a cop."

They were gathered in Farran's living room in the cottage/house hybrid she now called home. The floor and table were covered with books of flowers and decorations.

"I just want something simple," Ruth explained. "This isn't my first time, after all."

"But it will be your last," Lynn pointed out. "So we shouldn't hold back, should we, Jerry?"

"Like I said, no comment." He looked at Farran. "I came to see how you did so far with our friend Wallace. Any luck stirring up ghosts?"

Farran shook her head. "He's having a hard time absorbing the fact that Sam is dead, and has been for fifty years. They had a falling out before Sam disappeared, and Carl feels guilty that he didn't try to patch things up."

Jerry looked for a chair to sit down on, then thought better of it.

"How much of a falling out?"

"Family squabble," she shrugged. "Sam was getting thick with a guy named Rick Potts from the States. Carl said he was a bad influence. Sam quit the Hartshorne team to work with Potts moving earth on Iroquois Point, and moved out of the boarding house where he stayed with Carl. Said he and Potts had things to do."

"What did that mean?"

"Carl doesn't know for sure. And he never spoke to Sam again. But Sam said something odd that night. He said . . ." Farran hesitated. "He said he was going to show everybody real soon, and take care of everything. Carl has no idea what he meant, except if . . ."

She stopped.

"Sounds like he and Potts were up to something," said Lynn, "something he had to keep secret from his brother. Maybe something illegal." She ripped a page out of a magazine and added it to a growing pile. Carolyn picked it up to look it over.

"Could be," Jerry agreed. "Except if what?"

Farran hesitated.

"Except if . . . well . . . the only thing Carl could think of was a wild scheme of Potts to look for some lost gold according to a family story. Heard Potts trying to rope Sam in one night to help him look for it."

"Lost gold?" Jerry's face took on an impassive look. Farran's eyes dropped to the floor.

"Spanish gold doubloons, actually, lost during the War of 1812."

He opened his mouth to say the obvious, but Ruth cut him off.

"Fenton's fool's gold? *That* old story?" Ruth looked up at Jerry. "I'm sure your folks told you that one, Jerry. Handed down in the UEL mythology."

"I'm not UEL, remember? Fill me in on Spanish gold in the Lost Villages," he added dryly. "I have to admit, that's a new one."

Between Ruth and Farran, Jerry got the idea.

"So why Spanish gold doubloons? And why would it make Fenton seem a fool? I would think gold would be a better bet than silver."

"It was," Farran said, standing up to stretch her legs, "after the gold standard was adopted by England in the early 1800s. But before that, silver was worth more than gold. In fact, its value was inflated to the point where silver was overvalued to gold fifteen-to-one, and the silver was worth more as a pure metal than in coin form. So if you had silver, those coins could be melted down for a profit, and they had a hard time keeping silver coins in circulation because people hoarded them for that purpose. But not gold. At least not at the time of the War of 1812."

"So why Spanish money?" Carolyn echoed Jerry. "Where would they get that amount of Spanish gold coins?"

"Easy," Farran replied. "I spent some time on the Internet last night catching up on my Upper Canadian history. Seems we've had a stable currency in this country for less than a century. We've always had the minerals, but didn't have the mines or the mints to make the coins. Our first Canadian coins were minted in 1908, under the name of the Ottawa Branch of the British Royal Mint. It became the Canadian Mint in 1931." Farran was in her professor mode.

"At the time of the War of 1812," she continued, "Upper Canada used British coin when it could, but that was always in short supply. Halifax made some currency, but again nowhere near enough to supply the two Canadas. The war cut off the coinage supply from the States. Some forms of paper money were being used, like army bills to pay the soldiers; but, overall, civilians didn't trust the companies that guaranteed them, so coins or 'real' money was the first choice. A lot of coins had come into circulation from the States and Mexico, the most popular being the Spanish silver dollar. The gold doubloon was available, too. It would have been absolutely possible that Fenton got two chests of Spanish gold doubloons."

"Okay," Jerry eyed the one empty chair across the room with longing. "I accept that fact that the lost gold story might have some truth to it. But a motive for murder? Why would Potts kill Sam Wallace over an old story of lost gold?"

"Maybe it wasn't just a story," Lynn pointed out. "Maybe they found the gold. The old fort that Fenton never finished was on the Point, remember? Maybe he buried the gold there, and the guys found it while pushing landfill around. That must be why both Potts and Wallace wanted to work on the Point."

"Seems quite a stretch. I'm thinking there must be some other, more commonplace reason."

"Pollan says everybody working at Iroquois had reason to kill Potts," Farran said.

"Pollan?"

"Jeremy Pollan. I spoke with him yesterday at Carman House. He worked on the site with Potts and Sam during the Seaway. He stayed and worked on the lock after that. He's retired. I got his address and phone number for you from Mrs. Parmeter." She passed him a card.

Jerry looked at the card. "Why did everyone want Potts dead?"

"Gambling debts and women. The usual." Farran smiled. "But it's not Potts you found. It was Sam Wallace. You've positively ID'ed him, right? No chance it was Potts by mistake?"

"No. We finally found the dental records. It's Wallace, all right."

"The only other problem Carl could think of was some local woman named Vivienne that Sam had been involved with. Didn't mention her last name. Said she was trouble, too."

"Vivienne Dupuis." He really wanted to sit down and take a load off after the long day on the road, but he didn't dare. Somebody would pin something floral on him, or worse. "Born in Montreal and living with an aunt in Iroquois at the time of the Seaway. She disappeared in 1957, but never surfaced elsewhere after that. At least not as far as we can pin down yet."

"Were you able to trace Potts?" Farran asked.

"To Massena. Seems he went back to his wife around the time Sam disappeared. We're following that up right now."

Ruth got up and began to pace. "We need to make a decision on the colour scheme today. Shannon can do wonders with floral arrangements, but she needs to know the colours to order anything."

"I think the secondary colour should be rose," Carolyn cut in, oblivious again to the other conversation. She held a swatch up. Ruth looked unconvinced.

"Why don't you ask the groom his opinion?" Jerry suggested. Four pairs of eyes fastened on him. "I'm gone," he added, and left.

"Still nothing on Vivienne Dupuis." Wiley put a folder on Strauss's desk. "Her aunt that she was living with in Iroquois died some years ago. Her family in Montreal lost contact with her while she was here. Never heard from her again."

Jerry leaned back in his chair. He'd opted for the one at work instead of one at home. "Seems to be a lot of people who disappeared forever. Nobody disappears forever. Not today, anyway. Okay, we have Sam. We still need to find Potts and the girl. Maybe they're together. What did Massena say?"

"Not much. According to Potts's brother-in-law, the guy showed up in early fall of '57 and moved back in with his wife. Two weeks later, he was gone, and they've never heard from him since. Potts's wife, Charlotte, apparently had a breakdown over it and has lived with her brother and his family ever since. Apparently, not all there anymore. Just keeps saying over and over that Potts went to the dam the night he disappeared for good."

"Where there any children?"

"No. Not with Charlotte, anyway."

Jerry thought for a minute.

"Time to start the real dig. We need to find anyone still left from the American crew, the Iroquois Construction crew, and the neighbourhood." He passed Farran's card to Wiley. "We can start with Jeremy Pollan, thanks to Farran. Do some follow-up there. But Vivienne's family is a dead end. Let's find the people who owned the diner, if they are still here. Anyone who worked there and got to know Vivienne. Things seem to keep wrapping around her."

"Nope. Didn't know her."

Pollan was totally on the defensive and totally unsociable. The OPP had bearded the lion in his den on Davis Drive, a home that obviously had belonged to a bachelor for years. It was totally devoid of personal touches, but was, Strauss had to admit, unusually clean for a non-female habitation. He thought of his own house, and wondered if Farran would ever consider—

"From what we know," Wiley countered, "Vivienne Dupuis made a name for herself with the men of the area. Liked the attention. She worked at the Daffodil diner. Did you ever eat there, Mr. Pollan?"

"Yep." Pollan crossed his arms to stonewall, but saw something in Strauss's eyes that made him abandon the usual tactics. "'Course I did," he grumbled. "Everyone did at one point. It was the last restaurant in the old town site, before everything was destroyed in '57. I remember Vivienne, and I remember keeping my distance. She was trouble, like Potts."

"You just said you didn't know her." Jerry brought himself back to the conversation.

"I didn't know her as a person," Pollan corrected himself. "I usually made sure I sat where Shelley would serve me. I just wanted to do my job and be left alone."

"Shelley?" Wiley was taking notes in a small notebook.

"The other waitress that worked there. She was younger than Vivienne. Still in high school, I think."

"Last name?"

"Piper. Her family lived somewhere around here at the time. Haven't set eyes on her in fifty years, so can't help you there."

"What do you remember about Sam and Carl Wallace?" Jerry got up to walk around the spare living room. No pictures, no family, no grandchildren. Not unlike himself. *I just wanted to do my job and be left alone.* That's what they'd put on Pollan's tombstone. Did he want the same? He fingered Farran's card in his pocket.

"Not much. Only knew Carl to see him. Seemed like a regular guy. Sam, I worked with some on the Point, driving Euchs and pushing landfill around."

"Euchs?" Wiley looked up from his notes.

"Euclid trucks. And 'dozers. The kid had learned to handle these with the Hartshornes, and he worked well on the Point. Seemed a nice enough kid. Too bad he hooked up with Potts, though. I had a feeling that's why I didn't see Sam with his brother too often at the end. Couldn't say as I'd blame Carl. Potts was a bad egg."

"You told Dr. Mackenzie that Potts owed you money. How much?"

Pollan looked up at Strauss. "About a hundred dollars. A lot of money in those days. But Potts owed everybody at the end, at least that's what I remember. Ask me who would have wanted to put a gun to his head, I'd give you a list."

"Except that it wasn't Potts's body out there, Mr. Pollan. It was Sam Wallace."

Pollan fell silent for a minute. "Sam was a nice kid," he said finally. "Didn't make enemies. Unless Potts turned on him for some reason. Carl." He looked at Strauss again. "Your friend Mackenzie said that Carl Wallace was here. Is that true?"

"Came to identify the remains and effects. He's staying until he can take Sam home for burial. Did you want to talk to him?"

"Nope." The curtness was coming back. "Just thought this must be hard for him. Having this all dug up again."

Literally, thought Strauss.

"Shelley Frost? Shelley Piper Frost?"

The woman wiping down the table in the Hartford Retirement Centre in Morrisburg looked up at the two officers. Older woman, slim, attractive, with salt-and-pepper hair.

"Piper?" she repeated, straightening up. "No one has called me by that name for more years than I care to remember."

The younger officer explained. "We got your name from a Jeremy Pollan. Said you used to work at the Daffodil diner during the Seaway years. Remembers you serving him. If you could take a short break from your work, we'd like to ask you some questions about those days."

She blinked, then twisted the cloth in her hands.

"I . . . I suppose I could. I don't really work here. Retired. Just volunteer. What's this about, officer?"

Wiley introduced himself and Strauss. Shelley motioned to a small table with chairs. They sat.

"We're trying to find a woman you used to work with. A Vivienne Dupuis."

"Vivienne? But . . ." The woman seemed flustered. "I remember Vivienne. You don't forget a girl like that. Woman, really, I guess. She was a few years older than me. Why?"

"Do you know where she went after she left the diner?"

"The Daffodil? No. No. She just up and left. They were just about to tear it down, so I had to take the shifts she had left. They weren't going to hire anyone to replace her. I was glad to have the money, I suppose, but still, it was a lot of work for one person."

"When did she leave? Can you remember?"

"Just around Labour Day weekend. I remember, because I was ready to go back to school, and then she left, so I stayed on at the diner for the money. Moved with them to the new town after. Quit and moved to Morrisburg with my husband when we married." She thought for a moment. "Vivienne had an aunt in Iroquois . . ." Piper offered.

"Deceased, I'm afraid."

"What's this all about, Sergeant?"

"We're looking into the murder of Sam Wallace," Strauss said bluntly. "Do you remember him, too?"

"Sam?" The woman started to rise, hand to mouth, then sat down again. "Sam?"

"Did you know him, Mrs. Frost?" Wiley prodded gently.

Shelley closed her mouth into a grim line. "Yes. Nice boy. Too nice for that woman. Was he the one you found near the river in Iroquois?"

When Strauss nodded, she looked down at her hands still clutching the cloth. He wondered where she was, but let her stay there for a minute.

"What can you tell us about the Wallace brothers, Mrs. Frost? Carl Wallace says they both frequented the diner while working in Iroquois."

She perked up at that. "Carl? Carl Wallace? Is he still alive? Is he here?"

"Yes. He had to come to claim the remains."

"Yes," she said softly. "How is he? Carl must be almost eighty by now. It must be quite a shock for him. We all thought Sam and Vivienne had run off together. They were both nice men. Came from good family, you could tell. Sam was a bit wilder than Carl. Liked his drink, unfortunately, and that's how he got involved with Vivienne. She liked to drink, too, and didn't expect to pay for it. She had her pick of the litter," Shelley added gravely. "She should have left him alone. Stayed with someone more her type. Like Rick Potts. Both bad apples."

"Tell us about Potts. Sam and Rick became buddies, didn't they?"

"Unfortunately, yes," she sighed. "It was hard to watch. Carl tried to keep his brother out of harm's way, but the shifts were long and everybody was everywhere. Sam . . . Sam was a good man. He just got caught up with the wrong people."

RESUME WORK ON LONG SAULT COFFERDAM
CEREMONIES MARK DIAL SERVICE
TO STILL LONG SAULT RAPIDS IN A FEW DAYS
MERCHANTS START MOVE TO BIG SHOPPING CENTRE

IROQUOIS (Staff) — This week and next are big moving weeks for local merchants here as they take over their new quarters in an ultra modern shopping centre.

Mel Bradden, rehabilitation information officer for Ontario Hydro which built the centre, said today most of the merchants will have their stores open for Easter.

Spring 1957
Cornwall Standard Freeholder

"They're going to start tearing up this place next," said Carl as Shelley poured his coffee one morning at the diner. *The sun was getting up early now and so were the men. Not that they ever really stopped the work. The diner was packed as usual.*

"Haven't they done that?" the girl replied. *"The houses all moved, the schools going down. Everybody north in the new town. Not much left to tear up, I'd say."*

Carl smiled sadly at her. "Well, can't leave anything standing 'cause of the Seaway. All of the main street has to go. Every building left comes down this summer."

Shelley looked at him, then turned to put the coffee pot back on the burner.

"Even the town hall," she said over her shoulder. *"That beautiful old place."*

"Old is right," Vivenne sashayed past Shelley with a sniff. *"Rickety old place. Have you seen the new mall, yet? Gonna look great, kiddo."*

"Not everything new is better," the girl retorted. *"My great-grandfather helped build — "*

"Hey!" The door swung open and two men burst into the diner. One came up to Carl and slapped him on the shoulder. *"Hey, brother of mine, I'd like you to meet a new friend, here, Rick Potts. Ricky, this is my big brother Carl."* Sam winked at the other man. *"Keeps a close eye on me, you know."*

The second man, thin with slicked brown hair and watchful eyes, kept his distance from Carl. He nodded and put his hands in his pockets.

"Where you from, Potts?" Carl asked as Shelley set a plate of bacon and eggs in front of him.

"Massena," came the short reply.

"He's with the Americans come here to put the lock in the Point," Sam added.

"Where were you last night, Sam?" Carl changed the subject. *"You never come in to sleep."*

Sam shrugged. "I've been showing Rick around. A regular history buff, y' know."

"History?" Vivienne stood behind the counter, looking the
stranger over with interest. "There's lots here, but not for long, thank
God. Hydro's givin' us a whole new village. Ricky," she added softly,
meeting his eyes on her with a smile.
A dark look passed over Sam's face.

"The wrong people—like Potts." Strauss completed her thought.
"Sam eventually left the Hartshornes to work with Potts on the Point.
Do you know why?"

Shelley opened her mouth, then closed it again. She looked at
her watch. "No. No, I don't know. I figured he switched for better
money. The Americans paid well, I guess. I have to get back to work.
Is there anything else, gentlemen?"

She rose to her feet, Strauss and Wiley following suit.

"Just one thing," Strauss said. "You said that Vivienne left just
after Labour Day weekend, and that everyone thought Sam and Vivienne had run off together. He left the same time, I take it?"

Shelley chewed her lip. "Yes. That's what everyone said. One day
they were there and the next they were gone."

"And Potts?"

This time she had to think. "Rick was gone for a bit around the
same time, but he came back once to the village."

"To the diner?"

"No. Thought I saw him one day in the old town, at a distance.
Sure it was him. I remember being surprised and then forgot about it,
'cause I never saw him again. Guess he just came back for something.
He was from Massena, I think."

"Why are we back here?" Wiley stood with Strauss on the old
No. 2 where the road ran into the water. Just beside fluttered remnants of yellow tape from the crime scene. "Forensics and crime
scene are both done."

Strauss shook his head.

"I've got a bad feeling in my gut, Wiley. There is too much just
plain *wrong* with this case. Chests of gold in Upper Canada as a
motive bothers me on its own merits. Potts was the bad apple by all
accounts, yet it is Sam Wallace left under the ground for fifty years. If
Potts killed Sam for some reason, wouldn't Vivienne have raised the

alarm? All three—Potts, Sam, and Vivienne—disappear fifty years ago and never resurface until Sam does now. Sam and Vivienne were supposed to have run off together, but we find Sam here. Where is Potts? Potts's brother-in-law says he came home alone and moved back in with his wife, so no Vivienne with him. But where did Vivienne go to, then, if not with Potts?" He turned his grey eyes on to the riverfront and the wide expanse of field beside it.

Wiley followed suit. "You're thinking, Inspector . . ."

"Just what you are, Jordan." The grey eyes came around to Wiley. "That Vivienne did leave the same time as Sam, and like Sam, she never really left. She's been here with him all along."

EIGHT

THE ENEMY WITHIN

To be honest, I was more than a bit rattled by Jenn Farley's brief visit. I'm not sure why. I thought at the time it was because I saw so much of my old self in her—the self I had been before that summer in Oxford that had changed everything. There was also something in her eyes, something familiar that stirred up memories. I didn't like it.

"Ethan . . ." Professor Debra Hyde looked past Farran to a man coming in the door to her office. "Ethan, good timing. I want you to meet my star pupil. This is Farran Mackenzie from Ontario, Canada. Farran, this is . . ."

"Dr. Chamberlain." The handsome man smiled into her eyes, doing something to her knees she hadn't felt since high school. He was at least ten years older, but the curly brown hair and magazine smile seemed more important. "Professor of history, specializing in North American native oral culture." He shook her hand. "Please call me Ethan."

"Ethan," Farran said, blushing and looking at the floor.

Debra Hyde had fallen silent . . .

No, I didn't like it.

I kept myself busy the next day running errands for Ruth, getting things caught up for the wedding. We had only a few weeks left before the big day, Paul would be coming in ten days for a couple of weeks, the little church at the Lost Villages Museum was booked as was the hall at St. Matt's, Shannon had the floral order. Was I missing something?

I had nothing to wear.

I put in an emergency call to Diana Wiley, daughter of Detective Sergeant and Michelle Wiley, a teenager I actually considered a friend. She was smart, resourceful, intuitive—and had almost gotten herself killed last month when she got caught in the crossfire of a murder at the Sterling House B&B in Ingleside. If it hadn't been for Jerry's timing and my memory, things could have turned out quite different for everyone that day, Diana included.

She had just come in from school at Rothwell-Osnabruck in the village and was free that evening. With her mother's blessing, I scooped her up and drove into Cornwall. Under Diana's direction, we hit a number of ladies' stores in the Cornwall Square shopping centre, finally hitting pay dirt at Cleo's. Then she found me a pair of matching shoes at Payless. I treated for supper at St. Hubert's on the traffic circle, as I knew we were both chicken hawks at heart.

"Gold doubloons?" Diana gawked at me over her virgin Margarita. Oh, to be fourteen again. "Here? You're kidding me, right?"

"Nope." I thought of Jeremy Pollan and something flitted through my brain.

"That's as exciting as the Paul Revere necklace you found. Can I help with this one?"

I struggled to chase after the thought that was just out of reach. No good.

"Help?" I looked at the menu. "Well, I can bring you up to speed on the missing gold. The murder is still . . . well, all mixed up."

"I'll help with both," she replied cheerfully with the enthusiasm of the young. "Not a word to anyone, even Dad. Let's start with the gold."

"Not a word," I said pointedly, "and no activity like last time. Your mother would have my head on a platter."

"Okay," Diana agreed reluctantly. "Sounding board only. Fire away."

I decided on the rib and chicken combo and closed the menu. Starting with the lack of coinage in Upper Canada in the early 1800s, I brought Diana up to speed on Spanish gold doubloons, the War of 1812, Fenton's fool's gold, and the possibility of its discovery during the Seaway construction—all before we placed our order with the waitress.

Menus gone, Diana sat back in thought. "So, according to the legend, the gold disappeared around the time Fenton was murdered."

I took a sip of my red wine. "War was going on. Anything could disappear. Looting was a major pastime. But people seem to think it never left the area—at least at that time."

Diana nodded. "If you were a looter, how would you smuggle that much gold past all the soldiers or your commanding officer? One big problem would be simply the weight. I went to the Canadian

Mint in Ottawa in Grade 8, and they have a gold bar there for you to try lifting. It weighs a ton."

"Potts's ancestor must have said the gold stayed put because, according to Carl Wallace, Rick Potts was looking for it. At least that's what he told Sam, Carl's brother. Got him 'wound up' about finding the gold one night and Carl overheard him."

"What did he say, specifically?"

I shook my head. "I didn't push for details at the time. It seemed a wild story—still does, somehow—and the man was trying to piece together his memories about his brother. A brother he had just lost all over again."

"Well, that's first on the list, unless you think it's a wild goose chase."

"Problem is, Diana, right now it's the only goose we have. Except for Sam Wallace's remains, we have almost nothing to work with. It's funny." The creamy coleslaw appeared, and I let Diana divide it between us—a major gesture of trust on my part. "The other deaths from the past I've gotten involved in here have been from the Lost Villages, villages that were entirely eradicated and flooded out. Iroquois was moved one mile north of its original location, but most of the village was saved. Just the big buildings that couldn't be moved were destroyed. And most of the land is still above water. Yet this time I feel really up against it. Maybe it's the old story of the gold. That's almost two hundred years ago. I don't know. I just don't know how or if I can sort this out. And I want to," I tackled the wine again, "for Carl's sake. Can't imagine having something like this come at you at his age."

"But you're a professor of history," Diana reminded me. "This is what you do. Find out about the gold first, if that's the only goose you have. Find more people who remember Sam. I'm sure Dad and Uncle Jerry are on that. Then do what you told me once. Remove the impossible. Whatever is left, however improbable, must be true."

My old friend Leah Shadbourne had warned me once to watch what I said to my children, if I became a parent. Just when you think they weren't listening, she'd said, the words will come back to haunt you. You were right, Shad, I thought. I'll have to tell you next time I see you. Except this wasn't my child. This was a young friend . . . "borrowed" child, if you will. My real child, my little girl, was still out there somewhere and, for over a quarter century, I had success-fully avoided being her parent.

"Anything at all?" I was lying on my couch full of ribs and wine, new dress and shoes in bags in my bedroom.

"Nothing." Lynn was her usual self, straight to the point even though the subject was touchy. It was one of the things I valued in her. "I'm getting frustrated. I have to step carefully, but still. It's as though thirty days ago Stephanie Harrison vanished off the face of the earth."

I sat up, worried. "Is she missing? There's already been one attempt on her life, or so we think."

"Not as far as I can gather. It's still business as usual, and no one seems to be worried about anything. Nothing on the wire at least. Too quiet, though," she added carefully.

"Do you think something's happened and they're keeping it under wraps?" I didn't want to explore the thought that I might have waited too long to find Haley. But it hung in my emotional airspace just the same.

"It's possible," Lynn admitted. "But I don't feel any bad energy around. I know that's not very factual, but I've smelled my share of rats over the years and, so far, nothing here. She's just gone off the radar."

"Gone into hiding?" I suggested.

"Again, possible. You helped Alison do the same thing last year when she—"

Her voice broke off. Yes . . . yes, when she . . .

And then I was face down in the grass, feet torn out from under me, a terrible roar in my head. Confused, I sat up and looked around.

Confusion became horror.

The front of Alison's car was a fireball, windows blown out, driver's door hanging open. I spotted her lying motionless on the gravel road a few yards away, eyes closed. There was blood on her face.

"Alison!" I screamed. Somehow I got to my feet and stumbled toward her. It was a nightmare and my legs wouldn't run. "Help me! Please, somebody help me!" I called out uselessly. The cemetery was deserted.

I reached Alison and rolled her over. One hand clutched her chest and there was a terrible gash across her forehead, but she was alive. I held her and looked around, panic washing over me.

Dave.

He'd been getting in the car.

"Alison. Al." I shook her. "Wake up!" I shrieked in a voice that wasn't mine. "Where's Dave? Where is he?"

Her eyes flew open. She looked at me dully, tried to sit up and then saw the car. She started to scream.

"The car! The car! Get him out!" Alison made it to her knees, arm still wrapped around her chest. "Fan! Get him out!"

I followed her eyes in horror to where the car burned, flames shooting out from underneath the chassis.

The gas tank.

My mind gave orders and my body grabbed Alison, hauling her across the road. I threw her behind the nearest tombstone and fell on my knees beside her in the grass. Seconds later, hell opened. A blast of heat roared over us, its infernal fingers reaching . . . reaching.

I remember kneeling, screaming, hiding, praying.

Then voices, yelling, hands, sirens.

I remember terror turning to rage.

Now it was my war.

We both let it drop.

I called Carl Wallace the next morning at Sterling House B&B in Ingleside. Mildred Keeps, owner of the historic home, answered and told me Carl had left after breakfast.

"Said he was driving up to Iroquois. Going to Carman House for a look-see."

I headed that way myself after leaving a message for Jerry at the detachment. Both he and Wiley were out, and I wanted to know if he'd dug up anyone new to talk to. Hopefully, not literally.

Carman House was quiet when I arrived. There was a car with rental plates in the little parking lot and another vehicle just pulling out.

"Carl Wallace? Tall man, American accent?" I pointed to the rental car through the doorway. "I think that's his car right there."

"He was here," said Mrs. Parmeter, "but he must have left while I was talking to the couple from Balderson. They've left, too, I think."

"But his car is still here."

"Maybe he went over there to talk to the environmental people." Parmeter nodded toward a grey van with a group of people standing around near the river's edge, beside where the yellow tape still hung in. I looked, but saw no one with Carl's build.

"I'll just take a quick run-though the house, just in case," I said, then stopped myself to add, "Uh . . . any chance Jeremy Pollan will be in today?"

"Well," said Mrs. Parmeter with a shrug, "he *did* say yesterday that he would be in again this morning to take advantage of the sunny day for painting. Lord knows we haven't had much sun yet this summer. But I haven't seen him yet."

I walked through the few rooms quickly, passing an open door under the staircase that hadn't been open on my last visit. I saw desks and filing cabinets. An office. Off limits. No one in the kitchen. I wandered out the back door, around the back of the kitchen, and up the east side of the house.

The grey van had been joined by an OPP car and the group by two officers. Still no one at that distance resembled Carl Wallace, yet his car remained in the museum parking lot.

A little finger of worry began to poke me in the stomach.

Having no better option, I made my way across the field to the gathering. Coming up, I saw Wiley and another officer, Margaret Taylor, talking with a young blonde woman away from the others. Another officer was shepherding the rest of the Water People back behind a barricade going up: a young lady with red hair, two young men, and an older couple in Tilley hats and sunglasses. Fear poked me again. What, Farran? I wondered. Perimenopausal anxiety? I walked up to Wiley and waited. He finished with the blonde, turned, and saw me.

"Morning, Farran. What brings you here?"

The blonde stopped and turned back for a moment, as though she had remembered something. We locked eyes for a minute and I waited politely, but she changed her mind and joined her compatriots by the old road.

"I'm looking for Carl Wallace. Mildred Keeps said he came out here and his car is in the museum parking lot, but I have yet to lay eyes on him."

Wiley looked around and shook his head. "Haven't seen him walking around. Margaret?"

The female officer shook her head, too.

"So what brings *you* out here, Jordan? Great day for boating, but you're in uniform."

Wiley grinned. "Can't say a word officially, yet, Dr. Mackenzie, but you could call the boss and ask him. He might be in a more generous mood."

"Thanks," I said tartly, but left it. Protocol. "Are these the environmentalists?" I whispered, cocking a head slightly in their direction. Then I slowly rolled my eyes that way, only to meet the steady gaze of the blonde and redhead. If I hadn't known better, I would have said they were talking about me. Paranoia is one of my specialties.

"Yes. And they're not happy with us right now. We're blocking their access to the riverfront again."

"Why? I thought you were all done here last week?"

A man in grey overalls with POLICE on the back came up to Wiley.

"How far out, sir?"

"Let's start with ten metres in all directions." The man went back to the van.

"You have a nice day, now, Dr. Mackenzie." Wiley allowed himself half a smile.

I allowed him half a glare and headed off toward the museum. Carl's car was still there, and it still bothered me. Ignoring the feeling, I drove up to the viewing area of the international lock in case Carl had decided to walk up there. It was, after all, a nice day.

The viewing area and open park are adjacent to a cemetery that predated the Seaway. Some of the graves were quite old. Maybe a visit to check out the names would be in order. But not today. No sign of Carl anywhere around. With great personal control, I passed up an ice cream at the gift shop and drove back down to Carman House. Still the car. Still no Carl.

But the squad car and grey van were still there, as was a new and much larger ring of yellow tape.

I flipped open my cell phone and punched in Jerry's private number.

"Strauss here."

"What's with the new stakeout at the Point? Something you need to tell me?"

"Technically, no." Ah, the Bear was in a humorous mood.

"But you're going to tell me anyway, right? Seeing as I've been good enough to start chasing ghosts again on your behalf."

There was a calculated silence.

"Okay," came finally, "but there's nothing to tell—yet. And there might not be, if I'm wrong."

"I can't believe I'm going to say this to a man, but you're rarely wrong. So what's up?"

I almost heard the smile. "I should have that on tape for later. Anyway, we're back because I want to make sure that we didn't miss something . . . or someone."

"You think there might be someone else buried out here?"

"It's possible," he said, echoing Lynn.

"Who? Dupuis or Potts?"

"Either, or both. I have a problem with people who disappear forever. So," he altered course, "why are *you* back? Got some ideas?"

"Actually, no. I chased Carl Wallace up here to get more details about the lost gold."

"I'm not sold on that story being worth anything, let alone murder, but I guess we can't rule it out just yet. What did he say?"

"Nothing. I found his car, but I haven't found Carl. I'm actually getting wor—"

As if on cue, I suddenly heard yelling inside the museum.

"Something's wrong. Gotta go." I slapped the phone shut and ran up the front steps. Mrs. Parmeter came rushing at me out of the dining room.

"I think he's dead. I think he's dead," she babbled.

I grabbed her and held her still.

"Who?"

"That man that came this morning. The one you were looking for."

The finger of worry turned into a fist and headed for my stomach again.

"Where?"

"He's all bloody." She covered her face with her hands.

I shook her. "*Where?*"

Mrs. Parmeter blinked and then pointed in the direction of the dining room. "In the basement. Through that door."

I headed for the door underneath the stairs that I had noticed open earlier that morning. Barrelling through to the office, I looked around helplessly. Just a small room with a closed connecting door to the front parlour. Starting back towards Mrs. Parmeter, I noticed a small, dark stairway that ran downwards underneath the staircase to the second floor. I found the light switch and turned it on.

There was a huddled form at the bottom of the stairs. I gingerly made my way down and reached out to touch his face. It was Carl Wallace. He was breathing, but there was blood on his shirt. Rolling the elderly man over carefully, I drew in my breath sharply. There was a small handle protruding from his stomach, blood stains on the floor. I felt dizzy for a moment.

"Is he dead?"

The voice at the top of the stairs snapped me back.

"He's alive," I looked up at Mrs. Parmeter, "but he's badly hurt. Call 911. Then get over to the police across the field. Tell them we need help right away."

She disappeared. I cradled Carl's head on my lap, trying not to relive a similar moment I had worked hard to forget for several years now.

Making my way around to the side door, I found the knob and turned it. As the door gave way, it registered briefly on me that the knob had something sticky on it.

I was in the kitchen. I could hear the clock on the wall and see the tiny digital glow of the microwave.

"Carl?" I called softly. "Can you hear me?"

"*Gordon?*" *I called softly, doing what I'd told many TV characters they were idiots for doing—from the safety of my couch.* "*Are you . . .*"

My foot hit something soft. I didn't want to look down. I really, really did not want to look down. But I pointed the beam of light at the floor.

"Carl? It's Farran. You're going to be okay." I stroked his face, fighting the rising panic.

My uncle lay sprawled face downward on the ceramic floor, eyes closed. There was something dark on his head and neck, and beside him on the floor.

Trying to swallow my panic, I reached my hand out toward him and the flashlight picked up what I'd touched on the doorknob coming in.

Blood.

Carl's eyes fluttered open for a moment. He didn't seem to know I was there.

"Potts . . . Potts . . ." The words were so soft I had to lean over to hear. "Potts . . . you came back.

"You came back . . ."

Then Carl Wallace slumped and was still.

NINE

ERRAND OF MERCY

Ruth opened her back door to see Jerry Strauss standing in the yard, just out of range of the back porch light.

"Jerry," she smiled. "Don't just stand there. Come and have tea. I have some cake left from dessert tonight."

"I wish I could," he answered sincerely, "but this isn't a social call. Ruth, can you turn out the light?"

She looked puzzled, but did as she was asked. This was not a man who played games. Then she quietly came out on the back porch. He moved up to the railing.

"I need you to do me a favour, Ruth."

"Anything, Jerry."

"I need you to call Paul Vaughn and ask him to come home. Right away."

"But he is coming home in two weeks for the wedding."

"It can't wait. He needs to come home right now." He hesitated. "We've got trouble, Ruth. Farran's in trouble. Maybe big trouble. I can only stall so long, and I can't help her. Can't touch it with a ten-foot pole. I need Paul's help." He smiled grimly in the night air. "Tell him I said so. If my admitting that doesn't bring him home on the first red-eye flight, nothing will."

Ruth came down the steps to put a hand on Jerry's arm.

"You're scaring me, Jerry. What's wrong? What's happened?" When he only shook his head, she added, "Where is Farran? I haven't heard from her in a day or two, come to think of it."

"She's in the States, staying with that professor friend of hers. Shadbourne. And doing some more groundwork on the Wallace case."

"That poor man. Is he still . . . ?"

"Still hasn't come around, but he's stable. Farran would be still be there waiting for him, but I kicked her out and left a twenty-four-hour watch in place. I thought it best if she wasn't around for a few days."

Ruth nodded. "Good for her to get away. That was a bad moment for her."

"She's just gone for the weekend, Ruth. Then she's back here with the danger, and I can't protect her. Do whatever you have to, but get Paul here. Just tell him to get here, stick close to Farran, and be his usual diplomatic self." Jerry couldn't believe he was asking Paul Vaughn to stay close to Farran Mackenzie. But tough times mean tough decisions.

"I'll call him right now. Jerry . . . is Fan . . . ?"

It was his turn to put out a hand. "We'll take care of our girl, Ruth." He let out a deep breath. "Somehow. But I'm in a bad place with this. I need Vaughn to run interference." He squeezed her shoulder and turned to go.

"Not to worry, Ruth. Everything will be all right. It has to be. But," he added, stopping for a moment, "remember. As far as you and Paul Vaughn are concerned, this conversation never happened."

Then Ruth was alone in the dark.

TEN

DAGGER OF THE MIND

"It must have been awful." The hand the voice belonged to held a glass of brandy on ice. I accepted it gratefully.

I was doing something I did for several years back in my undergrad days — sit up late in my pyjamas and figure out life with brandy and Leah Shadbourne. We were sitting in the living room of her weekend retreat. Leah, or Shad as I still call her from the old days, is a professor at St. Lawrence University in Canton, New York. The retreat is an old farmhouse just southwest of Waddington that she has been fixing up for the past few years.

"It was." I took a stiff one, not quite as stiff as the one I'd had that night when I got home from the hospital — but close. Carl's bloody face with his glazed eyes came to me unbidden. "The poor man. He comes all this way from New Jersey to confirm it was his brother that was murdered so long ago and now he's attacked."

Wiley had arrived with Mrs. Parmeter before the paramedics. I had stayed with her while they brought Carl up from the basement. At one point, I was afraid the woman would need the medical aid almost as much as Carl. She was as white as a sheet and shaking. I took her into the kitchen to sit down, away from the sight of the gurney.

Wiley joined us shortly after.

"Can you tell us what happened, Mrs . . ."

"Parmeter," I supplied. I looked around for water, but with no success. It hadn't been a working kitchen in several decades. "Jordan, I think Mrs. Parmeter could use a drink of water." Actually, something stronger would have been the better choice, but I had even less hope for that. "Maybe in the office?"

"Crime scene," he answered briefly. "But the paramedics will check you out just as soon as they have Mr. Wallace on the way to the hospital, Mrs. Parmeter."

The woman looked white again and rubbed her hands together. I put my hand over them and gave them a squeeze. There was a question on the tip of my tongue.

"Mrs. Parmeter . . ."

"I have water."

The voice had come from the outside door behind Wiley. We all looked to see two of the Water People standing there. The blonde and the redhead. It was the blonde who had spoken. She held out a high-tech water bottle. Wiley glanced at Parmeter, then reached through the door. He handed it to me before heading outside to shepherd the ladies carefully back off the property. I heard him quizzing them while I found a cup for the drink of water. I also kept an ear bent toward the dining room.

"Who all came here today besides Carl Wallace?"

She shot the water back like Old Red Eye. We could hear the voices coming up from the basement.

"Just me, Mr. Wallace, and a young couple after him." She kept her eyes down, averted from the dining room door. "It's been a quiet day."

At that point, I had heard the gurney reach the main floor and went out to see Carl, white and still with blood on his face, strapped down and heading for the ambulance. I followed the gurney out to the ambulance.

"Taking him to Winchester Memorial," the one paramedic said briefly to Constable Taylor. She nodded and said something into a cell phone.

"I'm going to follow you," I said. "He's got no one here."

I went back into Carman House, through to the kitchen to tell Wiley that I was going. Poor Mrs. Parmeter still sat at the table.

"Are you going to be all right?" I asked her. "Is there someone I can call?"

She nodded, so I gave her hand a squeeze and headed out the kitchen door. Skirting Pollan's ladder and paint, I made it into my car. I looked through the front windshield and saw the new, larger area of yellow tape down by the river surrounded by various vehicles. A tent was going up again. The ambulance and I were waved past the barricades already set up, the yellow tape crew now hard at work shutting down Carman House.

Mrs. Parmeter said it had been a quiet day. Well, the place was crawling with people now. And at the rate we were going on this, I thought to myself, pretty soon we'd have the whole of Iroquois wrapped in yellow tape.

"Do they know what happened?" Shad asked me.

"Not yet," I admitted. "He was still unconscious when I left him at the hospital. Jerry posted a guard. Carl may have fallen, or he may have been pushed." I swirled the ice cubes in my glass (yes, I know, but it kills the taste), but they were no help.

"Didn't you say he was stabbed?" Shad sat on the floor, back against the couch, brandy with no ice. Her long legs were splayed out under the coffee table, her red hair with the first streaks of grey caught up in a Katherine Hepburn bun.

"Yes, but there were tools hanging along the wall. He could have grabbed one when he fell and fallen on it."

Shad shivered. "He's lucky to be alive."

"Yes. If Mrs. Parmeter hadn't found him when she did, she might have locked up and left him there all night. He would have died . . ." I trailed off.

"What?"

I shrugged. "I don't know. Something's weird about it . . . maybe . . . maybe I'm thinking of what he said to me."

"I thought he was unconscious when you found him."

"He was, but he opened his eyes for just a moment when I was waiting for the paramedics. I'd . . . I'd forgotten with all the upset."

"What did he say? Was it important?"

"I don't know. It didn't make sense at the time. I think he was delirious." I took another sip and let the cold ice blend with the burn of the brandy. "He thought I was Potts."

Shad giggled. "That's not delirious. You've been pots for years."

"You're a riot, Alice." I stuck my tongue out at her. "Not pots, *Potts*. Rick Potts, the weasely guy who worked with Carl's brother during the Seaway."

"Ah, the vanished husband of the batty lady you're going to see tomorrow. He thought you were that guy?"

I opened my mouth to defend Charlotte Potts, but let it go. From what Jerry had said, she *was* batty. Or pots, if you like. There are a lot of us around.

"He called me Potts and said—twice—that I'd come back."

"But Potts disappeared fifty years ago, just like Wallace's brother," Shad tried to keep up.

I nodded.

"Could he be alive and maybe returned to the area because they found those remains and he's spooked?"

I rolled that around my brain while I did the same with another sip of brandy in my mouth.

"Possible," I admitted. I was beginning to resent the word. *Remove the impossible*, Diana had reminded me. *Whatever is left, however improbable, must be true.* "The OPP is having a second look at the area where they found Sam. I'll do my best to pin that down tomorrow from this end."

"So your interview is tomorrow afternoon—"

"After I hit the Massena library to look at the old newspapers."

"Fine. Then we meet for supper in Waddington at Chris Fay's. Do you remember where it is?"

I hadn't been there in several years, but Waddington's Main Street just wasn't that big, north of the lights on Route 37, since they took part of her front with the flooding similar to Morrisburg on my side of the St. Lawrence.

"I'll find it."

"Speaking of finding," Shad got up to stretch her legs, "what's happening with Haley? You said you know who she is now. Have you made contact, yet?"

"No. Lynn's still looking for her, and she'll let me know when she has something solid."

"So all you can do right now is wait?"

The question irritated me, but it basically stated the truth.

"Yes," I said reluctantly. "First we have to find her, and she's gone off the radar right now for some reason. She's not actually missing or anything, but she's not around, either. Then I have to find a way past all the guard dogs to contact her directly. This isn't something I want to put in a letter that some secretary might read first."

"How long are you willing to wait?" Shad asked softly.

"As long as it takes." I punctuated my statement with the last of my brandy and passed the glass over for a refill. It was only my first, but the fatigue of the past week gave it the power of a third or fourth. Already I could feel the warmth spreading through me. I sighed. "She's waited for me for over twenty-six years. It's the least I can do."

"I thought you said she was in trouble." Shad passed the refilled glass back to me and sat down again. "If she is, then time is of the essence."

Trouble. *Trouble* . . . I was beginning to hate that word, too.

"Lynn is doing her best. It's a sticky situation."

"What about a private detective? I know one who is very good . . ."

"No. No." I shook my head emphatically. "Like I said, it's a sticky situation."

I fell silent and Shad did, too.

"Mack," Shad now used my name from the old days. "This is connected to that time in Oxford, isn't it?" When I didn't reply, she added, "Mack, are you ever going to tell me what the hell happened over there?"

"I don't know. I really don't. I'm not even sure I know myself."

It was a pitiful answer, and we both knew it. Thankfully, I was saved by the bell.

My cell phone rang.

"Hi, Ruth," I said, recognizing the number on my call display.

"Fan," she began.

"I'm in the States for the weekend, staying with a friend in Waddington."

"I know. Jer—umm. Listen, Fan. I have some news. Carl Wallace woke up this afternoon."

I sat up. "He did? How is he?"

"Weak, I guess, from the fall and the surgery. Jerry called to tell me. Said to let you know that Carl doesn't remember anything, other than arriving at the museum that morning."

Jerry called Ruth to tell her? Why not call me directly? I thought irritably.

"Nothing? Well, that may change once he feels better." I thought of Carl's words. *Potts . . . Potts . . . You came back . . . You came back.* The hair on my arms stood up and I shivered. What if the ghost of Rick Potts—

"Yes. Fan, when are you coming home? Sunday night?"

"Ruth, is everything all right? You sound funny."

"Yes . . . yes. Everything is fine. Call me when you get in?"

I agreed and shut the phone. Everything was not fine. I knew

Ruth well enough to hear the stress in her voice. Maybe it was just the approaching nuptials, but my stomach was telling me otherwise.

"Hey, Shad." I got up and followed her into the kitchen where she'd gone to give me some privacy. "What do you have for snacks?"

The town of Massena, New York, owes its name to the popularity of Emperor Napoleon's greatest general, André Massena. Appropriately, the first colonial settlers appeared in the late 1700s when the American army offered 200 acres of St. Lawrence River Valley land to anyone who enlisted. About a century later, almost as a harbinger of things to come, the St. Lawrence Power Company built a canal from the great river to the smaller Grasse River to bypass the Longue Sault Rapids, adding the area's first powerhouse to the new waterway.

Like its Canadian cousin across the river, Cornwall, Massena then used its access to cheap hydro power to grow an economy based on manufacturing, and soon outpaced its neighbouring agriculture-based communities. Unlike Cornwall, the town still has a substantial production economy and its own small international airport.

Also like Cornwall, Massena became a boom town during the Seaway years. Collectively, the Power Project hosted over 22,000 transient workers and Massena swelled with the migrants and their families. As Cornwall did, the town struggled to accommodate its new "settlers," who mostly had to stay in the work camps outside the town. Then they disappeared when the work did four years later. Massena now hosts a population of about 13,000 residents.

I ended up that afternoon at a small frame house tucked away on Pleasant Street. The name NEEDHAM was emblazoned on a floral plaque beside the front door, along with the house number. I rang the doorbell underneath it.

"Charles Needham?"

The older man in a golf shirt and slacks who answered my ring reminded me of a bit of Carl, with his tall, straight build. He was a bit younger, though—and not as friendly.

"Yah?"

"My name is Farran Mackenzie. I'm here to see your sister, Charlotte Potts."

"Why?"

Sensing another monosyllabic exchange coming my way (although one couldn't blame him), I cut to the chase.

"Sam Wallace, a man Charlotte's husband Rick once knew well, was found last week. Murdered fifty years ago."

"We know."

"His brother Carl came up to claim the remains. I'm here on his behalf. I'm sure you can understand the shock he's dealing with. Please," I added, "just a few questions."

"Charlotte ain't been herself since the day Ricky left. Don't know why. He was no good to start with. You won't get much help from her. She may be not'n to it today."

When I didn't move from the step, Needham shrugged and held the inner door open. I followed him into a large foyer that led into a front room, dining room, and stairs to the upper floor. He gestured to the living room.

"Have a seat. I'll get Charlotte."

Needham was gone for several minutes. I passed the time looking at framed photographs on the wall and on the side tables. Lots of children and grandchildren. One picture of a young Needham standing with a girl who looked very much like him. Charlotte?

I could hear voices down the hall in warm discussion. Evidently, Charlotte was not in to visitors at the moment. I strolled over to the doorway to try to listen when the voices grew louder, then scuttled back into the room and was sitting innocently on the couch when they entered.

"But why, Charley?" the woman was asking, rather childlike. And childlike, she stayed standing a bit behind him when he introduced us.

"Mrs. Ma—"

"Mackenzie." I stood up.

"Mrs. Mackenzie, this is my sister Charlotte Potts. Charlotte, say hi to Mrs. Mackenzie."

The woman, who looked just like Charley but with a tight bun at the back of her head, reluctantly took my offered hand and shook it. I should say, flapped it. Her hand was like a dead fish, and just as cold.

Charlotte Potts looked very much like her brother, except the grey hair was long and loosely caught up in a bun at the back of her head. She wore a floral shift dress that could have come from the Seaway days and just might have. The eyes were the greatest difference. Whereas Charles's eyes were watchful, his sister's were empty.

We all sat down. Charlotte sat with her brother, holding his hand. They looked like a set of salt and pepper shakers. Half of me wanted to talk to her alone, the other half wanted to leave. This was getting creepy.

"Charlotte, Mrs. Mackenzie has some questions for you about Ricky." She turned a worried face to her brother, who continued in a calming tone. "She's not here about Ricky, really. She wants to know as much as she can about one of Ricky's friends."

I had the feeling I was in a play, a well-rehearsed one. Unless I got the siblings away from each other, I wasn't going to get anything that the police hadn't already.

"Long time ago," Charlotte murmured and looked at the floor.

"This is very painful for her," Charley said.

"Charley and Charlotte?" I smiled.

"Twins," Charlotte told the carpet.

"Charlotte," I moved in carefully, "how long were you married to Rick Potts?"

"They married right out of high school," said Charley. "Ricky never really held a job. Worked at this and at that. Charlotte worked as a waitress. Kept the bills paid."

"Yes." Charlotte kept her eyes on the carpet. They were working up to a real conversation. I wondered for a second if they did that very often.

"Then he took work on the Seaway," I said.

"He went'n to the dam," Charlotte whispered. The carpet made no reply.

"She means the night he left," Charley took over again. "Ricky'd left for work on the Canadian side with an American firm doing work around Iroquois. Just up and left. I was hoping it was for good. He left in the spring of '57 and came back in the fall. Also just like that. Two weeks later, he was gone."

"Was he working on the dam, Charlotte?" I gave it another college try to pry her open.

"Went'n to it," she nodded.

"He got work around the main dam when he came back. There was still lots of work to be done, so that wasn't a problem. Still cement and masonry. Still needed drivers for big machines. He went to work one night and just never came back. Just like before; except this time, it was for good. Haven't seen him in fifty years. Sorry, Charlotte, but good riddance. You know how I've felt about that."

Charley fell silent. I veered away for a moment.

"Your family, Mr. Needham?" I waved at the pictures.

He smiled unexpectedly.

"Yes. My children and grandchildren. And my wife, Beverly." The smile left. "She died a few years ago."

"I'm sorry. You have a lovely family. Are any of them yours, Charlotte?" I already knew the answer, but thought it might add something to the carpet conversation.

Charlotte finally looked at me. "Sarah," she said simply.

"You have a daughter, Sarah?"

A single tear appeared and began to roll down her cheek. I suddenly felt like a troll.

"I'm sorry, Charlotte. I didn't mean to upset you."

"Miscarriage, Mrs. Mackenzie." Charley rose to his feet, with his sister following suit. "If you don't have any more questions for my sister, it's time for her nap. And mine, to be honest. We're both getting up there."

Naps are sacred, so I shook the dead fish and the brother's hand and left. I was in the car before I realized I hadn't asked about the gold story. Might have to drop by again tomorrow on the way to the bridge. Before I drove away, I placed a call to Jerry's cell. No answer, so I left a message. Pulling away from the curb, I took a last glance at the house. An upper window framed Charlotte's face before the curtain fell back to cut it off.

Bats. Pots. I found my way back to Route 37 and headed west to Waddington. Potty Potts. Charlotte Potts was bats, poor soul. What about twin brother Charley? They were both afraid of something, but what? I shook my head, convinced I'd never have the answer to that one.

At that point, I was about two hours away from understanding that I already did.

The meal had been, as usual, fabulous. It was Saturday night in Waddington, and Chris Fay's was packed—also as usual. Shad, who loved to pull strings, had pulled a few to get us this table. Saturday nights were too often booked up in advance.

Waddington is a small village of about 900 people, west of Massena on the river at the junction of Routes 37 and 345. The Seaway construction took not only its riverfront, but the river-based economy that had gone along with it. The village had also suffered losses of farms and some historic buildings for the flooding, only to have those lands remain above water. It is still charming, with many old storefronts on the main street and a small public dock for boaters from both sides of the river. Although quiet in the winter, Waddington now comes alive in the summer with a different type of river economy.

Three of us were lingering over coffee. David Trent, a good-looking man in his mid-forties, had joined us for the evening. He was a friend of Shad's, a specialist in St. Lawrence history—particularly the War of 1812. I was listening, but also trying to absorb the myriad antiques crammed into the little dining room.

"Well, that's one thing I don't understand," I broke into the update on the preparations for the bicentennial. "We say we won that war and you say that it was an American victory."

"It's complicated," Trent grinned. "Depends on which side of the history books you're looking from. Like so many other events, right?"

"We did send you packing from the St. Lawrence," I smiled back.

"We burnt your Parliament buildings in York."

"And we burnt your White House."

"Okay, okay. Time out." Shad picked up the wine bottle and refilled everyone's glass. "We don't need another continental scrap." She picked up her glass. "Here's to peace for almost 200 years."

"I'll drink to that." I raised my glass and Trent followed suit.

"*Status quo ante bellum*," he quoted, adding, "now, down to business."

"Business?" I echoed.

"Leah told me about the gold story. Asked if I could dig around a bit before tonight, see what I could find."

"Oh." I set my glass down, flashed a smile at Shad, and looked at Trent. "What did you find?"

"Absolutely nothing, I'm afraid. No mention anywhere, either in fact or rumour, that any sizable amount of gold coin or bullion was brought over here during the late fall or early winter of 1813–14. I looked in particular at Louisville Landing, the riverside hamlet we lost on this side to the Seaway."

"Why?" I asked.

"Because during the War of 1812, the people of the area weren't interested in fighting with their friends and neighbours across the river. They put together a small volunteer company of men for protection, but communication across the river continued quietly until peace was declared. I thought maybe something would have come across to the Landing itself."

"Any luck?" Shad prompted.

"Nothing surfaced," he said. "Not gold, at least. A lot of silver, though. The army tried to control the looting, but it went on anyway. Forsyth's men had a particularly bad reputation for that."

"Silver."

"Yes, anything they could get their hands on. Silver coin, silverware, silver plates. There are stories of what would be now priceless antiques being crushed between rocks to fit into army backpacks."

I winced and took a sip of wine.

"Why?" Shad asked.

"Because at the time of the war," I put in, "silver was far more valuable than gold, especially in its pure form. People hoarded silver coins. Because of the uneven values of the various currencies in North America, most silver dollars were worth more melted down into bullion. This made a vacuum that foreign coins had to fill."

"Hence the Spanish doubloons," she finished.

"And the Spanish silver dollar. That's what else Fenton had in the chests. A good amount of those, too. Enough to cover the gold."

"It's quite a story," said Trent.

"Do you believe it, David?" Shad asked what was on my tongue.

"Absolutely. Why not? This is a very old part of North America. It's full of great history. Looking at the facts, Fenton's fool's gold is totally possible. Your question is, where is it now, right?"

I nodded. "It's possible it was discovered during the Seaway construction in the 1950s. It might have ended up here."

"If it did, it's never surfaced legally or otherwise. 'Course, a lot of stuff disappeared during that project. People and things. Some of the stories are pretty wild. I'm sure you know that."

"I've heard some colourful tales," I admitted. "It would be an ideal place to disappear."

"Or be made to." David wiggled his eyebrows. "The old rumours are that some very nasty types used the construction sites more than once to dispose of inconvenient people and things. That there's more than just concrete in those dams."

I suddenly didn't feel so good. What a thought.

"Eewww. What a thought." Shad wrinkled her nose. "That's horrible."

My stomach inexplicably began doing the cha-cha. Carl's white face came to me again. And something else . . . but the light bulb didn't go on. It was all catching up to me, and I needed air.

David looked at his watch. "Regretfully, I have to go. Got to meet a friend at the train station."

I stood gratefully and shook his hand. No dead fish there.

"Thank you for looking into things for me," I said sincerely. "Ruling something out is just as important as finding something."

"I hope you do find the gold—or at least what happened to it. And let me know."

I promised to do so, and five minutes later Shad and I stood next to my car. The restaurant's outdoor lights went out.

"I guess we closed the place." I stared at the dark porch. The light . . . something about the light.

"Are you all right? You look funny."

"My stomach isn't happy. Nerves, I think."

""Was it Dave's story about the concrete? I'm trying to forget that one."

My stomach was now past the cha-cha and into a rendition suitable for *Dancing with the Stars*. What was my problem? Sure as hell wasn't the food.

Fear. I was afraid. Of what?

"Mack?" Shad's voice sounded far away.

The thought of the light bothered me again, but the band around my chest was new.

"Oh, my God," I whispered. "She told me. She told me to my face."

"Who?" Shad took my arm.

"Charlotte." My God, my God. I took a deep breath.

"I thought you said she was no help."

"She was. She told me everything. I just didn't understand." I turned to Shad. "We have to get back to Massena. Right now. You drive."

The front porch light was off, but there was a glow from the living room windows. I banged on the door.

"Mr. Needham. Charley. It's Farran Mackenzie. I need to talk to you."

At first there was no reply. I opened the screen door and banged on the inside one. It was late, but I couldn't take a chance on waiting.

Finally the porch light went on and the door opened. It was Charley Needham, standing in his pants and undershirt. I barged in with Shad on my heels. On the table beside the stairs was a tray with a bottle of sleeping pills and a glass of water.

"Shad, go upstairs and check on Charlotte."

"Uh," Shad hesitated, ". . . should I leave you alone?"

"Hurry." I never took my eyes off Charley. She took off up the stairs.

Charley sat heavily on the hall chair. "You don't have to. She's fine. I—I couldn't. But I don't know what else to do."

"I could give you a number of options, including calling the police. I can do that for you. But first we talk, and I'll start with one question.

"Rick Potts is still here," I said. "He never left. He's in the dam."

When Charley didn't reply, I asked, "Did Charlotte push him in?

"Or," I added slowly, "did you?"

ELEVEN

MASSENA 1957

LINES DRAWN FOR SEAWAY TOLLS FIGHT
POWER DAM 'PENTHOUSE' TAKING SHAPE
SOUTH CHANNEL DREDGING IS CAUSE OF CONCERN
FLOODING OF SEAWAY CHANNEL THROUGH GALOP
ISLAND STARTS
CANADIAN SEAWAY AN ALTERNATIVE TO TOLL
SITUATION
SEAWAY WORKER KILLED
SEAWAY TO SPARK BOOM

(Traverse City, Michigan): The president of the
Great Lakes Harbors Association says America's
next great industrial boom will come primarily
because of the St. Lawrence Seaway.

September 1957
Cornwall Standard-Freeholder

"C'mon, Charlotte." *Rick Potts scooped up his young wife
and twirled her around.* "We need to celebrate. I'm home and I'm
flush."

"And how long will either last?"

Potts put his wife down and looked behind her at the speaker.

"Party-pooper as usual, huh, Charley?" *Potts smirked at his
brother-in-law. The dislike was mutual.* "I've got money, and there's
more where it came from."

"Hope so, Ricky." *Charley Needham crossed his arms.* "You
never sent a cent to Charlotte the whole time you were gone. And we
had visitors a couple of times looking for you. Seems you owe some
guys from Jersey a lot of cash.'"

A shadow crossed Potts's face. "Yah, well, I'll be dealing with
them. It'll be fine. But now, Charlotte," *he added, turning back to his
wife,* "let's go out and do the town. There's a dance on somewhere,

and I start at the dam on Monday. As much work as I want. Moses has deadlines for everyone, and he's pushing it as usual."

"I . . . I couldn't," Charlotte murmured. "Besides, I have to work tonight. You go without me, Ricky."

Potts looked disgruntled. "Well, fine then. I will. I may not be back till late. Have a key for me?"

Charlotte looked uncertainly at her brother. Charley looked grim, then took a key off his own ring.

"That's for the back door. We keep both locked now with all the strangers in town."

Potts took the key. "What about our place?"

"Power Authority took it," she told him quietly. "Said they were going to condemn it if I didn't like their price, so I took what they gave me."

He looked at her, opened his mouth to say something, and then thought better of it. Shooting a glance at his brother-in-law, Potts gave his wife a quick kiss and was gone.

"Where would we find him?" The man at the door gave Charlotte the heebie-jeebies. There were more men in the expensive car parked on the road. Why did Ricky get involved with people like this? He'd promised her last year that he'd given up the gambling. This must be some mistake.

"There must be some mistake," she began, wishing that Charley were here to take care of these things, the way he usually did.

"If there is, ma'am, we'll sort it out with him." The man's tone of voice was as impassive as his face. Still, she couldn't stop the rapid beating of her heart. Ricky was in trouble again.

"Yes . . . well . . . he's working today, at the dam. I . . . I'm not sure exactly where. Did you want to leave a message?"

"When will he be home, Mrs. Potts?"

"I never really know. It's never the same time twice. Could be around suppertime, or as late as ten o'clock."

"We understand. We'll take a look for him, but tell him he really needs to talk to us. And not to take too much time doing it." The man handed her a paper with a phone number on it and touched the brim of his hat. "We'll be back."

When Charlotte left for her shift at the restaurant that night, she saw a man standing across the road looking at the house. When their eyes met, he turned away and gave lighting a cigarette his full attention.

When she came home several hours later, he was gone.

"Lucie says she saw you," Charlotte said softly. "It was you. With her. The blonde from the theatre."

"That's a load of shit and you know it," Ricky snapped. "Don't bother me with it now. I gotta think. If I could just go back. One more try. But I can't. Can't take the chance."

"Go back for what?" Charley loomed in the kitchen doorway.

"Nothing you'd be interested in," Potts got up and turned his back on his brother-in-law.

"You're talking about that goddamn gold again, aren't you, you stupid bugger?"

"Charley, please," Charlotte broke in.

"This is none of your business," said Potts over his shoulder.

"It is if it's under my roof." Charley was getting red in the face. "You'd have your own goddamn roof, if you weren't such an asshole!"

"Charley." Charlotte came around the kitchen table to him.

"And I heard what you said about that blonde, Charlotte. Believe it—don't believe him. He's just gonna hurt you again."

"He's my husband, Charley."

"He's a loser. You can do better than that."

At that remark, Potts whirled around to face his attacker.

"You leave her alone. She's my wife, and there's nothing you can do about it."

"You can get the hell out of my house!" Charley moved toward Ricky, but Charlotte stayed between them. "You and your nasty friends. Coming here when I'm not here. Watching the house and scaring Charlotte. I don't want them here, around my sister. Go live with your girlfriend."

Potts lunged toward his brother-in-law. Charley pushed Charlotte out of the way and landed the other man with a right cross to the jaw. Charlotte screamed as Potts went down.

"Charley—no!"

The sound of someone banging on the front door cut in.

"Potts!" came a male voice. "Are you in there? We need to talk."

Charley and Charlotte looked at each other in alarm.

"Do we answer the door?" she asked him.

They both turned to Rick, but the kitchen was empty. The back screen door hung open for a minute, then slowly swung shut.

"That's the last time I saw him," said Charley heavily.

"So you didn't push him in?"

The voice was not mine. It came from the doorway to the hall. Charlotte stood there in her housecoat, looking older with her long grey hair out of its bun. But the eyes were clear and the question was aimed at her brother, not the carpet.

'"No." The man slowly rose to face his sister. "God, no, Charlotte. I could never do that. I couldn't stand the man, but *kill him*? I thought—"

Her eyes stayed on him. She didn't seem to see me. She was having a conversation she'd waited half a century to have.

"You thought I did."

"I . . . I," he faltered. "I guess I didn't know what to think. You came home that night like a crazy woman. Yanking the curtains shut and switching off the lights. Hiding on the floor. I'd never seen you so frightened. And you ain't been yourself since then. Something awful happened that night. And we never saw Ricky again." Charley stopped and silence fell.

Charlotte stood like a statue, but I saw colour in her cheeks. I wondered how many years had passed since that had last happened.

"Charlotte," I said, rising to my feet and looking her in the eye, "you have to tell me what happened that night."

Shad came up behind her and guided her to a chair. Charlotte remained silent until both Shad and I had sat down. She looked at her hands and then rubbed them together as though she were washing them clean.

"Followed him. That night."

"I thought you were working that night," said Charley. I threw him a warning glance.

"Told them I was sick," she said softly. "I was. Thought he was going to meet *her*. Thought I was going to be sick. I had to know."

She stopped rubbing her hands and put them to her face.

"Not at the theatre, so I went to the dam." Charlotte closed her eyes and rocked a little. "So many people, so much noise. But not over there."

"Where?" I ventured.

"Where he was. On the scaffolding. Fighting with the man." The voice became a whisper. I could feel time twisting again. She was right back there, back fifty years, back to witnessing the gruesome death of someone she had loved.

"Went'n to the dam. Went into the dam." The rocking became worse, and sobs began to tear through her body. "*Threw him into the dam. He was screaming. I was screaming. Nobody came.*"

Charley got up and put his arms around Charlotte. I don't think I ever heard sobbing like that and hope I never do again. Gradually the sobs lessened.

"They were pouring concrete?" I asked.

Her head on Charley's chest nodded.

"Then you couldn't have saved him," I told her. "By the time anyone could have gotten there, it would have been too late."

"Ran away," came the muffled reply. "Ran away home."

Charley stroked her hair for a long time in our shared silence. Then he took her by the hand and led her upstairs.

When he came back down, Shad and I were standing by the front door. I had left two sleeping pills on the tray with the glass of water and held the bottle in my hand..

"I'll take these for tonight and bring them back tomorrow," I told him. "I have one or two last questions for Charlotte, but they can wait until she's had a good night's sleep. Are you going to be okay?"

Charley nodded slowly.

"She married him because she was pregnant," he told the hallway. "Then she lost the baby just a couple of months after that. That was the start of losing her."

We said nothing.

"After that terrible night," he continued, "she went inside somewhere so far I couldn't reach her. I had to protect her, so I did. I thought she'd finally snapped and done him in."

"Charley," I said, putting a hand out, "you need to call someone now, get some professional help for her. She deserves it—and so do you. First thing Monday morning.

"But tomorrow," I added before opening the door to leave, "you have to make the call you should have made that night. Call the Massena police department and report a possible murder."

TWELVE

THE DARKLING PLAIN

Monday morning brought a beautiful June day on the St. Lawrence. I'd made it home Sunday night from the States and gone straight to bed, dreaming about dark men chasing me through a massive construction site until I fell screaming into a pit—not filled with cement, but coins. Thousands of gold coins. And Jerry was there . . .

I woke up feeling that I had to call Jerry, but couldn't quite remember why. Padding out to the kitchen, I was filling the tea kettle when it all came back . . .

I had returned to Pleasant Street the afternoon following the very unpleasant evening of revelation in the Needham household. Charlotte looked much better, as did Charley. The Massena police had come and gone, taking with them the Needhams' statements, and a man introduced as Charley's lawyer sat noncommittally in the corner of the living room.

"Charlotte," I asked, "did you see the man who pushed Ricky that night?"

Charlotte shook her head slowly. "No. Lights too bright."

When I looked confused, Charley explained. "She told the police that the work lights up over the scaffolding were very bright. All she could see were the shapes of two men fighting."

"How did you know it was Ricky?" I asked the woman.

"Followed him. Saw the other man go up. Heard the voices."

"Did you know the other man?"

"Saw him before. Standing outside our house."

The man watching the house. Had he been a sentry for the guys in the car?

I put the kettle on the burner of my stove and turned the knob, looking out my patio doors to the St. Lawrence River. Well, my trip to Massena had been fruitful, but we now knew that Rick Potts was a dead end. If he had killed Sam Wallace, justice had already been served and horrifically so. I shivered despite the early heat of the day and picked up the phone to call Jerry with the news.

A knock on the door changed my plans. Only Jerry would be this early. But opening the door produced a different cop. Right profession, wrong man.

"Paul!" I threw my arms around Paul Vaughn. "Aren't you here early? We weren't expecting you until next week sometime."

Sergeant Paul Vaughn of the St. John's, Newfoundland, Police Service stood in my little hallway looking drop-dead handsome as usual. Prettier than Bloom Boy with the same dark curly hair, Paul had spun me around last summer when he'd arrived to find the truth about his parents. I'd helped him do that—putting together in the process that Paul had been born Stephen Hoffman, and revealing he was Ruth's long-lost son in my usual sensitive fashion.

We were cousins through my dead uncle Gordon, and the personal connection ran deep. For Paul, it had run deeper, but my feelings for Jerry Strauss stood in the way. Whatever they were. Whatever love means, like the man said.

"I got in on Saturday." He hugged me back. "Dropped by yesterday, but you weren't home yet. Ruth said you went stateside about the guy they found in Iroquois."

"I did."

"Any luck?"

The kettle started to whistle so we headed into the kitchen.

"Actually, yes and no." I made the tea and set cups on the table, while he sat down. It was nice and normal, so unlike another day we'd talked in my kitchen.

"Paul," I changed the subject to mask my own growing fear, "do you mind if I ask how your parents died?"

He looked back out into the rain and didn't answer. I was wishing I'd kept my big mouth shut when he quietly said, "Traffic accident. Head-on collision. Both killed instantly. Never knew what hit them."

"My God, I'm so sorry," I stumbled. "It must have been terrible."

"And then to find the box of clippings." Paul shook his head slowly. "That was the icing on the cake. That's what I mean, Farran," he turned to me. "It's enough to make you squirrelly. You had

a lot on your plate last year. When I decided to look for you, I dug up all the reports from the papers. Your father's body is found. Everyone thought he just left to go shipping and never returned. Your mother dies from a heart attack on hearing the news. And you come here cold trying to piece it together when everything is under water." His mouth went grim. "Stir in your uncle and a long-lost cousin. How did you handle it all without going a bit strange?"

Deep in my chest, I felt the small red glow of rage at his words, but I laughed it off. "I was strange to begin with, so I had the advantage."

I thought for a moment. "Hey, Paul—"

That's when he pulled me close and kissed me full on the lips.

The mind is a funny thing, isn't it? Well, at least mine is. I remember having an out-of-body moment then, half my mind saying, "Well, so this is how it feels to kiss him," while the other half said—

"No!"

I pushed him away with a violence that surprised us both. For a long moment, we stood squared off in embarrassed silence.

And then it had gone from bad to worse.

But not today, I told myself as I served the fresh tea. Today would be a good day.

"The no is about our suspect Rick Potts." I told Paul of Potts's gruesome end. "So Carl must have been referring to a time during the construction when Potts came back. I'll have to go see him today, see if he's feeling better. Tell him about Rick and ask what he meant by calling Potts's name that day."

"What is the yes?" Paul put three lumps in his tea. I refrained from comment.

"The yes is the full story of the gold as told by Rick Potts to his wife Charlotte. Not sure if it really helps, but at least one item on the list is complete. Have you had breakfast?"

Vaughn nodded. "Staying at Mother's. She wouldn't let me leave without it."

I smiled and dug out a fry pan. "That's Ruth all right." Bacon came out next and started to fill the kitchen with its wonderful cooking smell. Two eggs at the precise moment with the bacon and two slices of toast with butter.

"Well, the story boils down to this," I said, sitting down to eat.

Paul tried to slip one piece of bacon, but I slapped his hand away. "Hey, I offered. Pan's on the stove if you've changed your mind. Anyway, here's the scoop on Fenton's fool's gold according to one Private Henry Potts of the 4th U.S. Infantry. Took part in the Battle of Crysler's Farm. They were on the north end of the field when things got underway, and the 89th Regiment sent them into retreat—right into the 1st Infantry. Lots of confusion and everyone heading into the woods. Henry Potts saw that as his opportunity to make himself scarce. Didn't feel like sticking around to see how it turned out.

"That battle had over one hundred American soldiers listed as missing. Potts senior was one of them. Not only was he not interested in dying, he decided to use the distraction of the battle to return to Iroquois. When they had landed as advance guards, somebody had squealed about Fenton's chests of silver and gold—and about the unfinished fort. Forsyth's men had gone to check that site out and Potts followed his group to Cook's Tavern the night before the battle.

"When Henry Potts got back to Fenton's farm, he found Fenton dying and the place ransacked. Figuring some other 'missing men' had had the same idea and beaten him to it, he was looking around the house for anything left when he heard Fenton's voice. Somehow—details not really given and we can only imagine—he got Fenton to tell him where his money was before he died. Potts buried it and left, taking what he could in his pockets and setting the house on fire to give him time to make an escape. He later turned up in New York State, claiming amnesia from a head wound suffered on the battlefield."

Paul eyed my bacon again, but wisely thought better of it.

"Did he go back for it?"

"According to the family story, no. That's why the tale persisted. Henry left the gold behind. A year after returning home, he was thrown from his horse and killed. Shortly after that, the gold standard was put in place in England. Suddenly, those devalued coins were worth a lot more—if they could be found. But all the family had was a small sketch of Iroquois Point in Henry's diary and a notation of Fenton's dying words."

"Which were?"

"Very cryptic. Apparently he told Potts that you would have to see the gold in your own face in order to find it."

"'See the gold in your own face'? Whose? Potts's?" Paul shook his head. "Sounds mystical or something. Maybe he didn't know what he was saying. What did it mean?"

"Nobody knew. Not even Rick Potts. It stayed a riddle all those years. But Charlotte said Potts had the diary with the sketch. He loved the story as a boy, and, as a man deeply in debt to some very nasty people, I think it began to look like a way out."

"So you think the legend actually has something to do with the Wallace murder?"

"You sound as sceptical as Jerry Strauss. Just like the Paul Revere necklace, remember?"

Paul had the grace to blush. "Okay. Point made. I'll follow you on wild journey number two." He took his spoon and traced circles on the table. "So how is the inspector these days? Anything else interesting he's working on?"

"Not that I know of." I started to clear off my dishes. "Why don't you drop in and ask him? I haven't heard from him since Friday morning, but I'm heading west to the Winchester hospital. I want to see Carl first."

"Oh, yeah." Paul emptied his cup. "That reminds me. Mother said to tell you that Carl is out of the hospital. He's recovering at the Sterling House B&B."

Sterling House was in Ingleside, so I headed east instead of west. After that, I intended to go west again, to Iroquois, to see what-was-what at the crime scene. Maybe that's where Jerry was. He hadn't returned my message from Saturday night. Not that we were joined at the hip or anything, but it was uncharacteristic of him. The last time he'd disappeared on me was after Gordon's death, when there was a question he was not ready to ask.

The knowing is always better than the not knowing, right, Fan?

No, Alison, I told the car as I drove. Not always. There is always the exception that proves the rule. And maybe more than one.

"He's in the Gold Room," Mildred told me upon my arrival. "You can go on up. I'm bringing him a tea. Would you like one?"

Mildred Keeps looked years younger than in the spring when I had set eyes on her briefly on the lawn of Sterling House, swarming with equal parts police and reporters. I hadn't known who she was at the time, but her pink mules had set her apart from the rest. Today, she seemed a different person. But today there was no body in the Brass Room, no shootout in the living room. Today was a good day.

Carl also looked much better than when I saw him last, but that wouldn't be hard to do, considering. He also looked happy to see me.

"I hope I didn't scare you, Dr. Mackenzie." The elderly man took my hand as I sat down beside the bed. Three days after emergency surgery, he was already discharged, but with Mildred's no-nonsense attitude and background in nursing, this was the next best thing. "I saw the door open under the stairs and wandered in. I guess I got dizzy and fell." He put a hand on his stomach and raised the pyjama jacket enough to show the bandage. "Managed to impale myself, too. Fourteen stitches inside and out."

"Is that what you remember, Carl? And you should call me Farran."

"Okay, Farran," he smiled. "Yes, that's it. I don't remember actually falling, just going in the door. Why?"

"Was there anyone else around?"

"No. The lady who gave me a tour went into the front room. Heard someone come in the front door, I think. I was the only tourist there until then."

"Was Jeremy Pollan around? An elderly man doing work around the place? Mrs. Parmeter said she had expected him, but he hadn't shown up."

"Not that I saw. Why? It was just an accident. Wasn't it?"

Mildred brought the tea, so I changed the subject.

"I went to Massena over the weekend," I said once she had gone. "I found out what happened to Rick Potts after he returned home." I told him about Charley and Charlotte, and the horrible night at the Robert Moses Power House site so long ago.

"My God." Carl's hands started to shake so I took his cup. "How awful. I never liked Potts, but I would never have wished that on him. On anybody."

"I'm sorry, Carl. I didn't mean to upset you." I hesitated about going any further, then took a deep breath. "Carl, when I found you in the basement, you were still partly conscious. Your eyes opened for a minute and you said something . . . something strange."

He looked at me, puzzled. "I did? What did I say?"

"You called me Potts. You said 'Potts . . . you came back.'"

Carl stared at me for a minute. "Why the hell would I say that?"

"That's what I was hoping you could tell me. Did you remember something that morning about Potts coming back after Sam left?"

Carl looked lost. "No. No. I don't think so."

He was looking tired, so I veered away from the accident again, telling him the full Potts history of the lost gold.

"Well, Fenton wasn't the only fool about that gold, then," he muttered when I had finished. "Potts, I didn't care, but Sam—"

Mildred appeared at the door, announcing naptime. I dutifully left, promising to return the next day.

It wasn't until I drove off that I realized what was missing. The police guard. Evidently Strauss agreed with Carl that it was an accident. How could it be otherwise? Still, something bothered me about that day.

Then the light bulb went on.

Although I had questions for Jerry, who still had not called me back, I had one more important question for Mrs. Parmeter.

I turned the car around and headed for Iroquois. I didn't know if Carman House would be reopened yet, or if she would be there if it were, but I could also see who was at the crime scene they'd reopened in the field.

When I arrived, I couldn't drive in to the museum, as the road was blocked and the museum still closed. I continued around to where Carman Road intersected with what was now called Boat House Road. This, too, was blocked off, so I parked near the entrance and walked up.

A constable I didn't know stopped me when I got close to the police vehicles.

"Sorry, ma'am. This area is off limits."

"Is Sergeant Wiley here? Or Inspector Strauss?"

"Not at this time." He looked at me. "Did you need some assistance?"

I wanted to say yes, but couldn't. I turned to leave, and a woman in overalls and gloves came up to the constable.

"Call Wiley. I think we found what he was looking for."

I pretended not to listen but walked slowly away, ears straining. "Remains?"

"Yes. Thought he was crazy wanting to dig that deep. Tell Wiley—the Bear nailed it again."

The Bear, of course, refers to Inspector Jerry Strauss. It's his unofficial nickname in the detachment—unofficial, because no one in recent memory has ever said it to his face. However, only fools and angels would believe that Strauss didn't know about it.

So, The Bear was having a good day, too. He had been right about a second body. Must be Vivienne. Sam and Rick were both now accounted for, in terms of the missing people from Iroquois, 1957. If so, that was that. Rick killed Sam about the gold. Maybe he killed Vivienne, too. He was beyond the long arm of the law, and all that would be left was the location of the gold. If it still mattered to anyone. I doubted if Carl would care.

Yet, as I drove past the little road to Carman House, something still stuck in my craw. A small question for Mrs. Parmeter, but other than that—what? I braked and idled on the road for a moment, staring at the west side of the house with Pollan's ladder still standing against the wall ready for him to keep painting. Did Pollan ever show up? I wondered what he'd thought of all the police cars, if so. Maybe he'd just turned around and gone home. Not the type for crowds. Wishing I had marked down his address and phone from the card I gave Strauss, I slowly drove on.

Strauss was next on the list. I made it to the detachment in Long Sault in record time, perhaps fuelled on by more than a little female pique. As I said, not attached at the hip, but *still*. It had been a good day so far, and I wanted to keep that roll going.

I also, I told myself, had to tell Jerry about everything that had happened in the States. He or Wiley would want to contact the Massena police for official statements from both the Needhams. I wondered how it had gone this morning, with Charley calling the local mental health services. That wasn't something easy for that generation to do. Hopefully, the Needhams were also having a good day.

My luck ran out in Long Sault. Wiley had been called out (probably on his way to Iroquois), and Jerry wasn't in until after lunch. I tried his home phone, but there was no answer. I considered driving by the house, but nixed the idea for fear of looking like a clinging female. I knew the type. I'd been one in another lifetime.

The phone rang and rang. Finally, Farran hung up. She needed desperately to talk to Ethan, to feel safe. But she didn't dare call his house. If he wasn't in his office, she was out of luck.

Her big news would have to wait.

By that time, it was close to eleven o'clock. I had a feeling there was something I was supposed to do about then, but hunger ruled it out. I wanted to grab something at Jimmy's in Ingleside, but the Scottish half of me remembered the food that had been sitting in my fridge all weekend while I had treated myself to American food.

Home for lunch. And then the good day began to go very, very bad.

In retrospect, I can officially declare the beginning of the downward spiral of my good day was when a white car passed me on the road as I drove onto Ault Island. I sort of took notice as it went by, but was mentally thinking of what I had waiting for me for my meal. Food has always been one of my top priorities.

The second step into chaos was the card waiting for me in the crack between my front door and the doorframe. Ah, Jerry at last. He'd read my mind as usual. Humming, I put the key in the lock, pulled the card out and glanced at it as I pushed the door open.

It was not Jeremy Pollan's name.

It read *Stephanie A. Harrison.*

I sort of came to standing half in and half out of my doorway, card in hand. This couldn't be happening. After all the months of looking and trying to make contact, she'd been here. Here. *Right here.* On this doorstep.

My heart began to pound in my ears. Lynn. Had to call her. She had to know. I made my way to the phone and, after a couple tries with shaking hands, punched in her cell number. I got her voice mail.

"Lynn," I breathed. "She's been here. Left me her card. Haley . . . Stephanie. Call me right away."

I hung up and looked at the card again. I wasn't dreaming.

Stephanie A. Harrison. Harrison Media Inc. An address in Victoria, B.C. A 1-800 number underneath with e-mail.

I flipped it over. There was a cell phone number on the back.

I thought I was going to be sick. She was at the other end of that number, if I called right now. Haley. My little girl.

Somebody tell me what to do.

Ruth.

I punched in her number. God was merciful. She picked up right away.

"Farran?"

"Ruth. Ruth . . . I don't know what to do. Tell me what to do."

"Farran, what's wrong? Talk to me."

I heard another voice in the background.

"It's Haley. She was here and left her card. Do you understand? I have her phone number. But I can't do it. I can't call." I suddenly couldn't breathe, either.

"Her card? She left you her card?" Ruth gave a brief pause. "Well . . . you don't have to call right now," came the soothing reply. "I'll be there in a few minutes. We'll talk about it then, okay? Don't worry. It's going to be fine."

She hung up, and I followed suit. The card stayed in a death grip in my hand while I paced the living room, waiting to hear Ruth's car on the road.

Haley. Haley.

"We need to take her now, Miss Mackenzie. The new parents are waiting." The tiny cries echoed down the hall as the nurse took Haley away.

A knock came on the door. Ruth. I bolted from the living room and threw the door open.

Third bad moment. The Water People were standing there. The redhead stuck out her hand.

"Dr. Farran Mackenzie?"

"Uh, yes." I shook her hand in a daze. "Can I help you?"

I looked past her to where the blonde stood. The Tilley Hats were looking away, around the yard. The two young men were absent.

"May we come in?"

"Now . . . now isn't a very good time," I hesitated, just inside the door. *Ruth, where are you?*

The redhead looked at my other hand, still clutching Haley's card. "I see you found our card. We were here earlier, but you were out. Just thought we'd stop again on the way back to Iroquois. We need to speak to you."

"*Your* card?" I backed down the hallway to let them in.

The redhead led the way, then giving way for the blonde and the Tillies right behind. The man was laughing and talking with the woman as he entered, but the smile froze on his lips when he saw me.

The woman walked into him.

"What the—" Then she saw me, too.

"I believe introductions aren't necessary," said the blonde quietly.

All I remember from that moment is staring into those eyes I had once loved so deeply. His mouth opened and closed once, twice. "*Fanny?*" he whispered.

The woman said nothing. Her mouth became a straight edge, but I thought I saw fear flicker in her eyes.

"*Fanny?*" the man whispered again.

"Hello, Ethan." I heard the words come from my mouth, but didn't feel my lips move. Actually, I wasn't feeling much of anything right then.

We stood there in silence for a minute. Then I heard the sound of a car in the driveway.

"Farran?" Ruth called through the open doorway. "We're here."

She came in and stopped, looking at the Water People. Carolyn and Paul came right behind her.

"Farran, are you—?" He stopped, too. Nobody was moving. I felt like I was part of a scene at Madame Tussaud's.

Problem number five. I heard more cars stopping at my driveway. Turning to look out the front window, I saw a white car park behind Ruth's car, and a dark one follow suit behind it. Out of the white car came a strange man, and out of the dark one came Jerry Strauss.

Would I have room for more? I thought hysterically. Half of Ingleside was in my living room now.

"Farran?" I heard Jerry call through the door that was still open. For a crazy second, I wanted to run to the safety of his arms. But I was still made of wax.

Ethan ignored the voices, keeping his gaze on me. I had almost forgotten the two girls at the end of the room. We looked at each other across the small space, across the years.

"I thought you were dead," he said. We suddenly seemed to be the only two people in the world. "They said you were dead." His hand moved out toward me. "How . . . why . . . ?"

"That's a very good question, Professor Chamberlain." The stranger's voice cut into the fog. "One of many, I'd say, seeing you all here."

I turned to look at the speaker. A man about my age. He seemed familiar, but . . .

Then Jerry appeared behind him, looking like the Grim Reaper.

"A good question," the stranger repeated, "and I'm here for the answer. So tell us, Dr. Mackenzie."

I looked at him, the room reeling.

"No offense, Farran, but," he asked again, *"why aren't you dead?"*

PART THREE

"Finding the answers in life — finding yourself — is hard work. It's trial and error, and not for the faint of heart. I know that being a coward is easy. One size fits all. The only problem is that eventually you run out of places to hide."

—Farran Mackenzie
The Brother of Sleep

THIRTEEN

OXFORD

Oxford, England
Autumn 1981

It was early fall, and Oxford University looked beautiful. It always made her feel so very Canadian—just the age and history of the place.

I certainly came to the right place to study history, Farran Mackenzie often told herself. A long way from home, and she was homesick pretty much every day, but Oxford University . . .

Her mother had been so proud when Farran was accepted into the master's program here. Such an opportunity.

Now she had one year under her belt, thesis in place, supervisor signed up. Getting Debra Hyde was also a coup. Hyde was younger and more innovative in her approaches to the study of the past than most of the other profs.

Today was tea and more discussion. Farran had dropped by Debra's office with the rough work she had done over the summer.

"Ethan . . ." Professor Hyde looked up and past Farran to a man coming in the office door. "Ethan, good timing. I want you to meet my star pupil. This is Farran Mackenzie from Ontario, Canada. Farran, this is . . ."

"Dr. Chamberlain." The handsome man smiled into her eyes, doing something to her knees she hadn't felt since high school. He was at least ten years older, but the curly brown hair and magazine smile seemed more important. "Professor of history, specializing in North American native oral culture." He shook her hand. "Please call me Ethan."

"Ethan," Farran said, blushing and looking at the floor.

Debra Hyde had fallen silent.

Winter

She'd finally managed to work in one of Chamberlain's courses, even though their fields of interest were—literally—worlds apart. Spotting him in the various hallways was always a bright moment in the day. He was so funny, so handsome, so intelligent. Shame he'd been on sabbatical for her first year, but at least she had him now for one class. That should make the dreary British winter go a bit faster. How she longed for the fluffy whiteness of a Canadian winter!

"You look a little homesick, Farran."

Ethan stood over her desk, the others all empty.

Farran started and stood to collect her books, blushing a little. She'd been daydreaming and hadn't noticed that the others had gone. Not that she wasn't inclined to dawdle behind on occasion . . .

"I guess it shows on my face."

"Winter is when it hits hardest for most," he smiled. It reminded her of the smile in the picture of a young man, hidden in a bracelet in her mother's jewellery box—until she'd discovered it. Then the bracelet had vanished. But the memory of the young man remained.

"Along with my mother," Farran smiled back, "I'm missing our Canadian snow the most. Can't believe that."

"What city do you come from?"

"Preston . . . well, it was Preston. Now it's part of Cambridge. Don't think I've ever really gotten used to that."

"Ah! Named after Cambridge, England?"

"No, actually. Named after Cambridge Mills, Preston's original name."

They had had tea that day after class, in his office. He'd asked her all kinds of questions about home, about her mother, about life. It had been so . . . so nice. Nice to talk to a man about things. There hadn't been anyone special in high school, and it had been almost ten years since John Perry died.

But he was her teacher, after all.

"Why not?" the man whispered. "You're such a bookworm. Live a little."

Peter Simons didn't give up easily. He'd been asking Farran for a date for weeks now, but they were also direct rivals for the same PhD seat in the fall. She just preferred to keep her distance. Keep her focus.

"Thanks, but I have to pass." She gathered up her books to leave the library. "I have a paper due on Monday."

"I have the same paper, remember? Besides, I'm sure old Chamberlain would give his favourite pupil an extension if she asked for one."

"What is that supposed to mean?" she hissed back. The librarian with the book cart was starting to look over.

"Nothing, nothing. Just saying." Simons grinned. "We're going to London for the weekend. We've got room for you."

Farran suddenly wanted to be alone.

"I appreciate the offer, but I'm too snowed under. Maybe next time."

Simons did not reply. Farran escaped.

"Just saying," Farran said to herself. Who else was "just saying"?

She cut Friday's class and stayed in bed. Couldn't call Mom. This was just stupid high school stuff. She turned on the radio and the Human League's "Don't You Want Me" came on. She snapped it off again. Never mind that it was such a big hit. The constant airplay seemed personally cruel.

Alison and Jeanie. Their faces came to her suddenly. Both gone. And why? No goodbyes. Just gone.

Was there something in her that brought that into her life? Certainly the student cliques and social positioning here at Oxford guaranteed her a bottom rung and little company. Peter Simons came to mind, along with her latest brush-off. Was she a loner like her mother? At least her mother had married. It just had ended so soon, so tragically.

But there was something else there . . . something that had hurt or frightened her mother so badly that the door was forever closed. Even to Farran.

When it felt safe, she dressed and headed out to get her mail before the postal station closed for the weekend. The skies threatened, but she hoped for a letter from home. There had been nothing in two weeks, so unlike her mother.

The letter was there, as expected, but its contents unexpected.

"Don't worry," Leslie wrote, "because everything is fine now.

It was all so sudden that it was over before anyone could call. Then I told them not to because it would just upset you for nothing."

Gall bladder. Surgery. *Leslie was recovering now at home with a daily nurse.*

Farran sat down on a nearby bench under a tree.

"Farran. There you are. When you weren't in class, I was a bit worried. You've never missed before."

She looked up into Ethan's eyes and her own filled.

"What's wrong?" He sat down beside her. "You're pale as a ghost."

"She was sick. My mom. Had to have emergency surgery, and it might have gone badly. I should be home. I should be home . . . we only have each other."

The tears were falling now as freely as the rain that had finally arrived. They sat together protected by the tree. It was as if the rest of the world had vanished.

"May I?" When she held out the letter, he took it and read it through. "But she's fine now, Fan," he added, using her nickname for the first time. "Everything's fine. And your mother is right. You couldn't have done anything except be upset by it all."

"Then why can't I stop crying?" Farran wiped more tears out of her eyes, feeling such a ninny in front of him.

He put a comforting arm around her. "Because you're tired, you're homesick, and you've just had a shock. Why don't you let me buy you a drink?"

She took the letter back from him—and a tissue as well.

"Come on. It'll make you feel better."

Ethan stood and gave her a hand. Rising, Farran heard Peter's voice from the other day. Just saying . . .

"I—I can't. But thank you. Really." Farran walked away into the rain. It was really coming down now.

"Farran. Fan. Please wait."

Right then, Farran made the mistake of stopping and turning around. She hadn't been brought up to be rude, but she should have kept going. Then life might have turned out so differently.

Ethan stood there in the rain, soaking wet, hand out. "Let me help."

She shook her head. "No, it doesn't look good. People are think-ing—"

"Thinking what?" he answered over the downpour. By now they were the only two figures left on the commons. "Thinking that I care?" He let his hand drop. "I do, Fan. What do you want me to say?"

For a few minutes, they stood looking at each other, oblivious to the pouring rain. Finally, he walked up to her and stopped just in front, not touching.

"Let's go for a drive," he said. "Let's talk."

So they did. They drove and talked for an hour, ending up in Southampton for supper, for the evening, for the night.

Spring

"So we get to see the big house finally." Simons was driving, his little car full of soon-to-be graduates. "Heard that Hyde is loaded. Family money."

"I heard it was him, not her," someone replied. "Supposed to be related to Old Neville himself somehow."

Neville? Farran wondered who they were talking about. She was so out of the loop, but it was her fault or choice—depending how you looked at it. First it had been the books and now any spare moment she secretly spent with Ethan. It wasn't right, but it was wonderful. For the first time in her life, she felt whole. Not the half person wandering around like usual.

She'd never met Debra's husband. Debra rarely mentioned her private life, so it would be interesting to meet the man in her supervisor's life. It suddenly hit her how little she knew about Debra Hyde. Was it her indifference or Debra's privacy?

The students were all dressed up for the big wine and cheese celebration. It was a beautiful evening. Maybe Ethan would be there. In a few weeks, she would be going home for good. But no need to think about that tonight.

At that moment , Farran Mackenzie was truly happy.

Ethan was married.
He was married to Debra.
Farran sat deaf to the conversations around her in the big house. She refused to meet Ethan's questioning eyes.

Home. Need to go home. Right now.

Want to die. Right now.

She stretched her granite features into what she hoped was a smile, and drank her wine.

"Farran, I seem to have forgotten your paper in my office." *Ethan looked at his student over the batch of papers he was handing out to the class. "I'll be there shortly after class, if you want to pick it up."*

It was a ploy to speak to her alone, of course. She'd purposely avoided him for the past week, since the wine and cheese. Did everything in her room—write her final papers, eat what she could smuggle in, do her readings, get ready for her thesis defence. Fortunately, her research was complete and she didn't have to make a dash for the library. He would never come to her room.

Farran made no reply, but nodded slowly. She had no legitimate reason not to go, so she would.

Just go and get it over with.

An hour later, she stood in the doorway of his office. Ethan looked up.

"Close the door behind you, Farran, and have a seat."

She did as she was told, except to remain standing, silent.

"What's happened, Fan?" he asked quietly. "Something happened the night of the party, didn't it?"

"Yes," Farran said dryly, looking at his desk. If she met his eyes, she knew she'd throw up. "I met your wife. Small detail you never mentioned."

"But I thought you knew." Ethan rose to his feet. "You've been working with Debra all these months . . ."

"I don't ask my professors questions about their personal lives, Ethan. Maybe that's a policy I should change, considering. But not to worry. I'm gone in three weeks. No mess. No cleanup. Can I have my paper, please?"

He came around the desk. "I never mentioned it because I thought you knew. And I wouldn't be thinking of discussing my wife with—"

"Your mistress." The words came out like bullets. Farran Mackenzie, the other woman. This was something she couldn't tell her

mother. She could barely say the words to herself.

"My best friend. Farran," he reached out for her, but she moved away, "I never meant for this to happen. I've been so . . . so lonely in my marriage. I guess I just let it. Bloody selfish of me, but you just made me feel alive again and I couldn't stay away."

Still she avoided his eyes. "Well, like I said. I'm gone in a few weeks. And I think that's best." Finally she looked up. "I love you, Ethan. But I can't do this. I just can't."

Farran splashed cold water on her face and looked in the mirror. She was pale with dark circles under her eyes. She'd barely eaten in the two weeks since walking into the truth about Ethan's personal life. But the nausea was now as regular as clockwork every morning.

It was just the stress, she told herself again. And depression. She could barely get out of bed in the morning.

But for someone who wasn't eating, her pants weren't fitting so well any more.

Just stress.

In a few weeks, she'd be home.

The phone rang and rang. Finally, Farran hung up. She needed desperately to talk to Ethan, to feel safe. But she didn't dare call his house. If he wasn't in his office, she was out of luck.

The news would have to wait.

"We're going to have a baby?" Ethan ran his fingers through his hair, making his curls stand up.

Farran longed to do the same, but closed her eyes and kept her distance. She had to start taking care of herself for her baby's sake.

"I'm going to have a baby," she repeated. "I'm keeping the baby, and I expect nothing from you. You're free and clear. I just thought it was right you should know."

They were standing in a little park in Brighton, where Farran had thought it would be safe from prying eyes. She'd rented a car for the day and met him there.

"We're going to have a baby," he said again, letting the words sink in.

"Ethan, I said — "

He grabbed her by the arms and broke into a grin. "Fan, we're going to have a baby. We'll be parents. I'm going to be a father. I never thought I would."

Of all reactions she'd imagined, this one had never crossed her mind. Unsure what to say, Farran said nothing.

"Debra can't have children, Fanny. I've begged more than once to adopt, but she won't. Now she's really married to her career. I thought I'd never . . ." He sat down on a bench.

"You're a married man." The blunt statement was as much for her as for him. His happiness was intoxicating to her fear and loneliness, but she needed to keep her head.

Ethan looked up. "Yes . . . yes, I know. And right now I don't know what to do. But you'll keep the baby. And you won't tell Debra?"

"Of course not." Giving in to her body, Farran sat down next to him. It was too close.

"I need time to think. Can you give me that, Fan?"

"Yes." It was barely above a whisper. She longed to hold him, be held, be safe. But that would be a long time coming.

Ethan took her hand. "Parents . . ." he said softly.

"Your funding has been confirmed. Well, congratulations."

Debra Hyde's voice did not match the occasion. She passed the letter back to Farran, her eyes as flat as her words.

"Thank you." Farran's head was spinning. Before, this would have been incredible news. But now . . . The baby complicated everything. She hadn't even called her mother, yet. Like Ethan, she needed time to think.

She was miserable in Debra's presence. Although Farran was still able to wear regular clothing, switching to looser tops and stretch pants that made it look only that she was putting on a few pounds, she knew that would be the case for much longer.

"Ethan." Debra rose from her chair at his entrance. Farran froze.

"Oh . . . Sorry. Didn't mean to interrupt." Ethan stole a glance at Farran.

"Not at all. I was just leaving."

"*Farran has received her funding.*" Debra's words cut off her escape. "*She'll be back in the fall in the PhD program.*"

"*That's . . . that's wonderful news,*" Ethan said without looking at her. "*Congratulations, Farran.*"

Farran suddenly wanted to be in her living room back home in Cambridge. Just home. Just herself again.

"*Thanks.*" She flashed them each a brief smile and made her escape. You could have cut the tension between them with a knife.

"*She won't give me a divorce.*" Ethan finished his beer at one draught. "*She said if I pursue it, she'll take me for everything. Money. Scandal. My job.*"

"*You told her about me?*"

"*No, not by name, but she guessed that there was someone else, and that it was a student. Said she'd wondered for some time. I never mentioned the baby, either. Don't want to at this point. It would really upset her.*"

Ethan became grave. "*She's always been possessive, controlling. It didn't used to bother me. Thought it was love. But she scares me . . .*"

"*You're scaring me.*"

Ethan looked up and put his hand on hers. This time, they were in a pub in Northampton. Safe.

"*Don't be scared. I can look after myself. Debra was just sounding off when she said—*" He broke off, then looked for the waiter. "*I could use another.*"

"*Said what?*" Farran put her hand on his.

Ethan didn't reply.

"*Said what, Ethan?*"

"*That,*" he answered slowly, "*she'd rather see me dead . . .*"

"*I understand you're leaving tomorrow.*"

Debra and Farran stood, faced off, over the desk in Debra's office. Debra had summoned Farran and, as tempting as it was for the younger woman to escape home with any further contact, the student dutifully appeared.

There was a package on the top of the desk with Farran's name on it.

"Yes," Farran replied. "My flight out is tomorrow afternoon."

"Heathrow or Gatwick?"

"Gatwick."

The social amenities over, Debra indicated the package.

"There's the final draft of your thesis, with all the notes I've made attached. I suggest you take the time this summer to get it ready for publishing. Don't dawdle. Get it out from under before starting the other program. And congratulations again."

"Thank you." Farran picked up the parcel. The thesis paper was in a cardboard box she could feel under the brown paper wrap and string. This was a moment she had worked toward so long, yet all she could feel was a cold ball of fear in the pit of her stomach.

There was an awkward pause.

"Have a safe trip home," Debra said. And smiled.

The voice on the phone was so agitated that, for a moment, Farran didn't recognize it.

"Ethan?" she whispered.

"You have to be careful at the airport . . . We argued . . . It came out. She knows it's you and about the baby."

The cold ball of fear still with her began to take over her lungs.

"Ethan—"

"No time," he cut in. "I can't see you off. Just do what we planned. Wait to hear from me. I'll take care of things here."

"You're scaring me again."

"Don't be frightened. I'll make everything okay. I'll keep you both safe."

"What do you mean?"

"She's . . . she's . . . not right. I knew she was possessive, but—"

She'd rather see me dead. Ethan's words from the other week surfaced through the growing fear.

"Ethan, are you safe there? Come with me. No matter what, we'll be fine," Farran babbled into the phone. "We'll make do. Nothing is worth this."

"It's you, Fanny." Ethan's voice grew very calm. Too calm. "She won't hurt me. She'll hurt you. And the baby. It's the baby she wants. Our baby.

"Get out of here. Do what we planned. I'll meet up with you when it's safe.

"And I'll make it safe. I promise you that. For both of us. Whatever it takes.

"I love you, Farran."

The line went dead in her hand.

FOURTEEN

THE NAKED TIME

Why aren't you dead?

That's the moment my life began to come apart.

Like in the old demo films about atomic bombs, I could feel the pieces of my times, shards of living, miles of running, hundreds of moments carefully placed—all disintegrating in the blast from the past I had worked my adult life to escape.

I did what any trapped animal does that sees no way out.

I played dead.

Suddenly, everyone else came to life. I alone remained of wax, painfully aware of the presence of Someone I had to protect from this mess.

Keep the child safe, lass.

Yes. Safe.

"What the hell do you mean by that?" Paul kicked into police mode. It registered in me that he exchanged a meaningful glance with Jerry, who still stood by the door. Then he moved between me and the stranger.

"Your friend has a weird sense of humour, Strauss," he said.

The stranger ignored Paul's question and looked at me again.

"Do you know me, Farran?" he asked quietly. "It's been a long time."

Unconsciously, I also moved, putting myself between the stranger and the two girls from the Water People.

"Peter," I said simply. "Peter Simons. Oxford, a lifetime ago." My voice sounded as though it came from far away. "What are you doing here?"

"Another good question, I'd say, except for seeing Ethan and Debra here. Quite the gathering." Peter turned to the Water People. "I apologize for the interruption. I do need to talk to Dr. Mackenzie."

"Farran, who is this guy?" Paul put his hand on my arm. "Comes marching in here—"

Peter dug into his jacket and pulled out a badge. Paul looked at it then at me.

"Scotland Yard?"

"You're police?" I asked Peter.

"I think we've come at a bad time, Dr. Mackenzie." The voice came from behind me. For the first time, the blonde girl spoke. "We should go and let you have some privacy."

I snapped around. "Yes, you need to go. Tomorrow would be better."

"I'd like an answer to Peter's question, Farran." Debra Hyde took a step closer to her husband. "All these years we thought you were dead."

"Is that why you're here?" Peter asked.

"They're here for research," I cut in, turning my back to the blonde again.

Ruth had been staring at Jerry for some minutes, but he'd avoided her gaze. Finally, she looked at me. "Fan, what is this all about?"

"I don't know," I hedged.

"Then let me refresh your memory," said Peter. "On May twenty-third, 1982, you boarded Flight 39 from Gatwick Airport outside London to return home from Oxford University. The flight left on schedule, but never made it to Toronto. Forty-five minutes into the flight, the plane exploded over the Atlantic, killing all passengers and crew. All 115—except you. It's great to see you again, Farran, but why aren't you dead?"

"I don't know," I repeated, passing my hand over my face.

Paul steered me toward a chair.

"What do you mean you don't know?"

"This is over," Paul straightened up and looked at Jerry. Right then, it occurred to me that Jerry had not spoken since calling my name when he'd arrived.

"It is," Jerry concurred briefly, "unless you want to continue in an official capacity, Inspector Simons."

"Not now," said Paul. "She's white as a sheet."

"That's right, Jerry," Ruth stepped up to bat. "I don't understand everything that's going on here, but if anyone wants to talk to Farran, they can call me tomorrow."

"This afternoon would be better, ma'am," said Peter.

"Tomorrow," Ruth repeated firmly.

The inspector backed down.

"Okay, show's over," Carolyn said with her usual social diplomacy. "Everybody out."

Ethan made a move toward me, but Debra put a hand on his arm. I avoided his eyes.

They filed out, Jerry included. Paul went out with him for a few seconds and then returned. I snuck a glance as the Water People left the room. I had waited over twenty-five years to see my little girl and now had to let her walk out of my house without exchanging so much as a hello. I couldn't let anyone know who she was, that she was there.

I wondered if she knew about me, or if the meeting was only cruel chance.

Finally, I was alone with Paul, Ruth, and Carolyn. Someone put a shot of something stiff in my hand and I instinctively drank it back.

I heard Paul tell Ruth that she should call my lawyer this afternoon. *This isn't happening*, I told myself. But it was. And in a really bizarre way, it felt as though there was no way I could have avoided this day, this scenario. That it was part of a greater plan.

You lying bastard . . .

"Shut up," I muttered.

They all sat down around me as if waiting for something. Then Paul leaned forward.

"Farran," he said carefully, "what's this all about? What happened on that flight?"

"I don't know," I said mechanically.

"You need to," Paul persisted. "I don't know where this Simons guy is going with it, but I don't like it. You need to think and get your statement clear, and talk to your lawyer. They're going to want to speak to you soon."

"Won't matter." I stared into the bottom of the empty glass. "Won't matter at all."

"Why?" asked Carolyn.

"I can't answer their questions," I shrugged. The drink was taking effect.

"You have to, and you have to do it right. And soon, or it will look like—"

"*I can't!*" Haley's face from the photo came to me. For some reason, I couldn't remember her face from today. "I just can't."

"Why?" Paul rose to stand over me.

"Because," I looked him right in the eye, "*I don't remember.*"

"What a mess. What a goddamn mess." Carolyn had joined me in the stiff drink. I guessed she was the one to start me off in the first place. "Even for you, Mackenzie, this is a hell of a mess."

"And I don't like where the questions are heading," Paul put in. "I admit it doesn't look good with you leaving the plane and then it's destroyed, but . . ."

"Yeah, really," Carolyn added. "I know you're a flake, but a terrorist?"

"Jerry thinks I am — or at least thinks it's possible," I told my empty glass and then waved it at Carolyn, who took it to refill it.

"Why do you say that?" asked Paul. "He didn't say that."

"He didn't say *anything.*" I gratefully took the refill from Carolyn. She mumbled something about it being my last because she wasn't volunteering to put me to bed this early in the afternoon. "With Strauss, silence is a conversation in itself."

"Not this time," Paul disagreed. "If this Scotland Yard guy is looking into this officially or even unofficially, Jerry has to back right away from you and be squeaky clean about how the investigation is handled. If it looks like there's been one iota of favouritism or special treatment from his office in something like this, they'll have his head on a platter. And yours. He can't be involved, especially if they know that he and you are . . . well . . . you *are*, aren't you?"

Believe it or not, at that moment I was saved by the bell. The doorbell, actually.

Jenn Farley stood there when I opened the door (despite Carolyn's protestations about my ability to perform simple tasks).

"Oh, my God." I put my hand to my mouth. "It's Monday afternoon. I forgot. I'm so sorry, Ms. Farley."

"Are you all right, Dr. Mackenzie?" she asked. "You don't look well."

"She's had a shock." Carolyn materialized at my elbow, taking hold of it. "Some bad news, I'm afraid. I think you need to lie down, Dr. Mackenzie."

"I do?"

"You do." Carolyn turned to Jenn. "Can she meet with you in a day or two? Can she call you?"

"Oh, yes. I'm sorry you've had bad news."

"Me, too." Suddenly, I did actually want to lie down. "I still have your number. I promise to call you tomorrow."

Jenn shrugged and smiled. "I'm here for the week. No rush, Dr. Mackenzie. When you are up to it."

I wanted to lie down, but for some reason I was loath to let Jennifer Farley leave. Maybe it was the stiff ones I'd had. I watched her pull out of the driveway and realized I was sad. Sad? Feeling guilty, I guess.

"You need to lie down." Carolyn steered me back into the living room. Obediently, I lay down on the couch. Exhausted, I fell asleep.

When I awoke, the sun had moved around to the other side of the house. I must have slept a couple of hours. I could smell something good coming from the kitchen and hear Ruth humming to herself. For just a moment, in my drowsy state, I was back in the old house in Preston with Mom.

"Mom?" I murmured.

Trouble . . . Haley

My eyes snapped open.

Hurry . . .

I sat up. "Why?" I asked the room.

"Why what?" Ruth came in with a cup of tea.

"I . . . I was dreaming, I guess. Thought I heard Mom's voice."

Ruth handed me the cup. "What did she say?"

"She said that Haley was in trouble and to hurry."

"Drink that and then we'll talk."

I did as I was told. I can do that when I have to.

Ruth came back in with a cup for herself and sat down. "Supper will be ready in about twenty minutes. But we need to talk first." She set the cup down and took both my hands, looking me right in the eyes.

"We'll start by getting one question out of the way. Farran Mackenzie, did you have anything at all to do with the bombing of that plane?"

"What?" I half rose. "Do you think—"

"Sit down, Fan. I'm not thinking, yet. I'm only listening. You have quite the situation right now with this Inspector Simons coming here and Haley arriving on your doorstep. You need to talk to someone about everything, to sort it out and see what we should do. You can't talk to Lynn because of her professional position at the *Ottawa Citizen*. The same goes for Paul. He's not here officially, but he's still a police officer. That puts him in a difficult position.

"I'm the only one who can walk into this. I'm not anybody special—"

"Yes, you are. You're special to me, and I'm not letting any of this fall on you. Christ, Ruth, you're getting married in ten days. There's no way I'm going to mess *that* up. You need to stay away, too. I'll call my lawyer," I added, but Ruth was shaking her head.

"Paul called her, and you have an appointment tomorrow after lunch. But I'm not going to let you go through this alone. You're Leslie's child, and I owe her that. She would have done the same for me without batting an eye."

I couldn't argue with that.

"Now," Ruth got up, "let's sit down and eat, and you can tell me everything. And maybe I can help you call Haley tonight."

"You don't have to," I said flippantly. "She was here."

Ruth spun around. "She was *here*? You met her?"

"I think so. We weren't really introduced. Right after I called you, those environmental people who've been doing tests in Iroquois showed up at the door. The one woman said that they had left the card. They were here when you arrived. There were two women the right age, one blonde. I assume she is Stephanie Harrison, a.k.a. Haley Mackenzie."

"Did you speak to her?"

"Not really, only once in reply when she said they should leave, remember?"

"So she was here and then gone?"

"Oh, that's only the half of it. The older man standing with them was Ethan Chamberlain, Haley's father."

"*What?*"

"Oh, yeah. A freakin' three-ring circus in here today with my long-lost daughter, her biological father and his wife, and then

Hercule Poirot with his bombshell about a bomb." Alison. Will I ever get past that? "I don't want to talk about bombs, Ruth."

We sat down to a chicken supper with dumplings and lots of gravy. Soul food. Ruth and I talked about the wedding, about Paul, about Celebration 50, about everything but the mess I was in. Finally, over dessert, Ruth looked at me.

"So, you're telling me that your daughter walked in your door accompanied by her biological father."

"Yes."

"That's bizarre. Absolutely bizarre."

"I don't know, Ruth. In my life, that would qualify as just another day."

"She must know who he is and brought him here. Coincidence can't go that far."

"I don't know why Ethan would be involved with an environmental study. I haven't seen him in twenty-six years, but his field was North American native studies."

"Are you going to call her tomorrow?"

"I don't know. I don't want to make any connection until this thing with Simons is cleared up. I don't want to walk back into her life with this going on."

"She may disappear again," Ruth warned. "And she's in trouble, remember?"

"Maybe I'm the trouble. I have been for a lot of people the last few years."

Ruth put her hand on mine. "You are her mother," she said simply. "Now, begin at the beginning and tell me everything you do remember."

So I did. It took two helpings of dessert to make it through, but I filled Ruth in on the whole story of my life in Oxford, ending with that horrid day at Gatwick airport.

"And then nothing," I finished. "I remember seeing the bulletin on the television at the airport, and then I don't remember anything until calling Mom from somewhere on the coast, telling her I was alive, but she couldn't tell anyone for a bit."

"Did Leslie know about Ethan and the baby?"

"No." I shook my head. "No. I couldn't tell her. I'd made such a mess of things and then actually considered flying out and letting

Ethan . . . get rid of Debra."

"But you didn't," Ruth pointed out. "You got off the plane and called the police. Why did you think he meant to kill her?"

"I heard the desperation in his voice. She was going to ruin his life. But he said she threatened me and the baby. He said 'It's the baby she wants.' Apparently Debra couldn't have children, and Ethan leaving her for a life with me and our baby pushed her over the edge."

"But they are still together. You said that it was Debra with him today."

I nodded. "Also bizarre." I ran my fingers through my hair. "God, I wish I could talk to Jerry about all this. He'd know what to do. Cut through the crap. I'm too deeply involved emotionally to work this out."

Ruth patted my hand again. "Trust me. Jerry is following protocol to the letter on this, but if know him—and I do—he's not sitting idly by. But there is this whole side he doesn't know. That's the dilemma."

"So, what next?"

"See your lawyer and then talk to Simons. Get it over with. There is no reason to connect you to a terrorist bombing in 1982. Then call your daughter. Meet with her. Avoid Ethan and Debra, if you want. You owe them nothing, and it's Haley's choice if she wants to connect with her father. Take care of Farran Mackenzie."

Maybe it was the dumplings or the two pieces of cake. Or both. I suddenly felt better. It seemed so simple and doable.

"Have I told you I love you, Ruth? What would I do without you?"

She smiled. "I have no idea," she replied.

Shall we talk about sleep that night? If we did, it would be a short conversation. In terms of haunting, Hamlet had nothing on me. Once the dumplings and cake wore off and Ruth had gone home, I was alone with all my demons.

How anyone could point the finger at me about the bombing of Flight 39 was beyond me. The only thing was, I had left the plane. And I had left suddenly and without my baggage. Question for Simons: Did they know where the bomb had been? And how did it get past security?

Haley. My little girl. Now all grown up as Stephanie Harrison. And just a few hours ago, standing in my living room. I could have reached out and touched her. I should have, in retrospect. But then the wax feeling in me that had kept me together would have melted from the touch, and I would have lost it in front of an audience.

I didn't know what she knew, if that was why she had come. She said it was research, and it could still be that simple. And who's to say she wants to know me? Especially now that it looks like I had a former career as a terrorist. I needed to keep her safe, and the story of her parents was the only reason I had to run off that plane twenty-six years ago. It was a reason I would have to keep to myself.

Parents.

Fan, we're going to have a baby. We'll be parents. I'm going to be a father. I never thought I would.

Ruth said I owed nothing to Ethan, or Debra. For the most part, that was true. However, Ethan had a daughter he didn't know—as far as I knew. But again the balancing act. Do I tell him? What was the state of Ethan and Debra's marriage? After my "death," they obviously had sorted things out. Was she still possessive and unstable? Did Debra still harbour a hatred for Haley and me deep down, one that threatened my safety and that of my little girl? Why were they here at all? And in Iroquois of all places—doing water tests, or whatever?

Iroquois brought Carl Wallace. I needed to check in with Jerry about what they had found out near the original crime scene, and bring him up to speed on the Massena situation. See where it all stood. I'm sure Carl was ready to go home. But could I talk to Jerry?

I did need to talk to Mrs. Parmeter. Something about the light . . .

The phone rang and I jumped. By this time, it was 3:00 a.m. Hoping it was Jerry caving in to make one clandestine call, I looked at the call display. It was an unfamiliar cell number. Feeling queasy, I answered.

"Hello, Farran," came his voice.

One of the great cruelties of life is that—barring extreme old age or serious illness—our voices never change. Ethan came across the wire exactly as I remembered him from the past. Without the arena of spectators and gladiators in my living room, I was alone with the voice and the memories and the emotions attached. I was afraid to close my eyes in case this was some Twilight Zone moment and I would wake up back in Oxford, unable to find my way home again.

"Ethan." It was just above a whisper.

"I thought I'd never hear your voice again, Fan." He paused. "What . . . what happened? How?"

"I just didn't get on the plane." It sounded so inane and ridiculous, even to me. *No shit, Sherlock,* would be the appropriate reply.

"You never called . . . All these years . . ."

I didn't reply. There was so much explanation I owed this man, so much he owed me. *I thought you were going to protect me by killing your wife. She seems very much alive. Did I stop you in time with my call to the police? Why are you still together?*

"Our baby, Fanny. What about him?" I remembered Ethan had talked about our having a son, referring to the baby as male even though it had been too early to find out.

"I can't talk about . . . him . . . about that. This is all a lot for me to take in, and Peter is here making insinuations about the bombing of that plane. I can't talk to you."

"Is he alive?" Now Ethan was just short of a whisper.

"Yes. Our baby is alive, Ethan." *And you were standing right beside her today . . .*

"We need to meet—"

"Ethan," I cut in. "We will sit down and talk this through at some point. But right now, I can't. You asked me for time years ago in Oxford, and I gave it to you," I added. "Now you need to give it to me."

He gave me his number. "I'll wait for your call. I won't bother you again for a bit, but I won't leave here until we talk, Debra notwithstanding."

I wanted to ask him exactly what he meant by his last remark, but guessed the obvious and took my cue to hang up. My Great Love Affair, over and out.

Every moment of every day since I lost her, I have missed Leslie Evian Mackenzie in my life—but never as I did in the wee hours of that morning. I had never told my mother the details of my escape from Oxford, about Ethan or Haley. In retrospect, I understood that part of that tacit agreement to not pry was that she had secrets of her own, secrets, that, in her mind—and correctly so, as my personal history has now made clear—decided the safety of her only child.

Yet another reason I so needed to talk to my mother: I needed her experience with this, her Scottish common sense, her infallible intuition from the Gypsy blood of my grandmother Evian, her unconditional love, her loyalty, and . . . just her. The presence, the physical space she once occupied, her voice, her hand on my shoulder. Despite all the challenges in my lifetime and the times I chose to walk away from relationships, I had never felt more alone in my life than I did right then.

And if I needed my mother at the age of almost fifty, what was my daughter feeling about her own dead mother, the woman who raised her and was now gone? What did Haley have left? A name in a file and, now, a glance at a face. Five seconds of conversation in over a quarter of a century. Did she need me? Did she want me? She had come here, but what was it about? Did she know our connection, or was it just bizarre chance she's here? And with Ethan?

I took the business card with Haley/Stephanie's cell phone written on it from where it lay on my nightstand. I hadn't let it out of my possession since I found it in my door a million years ago. But my sense of decency (or, rather, lack of nerve) won over at that time of the morning, and I set it back down without calling.

Three o'clock that afternoon found me and my lawyer, Lenore Delaney, in Jerry's office with the man himself and Peter Simons. Just as I was getting settled, Constable Taylor quietly entered and sat down in the corner.

"First of all," Jerry began as he leaned back in his desk chair, "as far as the OPP is concerned at this point, this is not an official investigation and the RCMP has not been brought in as yet. This is just a Q&A session."

"What about Scotland Yard?" I asked Peter.

"I'm on vacation," said Peter. Out of the corner of my eye, I saw Jerry begin to flip a pencil end over end on his desk, and I smothered a smile. "And I haven't," Peter continued, "officially reopened this case—yet. I won't get 115 families all worked up again unless I have a solid reason for doing so. It's just that when I saw the news last fall about your surviving the attack that killed Alison Standish, I was shocked to know you were alive after all. I started to dig around the files about Flight 39."

"So, officially, we all know what we aren't doing," my lawyer cut in. "What *do* you want from Dr. Mackenzie?"

"I want to know why she left Flight 39," he shot back. "Ran off, to be exact, minutes before takeoff. Left any carry-on luggage she had on the plane. Had only her purse in hand. One hour later, every person on board that flight was dead. What was in your luggage, Farran?"

I opened my mouth, but my lawyer raised her hand so I shut up.

"How do you know she 'ran' off and without her carry-on baggage?" Lenore asked the question I had started.

Instead of answering, Peter flipped open a small laptop. Seconds later, a grainy film appeared on the screen. And there I was, twenty-four years old, running past the airline staff at the desk and out of the boarding area, purse clutched to my chest. Peter played it a second time, then closed the computer.

"Security cameras caught it at the time," he explained, "but no one could identify the woman. No one came forward to say they had not been on the plane and were still alive. I wasn't on the force then; I was still at school. Never saw the tape, and if they put it on the news, I didn't see it. We all thought you were dead, Farran. And you never came forward to say otherwise. Why not?"

I shot a look at Lenore, who gave me a slight nod. We'd had a quick once-over in her office just after lunch to get ready for the tea party here.

"To be perfectly honest, Peter," I said, turning to him, "there is not a lot I remember following my seeing the news report of the accident. I remember the report, the shock, and the impact of realizing that I should have been on that plane. I should have been dead at that moment." I wanted to look at Jerry, but didn't dare. Not yet. "After that, it's a fog for a bit. Then I went home to Canada, by boat, as I'm sure you can understand.

"The reason I left the plane and the reason I later did not come forward are one and the same—a personal crisis that had nothing to do with that bombing, and as it involves other people even now, I will not talk about it unless I'm subpoenaed to do so. I'm not a terrorist. I had no reason to kill over a hundred innocent people I didn't even know. Unless you have something more damning on me, there is no case here. No connection except that I am sitting here now, alive."

"Do you have anything else we should know about, Inspector Simons?" Lenore asked, in a tone that said we were done.

There was a pregnant pause in the room. Jerry stopped flipping the pencil and looked at Peter. The latter shook his head.

"No, not for now. Off the record, Farran, I don't see you doing anything like that," said Peter. "But it is a new blip on the screen, and all these years, there has been nothing with this case. No group ever claimed responsibility."

"Are you going to keep following me around?" I asked dryly. "I know your white car to see it, now. You'll have to rent something else."

"I'll be around for a little bit, yet," he smiled back. "I'll be in touch."

"Well," I got to my feet and Lenore followed suit. "One of my best friends is getting married in just over a week, and I don't want any mess around that, Peter. I'm not going anywhere. I live here now. When Ruth is safely married, if you want to hash this out again, we can do it. But nothing until after the twenty-first, okay?"

With Lenore on her way back to Cornwall, I stuck my head in another office door just down the hall from Jerry's.

"Hi, Jordan."

Detective Sergeant Wiley looked up from his desk.

"Dr. Mackenzie. What can I do for you?"

I let the formality of "Dr." pass. Probably on orders from Strauss.

"I just asked the inspector about an update on the Sam Wallace murder, and he sent me to you. What did you find out there? Vivienne?"

When he hedged, I told him of the conversation with the crime scene officer the day before. Was it only a day?

"There was a second body found," Wiley admitted. "Possibly female, but we're still waiting for the report from Toronto."

"So that pretty much wraps it up, I guess," I responded. "I had a very interesting weekend in Massena." Taking a chair, I gave Wiley my statement about Charley, Charlotte, and the late Ricky Potts. Wiley wrote it all down, but I noticed he didn't say much about it except that they would follow up with the Massena police.

"Is Carman House open again, now?" I asked, getting ready to leave.

"Yes, it should be," said Wiley. "We were out of there last week. Not much to do with an accidental fall."

I shook my head. "I'm not so sure. There's something wrong with it all, but I just can't put my finger on it. I'm going to head out there this afternoon and talk to Mrs. Parmeter about it. Haven't spoken to her since it happened.

"Give my love to Michelle and Diana, okay?" I added, and was gone.

I stopped in at Sterling House on my way through, to check up on Carl and let him know about the second body. He wasn't there, but Millie was — unimpressed with Carl's early gallivanting after surgery.

"He's out driving around?"

"That's what I said," she sniffed. "You have to get moving after surgery, but driving around isn't good. I tried to stop him, but he slipped out and left me a note. Said he had something to do."

I had Millie promise to call me when he got back and continued upriver along the No. 2. Next stop, Carman House, hopefully before they closed for the day and hopefully to find Mrs. Parmeter on the job.

I arrived to see her little car behind the museum and the flag still out. Score on both points. There were no cars in the guest parking when I pulled in, and I shot a glance across the field to where the police tape had been extended. There had been digging and there was still a patrol car blocking the road in. No sign of the Water People.

It had been quiet with the Water People on my front since Ethan's 3:00 a.m. call. No more visits or any calls from the Harrison contingent. I still hesitated to contact anyone, but carried the card with the number on my person like a talisman. For a second, I was frightened. What if the continued investigations in that area had discouraged the studies being done and my daughter had vanished once again into the void, out of reach? I fingered the card in my pocket and decided that, hell or high water, I would call her that night after supper.

The door to Carman House stood open. I suddenly felt that anxiety again. Perimenopause is not for the faint of heart, I figured, and headed up the porch stairs. The house was very quiet, with only a breeze rippling some pamphlets near the door. The donation bowl was empty.

"Mrs. Parmeter?" My voice echoed in the dining room, as I made my way to the back of the house. Kitchen empty, too. I went out the kitchen door and circled around the house. Car still there, no sign of its owner. Odd. By now it was almost five o'clock and probably closing time for Carman House.

I heard the phone ringing inside and remembered the office. She was probably there, doing some paperwork. The phone had stopped by the time I made it back in, so I knocked on the door under the stairs so as not to walk in on the conversation. But there was no reply, and no sound of anyone talking on the other side of the door.

"Mrs. Parmeter?" I slowly opened the door and stuck my head in. By this time, my perimenopausal anxiety had graduated to a more ominous dread moving up the back of my neck. The stairwell to the basement was in darkness, as it had been when I found Carl lying at the bottom. *That* had been the problem, the question that had been bothering me since that day. Let's see what Parmeter had to say about that, right now.

But it was not to be.

It wasn't red paint. And it wasn't a pile of clothes.

Blood and foam and Meredith's horribly mangled body churned in the water around the gears. I shall see it till I die—the red print dress turning over and over like grotesque laundry in a wringer washer. And the gears slamming relentlessly, threatening to grind her in.

The dread in my neck took over my throat and lungs as I walked over to the clothing.

It was Mrs. Parmeter, in her tour guide dress, eyes staring sightlessly, with blood seeping from a large, dark patch on the side of her head.

Question Period was over before it had begun—forever.

FIFTEEN

PATTERNS OF FORCE

"Dearly beloved, we are gathered here today in the sight of God for a life celebration—to join this man and this woman in holy matrimony."

Jerry Strauss sat quietly in the pew, enjoying the temporary suspension of general chaos. As with so many weddings, it was a beautiful ceremony with absolutely no indication of the turmoil leading up to it. With this group, however, the turmoil had a capital "T".

St. Matthew's Presbyterian in Ingleside was almost full for the marriage of Ruth Hoffman and Ernie Black. Jerry surveyed the attendees thoughtfully. On Ruth's side of the church were all five of her children, including Paul, who sat with Lynn and Farran. Buck Bradshaw, his old nemesis, sat beside Lynn. The man had flashed him his usual cocky smile on his way into the church, and Strauss had made a personal sticky note to avoid any Q&A with him today. The man was a natural bloodhound, and Jerry wondered if Lynn had said anything to Buck after she'd talked to him.

"Talked" was a relative term in this case. In the past week leading up to the wedding, Jerry had gone a few rounds with each of them except Buck. With all hell breaking loose around the Sam Wallace murder and Peter Simons hitting town, it was nothing short of a miracle that they were here, sitting peacefully in the church watching Ruth take her vows for the second time in her life.

Strauss had thought to have a lull these past few days. Listening to the ceremony, he ran it all through his mind again . . .

"Well," Farran had said to Peter Simons as she and her lawyer rose to leave Jerry's office, "one of my best friends is getting married in just over a week and I don't want any mess around that, Peter. I'm not going anywhere. I live here now. When Ruth is safely married, if you want to hash this out again we can do it. But nothing until after the twenty-first, okay?"

Simons had agreed. The man was around on vacation for two

weeks and seemed in no haste to pursue this. Either he had no case, or he had more up his sleeve that needed confirmation. Either way, Jerry's spider senses told him, it was far from over.

After Simons had left his office, Jerry could hear Farran's voice with Wiley's talking about the Wallace case. He longed to go and join in, to talk to her about the case and listen to her paranoid (and usually dead-on) feelings, to be with her even officially. But the situation wouldn't let him. Kept him at arm's length until further notice. At least until they danced at Ruth's wedding.

What was the personal crisis Farran had responded to by fleeing the plane? Did it have anything to do with her daughter? They had talked about Oxford and her daughter in general terms a couple of times, but she had given no clues as to the identity of the father. She had been tight-lipped about that, not in a secretive way, but only in terms of reluctance to talk about it at all.

Weren't two of the Water People British?

And hadn't Simons recognized them? What was that name . . . Chamberlain. Dr. Chamberlain.

Strauss pulled up the Internet and in a few minutes had the full name and profile:

Dr. Ethan Chamberlain, full professor at Oxford University. Faculty since 1976. Married to Dr. Debra Hyde, also at Oxford. Specialty: North American native oral culture and colonial interface. Currently on loan to the University of British Columbia as consultant to the Iroquois Project: a multidisciplinary assessment of environmental, historical, and cultural impact of dams and flooded lands on native peoples as part of the follow-up to B.C.'s River Recovery Project. Major sponsor was Harrison Media, Inc.

He heard Farran leave the building, and sat for some time, pencil going end over end. Oxford. It was too late to ask now. And she hadn't told him.

"*I need to ask about the bombing that killed Alison Perry Standish and almost killed Farran Mackenzie,*" *Simons had said when he'd first turned up at the Long Sault detachment.*

"*What about it?*" *Strauss had stonewalled.* "*That was last year.*"

"*It was a bomb and it happened in Dr. Mackenzie's driveway, did it not?*'

"Yes, but I don't see—"

"Has anyone been arrested for that crime?"

"No. It was linked to an earlier murder in Cambridge of a retired police officer named Dave Carlson." Strauss had sat back, hoping to look unconcerned. "Standish had been receiving threats about her return to politics, and it looked as though the bomb that killed Carlson was meant for Standish. At this point, it has been ruled murder by person or persons unknown. And there is an associated investigation into a group affiliated with organized crime. You'll need to talk to the Cambridge police about that."

He'd hoped he had shut that down. Certainly, Farran's growing hobby of being around for bomb blasts didn't look good in Simons' eyes, considering the fate of Flight 39. And he would never tell Scotland Yard what Farran thought about the death of Alison Perry Standish.

He shot back his drink and put the glass down. Then he finally looked at Farran. "That's not an excuse. Just an explanation. When the news came about the arrests in Cambridge, I pulled the security detail off. I thought it would be safe, then, with Alison's story all over the wire. I should have known . . ." He struggled for a moment. "I let Alison down. I let you down. I'm sorry."

"No," said Farran. "No, Jerry—"

"I should go," he said abruptly and headed for the door.

"The bomb wasn't meant for Alison. It was meant for me."

Jerry stopped dead in his tracks and carefully turned to face her. "What did you say?"

"I said the bomb was meant for me. Not for Alison. You couldn't have saved her if you'd tried. Alison killed Dave Carlson for killing her father, and once she knew I'd figured it out she planned to kill me, too."

"But that's imposs—"

"I said it was meant for me!" she screamed and hurled her glass across the room. It hit a framed print on the far wall, glass meeting glass, exploding into a thousand fragments. The silence that followed was deafening.

But no proof. No evidence.

Farran had told him about that, but not about Ethan. Was it just not offered until it was too late? Or was there something else? If he were right about Ethan Chamberlain, the father of Farran's baby had been standing right in her living room. And she hadn't told him the man was here, let alone who he was.

Paranoia isn't all it's cracked up to be, he thought.

"Sir?" Wiley appeared at the door.

"Yes, Jordan?" The first name had stuck since its inaugural use when the younger office had been gunned down in Sterling House, trying to protect his daughter from a killer. For a moment, Strauss had thought he'd lost Wiley, one of his best officers as well as a friend. "What is it?"

"A call from Toronto. The second remains found in Iroquois are female and are confirmed as one Vivienne Dupuis, according to dental records provided by her family in Montreal. The gun we're still working on, but waiting to hear from the U.S. military records."

"Military?"

"Yes, sir. We've identified it as a Colt .45, or M1911A1 .45 calibre pistol. Been issued to American troops since World War I. Has a number on it. Hopefully, the military can tell us who it belonged to last."

Wiley handed over an envelope.

"Crime scene also found this in with the remains. Seems to be a coin. Early 1800s."

Strauss turned the envelope upside down and dropped its contents into his hand.

"I also took a statement from Dr. Mackenzie just now," Wiley continued. "Seems she found out what happened to Rick Potts when he returned to Massena that fall." He passed Strauss a folder. "I guess that will wrap it up, if we can conclude that Potts killed both Dupuis and Wallace for the gold."

Gold. Strauss looked at the coin in his hand.

Then his cell phone had rung.

"You'd think I would be getting used to this by now."

Farran had sat in Jerry's office, white-faced, with her hands wrapped around a coffee mug. Paul Vaughn was with her, having shown up at Carman House not long after the squad car and ambulance. She must have called him. Did she call Paul before calling his cell, Jerry wondered? Then got a grip on himself.

"Let's hope you don't have to." Jerry sat down at his desk, remembering the first time he'd done that with Farran in that chair. Meredith had just been murdered, Gordon didn't yet know about being Farran's uncle, and Jerry had been about to find out his personal connection to this beautiful, flakey, and enigmatic woman facing off with him in his office. "Tell me again why you went out there."

"To talk to Mrs. Parmeter." Farran looked down into her coffee and swallowed.

"About what?"

"About Carl's accident. About why the light was switched off."

Jerry sat back in his chair. "What light?"

She looked up at him, and he wished for a moment that Vaughn wasn't in the room.

"The basement light. It was off when I found Carl. I remembered having to switch it on, and that bothered me. I wanted to ask her about that." Farran managed a swallow of coffee and Paul put his hand on her shoulder. "That was all wrong."

Strauss studiously avoided looking at the hand on the shoulder. "Why?"

"Because Mrs. Parmeter came yelling and running out of the museum that day, all upset about finding Carl at the bottom of the basement stairs. When I went to find him, I had to turn the light on at the top of the stairs to see him. She must have had to, too. So why was the light off again? If you find something that upsetting, I don't think you would bother stopping to switch the light off before heading out to yell for help."

"You've got a point," said Paul. "What do you think it means?"

"I don't know," she shook her head slowly. "But I have an awful feeling that if I had asked her earlier, this might not have happened."

"You think Julia Parmeter was murdered because she knew something about the day Carl Wallace fell down the stairs?" Strauss leaned forward. "That it wasn't an accident?"

"I don't know," Farran repeated miserably. "There is something else but, . . ." Her voice trailed off, and both men waited expectantly. Finally, she shook her head again. "Something else. But I can't remember what it is."

"If that's true, then so much for wrapping it up with Rick Potts," said Strauss. "He's been under several tons of cement for fifty years."

"No chance Parmeter was an accident, too?" Paul ventured.

"No." Strauss said shortly. "Still have to wait for the autopsy, but there was nothing in the office that could account for the head wound. In fact, if it confirms as homicide, we have no murder weapon. Yet."

"The office had been ransacked," Farran remembered. "And the donation bowl near the door was empty."

"Looks like someone was looking for something, got caught by Parmeter, killed her, and then cleaned out the donation bowl to help make it look like robbery." Strauss picked up his pencil. "But a museum?"

"Looking for what?" said Paul.

"Anybody's guess," was Strauss's reply, and then he pulled open a drawer. Taking out a small brown envelope, he passed it to Farran.

"Speaking of robbery, I thought you might find this interesting, Dr. Mackenzie."

Farran dumped the contents into her hand. She looked at it closely, then rubbed the surface with her fingers. "1798," she read carefully, then looked up at Strauss. "Is this what I think it is?"

"Apparently so," he nodded. "It's a Spanish gold coin, commonly referred to as a doubloon."

"Where did you get this?"

"From Vivienne Dupuis." Age must be bringing the dramatist out in him, Strauss thought. "Crime Scene found that in the bones of one of her hands. She must have been clutching it when she was killed and buried."

"So you did find Vivienne?" Farran asked thoughtfully.

"Toronto just confirmed it this afternoon."

Farran set the coffee down and put her head in her hands. "This is getting all so muddled, now. I thought Potts killed them when he left for Massena. That maybe they fought over the gold."

"That hasn't been ruled out," said Paul. His hand remained on her shoulder.

"Then why is Julia Parmeter dead?" Farran raised her head.

"This is either going to help, or make it more muddled."

At the voice, all three looked at the door where Wiley stood with a paper in his hand. He walked over and laid it on Strauss's desk.

"Preliminary background on Julia Parmeter," he told Strauss. "I'm calling Shelley Frost back in for more questions. Seems the deceased's maiden name was Piper. Julia Piper Parmeter was Shelley Piper Frost's older sister."

Shelley Piper Frost kept wiping her eyes with a tissue. Sitting in the chair in Wiley's office, she seemed much smaller than Strauss remembered from his visit with Wiley to the Hartford.

"I don't know who would want to kill Julia," she repeated. "Julia never hurt anybody. Always giving. Always volunteering. Can't believe it. Seems like a nightmare. Maybe it's a mistake? An accident?" Her voice trailed off.

"I wish it were, Mrs. Frost," Wiley said kindly.

"And all that upset with that poor man who fell."

"Carl Wallace."

Her eyes grew round. "It was *Carl* who fell? I didn't know. Julia never said the name. How is he?"

"He's recovering. Did your sister talk much about that day?" Wiley added.

"Well, she was upset by it all, of course. And she seemed . . . well . . . worried, I guess."

"About what, Mrs. Frost?" Strauss asked. "About the accident?"

"Sort of, I think." Shelley hesitated. "She was worried after the accident, but I had a feeling it wasn't about Carl. If you know what I mean."

Strauss looked at Wiley, who smiled a brilliant smile at the woman.

"We do, but why don't you put it into words? For our statement, Mrs. Frost."

"Well," she began, "she felt bad for Carl, but she kept talking to herself about if it was right or not."

"That Carl fell," Wiley prompted.

"I guess. I think she was worried about Carman House, and maybe Mr. Pollan. He does most of the repairs around there, and she was kind of sweet on him."

"I'm not sure I follow, Mrs. Frost," Wiley admitted. Strauss covered his mouth with his hand.

"I had a feeling she was afraid that Mr. Pollan would get in trouble because that man had an accident, that maybe he tripped on something left in the way or something like that."

"And Mrs. Parmeter was sweet on Jeremy Pollan?"

Shelley blushed.

"I thought so. She never really said anything, but she talked about him a lot. Been lonely since her husband John died a few years ago. I know what that's like."

"What do you think about Jeremy Pollan?" Strauss asked unexpectedly.

"I don't really know," came the answer. "Never met him. Just heard about him. He never seemed to be around any days that I would show up. Comes and goes on his own schedule, Julia said."

At the mention of her sister, Shelley's eyes filled again.

"Is there anyone you can think of who might have wanted your sister dead?" Wiley asked gently.

The woman wiped her eyes again and shook her head.

"No," she whispered. "Like I said, Julia never hurt anybody."

"Then it must have been robbery."

Wiley sat where the now departed Shelley Piper Frost had sat. Strauss was up and pacing.

"Why don't I believe that, Wiley? Doesn't feel like a robbery, the apparent looting notwithstanding." Strauss thought about Farran's question about the light. "It doesn't add up. And the issue of the light being switched off—Farran's right. That bugs me, too."

"Sounds like you think Carl's fall wasn't an accident. Do you think he was pushed?"

"Possibly."

"He doesn't remember it that way."

Strauss sighed. "He doesn't remember it at all." He shook his head and continued pacing. "We've been sloppy with this, Jordan. We should have spotted the connection between Parmeter and Frost. Maybe Farran's right about that, too. She said she felt that if she'd asked Julia Parmeter about the light earlier, she might be alive now.

"It's my fault. This business with Scotland Yard—" Strauss broke off.

Wiley hesitated, obviously wondering if he should pursue

Strauss's thoughts on that—then thought better of it.

"Muddled," he said instead.

"What?"

"Farran said it was all muddled in her head, and I agree. There's no pattern coming clear here, yet. We have two dead people in Iroquois, a dead alleged murderer in the dam near Massena, one wounded or attacked elderly brother of a victim, a newly murdered woman, and her sister that used to know the Iroquois victims and the murderer during the Seaway."

The two men were silent for a minute.

"Farran also asked a good question, I think," Wiley continued. "Why *is* Julia Parmeter dead? If this is all somehow connected to that summer of 1957, then it should be Shelley who was killed. It was Shelley, not Julia, who worked at the diner and knew the Wallace brothers."

Silence again. Then Constable Margaret Taylor poked her head through the door.

"Sergeant Wiley?" she asked. "You wanted to know when this came through."

Wiley took the paper from her hand, scanned it quickly and turned to Strauss.

"More and more muddled, sir. It's a reply from the U.S. Military Department of Records. According to the registration number, the gun we found was last issued for military service during the Korean War and then reported missing by its owner."

Wiley held the paper out to Strauss. "Guess who?"

"Come in, son." Daniel Sterling stood with military erectness despite his years. "It's good to see you."

After speaking with Shelley Frost, it had been too late in the day to drop by, so Wiley had called Sterling House to set up a meeting the following morning.

Jerry's own father, Bill Strauss, had died suddenly during the Seaway years, leaving his twelve-year-old son angry and lost. For a brief time the summer after, Daniel Sterling had been like a father to the boy. Finding each other again unexpectedly after fifty years was something Strauss was still absorbing. He realized with more than a little guilt that he hadn't been back to Sterling House since the murder and its time-sensitive investigation.

"This is business, Daniel," Strauss explained, "but I'd like to drop by for a tea sometime soon if you can."

Sterling grinned, the face looking so different from the old days, but the eyes not at all. "You're the working stiff, Jerry. I have no schedule. Name the day and we'll do it. Hello, Sergeant Wiley," he added as Jordon came through the door behind Strauss. "How is that lovely daughter of yours?"

"Just fine, thanks to you, Mr. Sterling," Wiley answered, taking his hat off. He looked from the hallway into the living room and grew grim in remembering that morning.

"Carl is waiting for you in the dining room. Millie made some tea." Daniel led the way through the swing door. "I'll join Millie in the garden and leave you three to it."

Carl Wallace sat at the dining room table, nodding a greeting as they entered.

"How are you feeling, Mr. Wallace?" Strauss took a seat and accepted a cup of tea from the man.

"Still sore, but much better." Carl passed a cup to Wiley. "Stabbing myself seems a bit overdone, I'd say," he added, smiling sheepishly. "Could have just broke my fool neck in the fall and been done with."

"What do you remember about the fall?" Wiley asked.

"No more than before. Don't know what possessed me to go in that doorway, but I don't remember anything after opening the door. Is this what you need to see me about?"

"No, I'm afraid not." Wiley put a small parcel on the table and unwrapped it. "Mr. Wallace, do you recognize this gun?"

Carl slowly set his tea down and picked up the weapon. He held it gingerly in his hands, turning it over several times. Then his face cleared.

"My God," he looked at Wiley. "This is my gun from the army. Korea. Lost it a long time ago. Wherever did you find it?"

"Near where we found your brother's remains," came the grim reply. "Along with the remains of Vivienne Dupuis."

"What?"

"When we ran into a dead end for Dupuis and Potts," Strauss said quietly, "we went back for a second look in Iroquois. Couldn't see how all those people could just disappear off the face of the earth. We found Vivienne's remains near those of your brother. Potts, we've learned since, died in Massena on the dam site."

"Yes," murmured Wallace. "Dr. Mackenzie told me."

"That gun was reported lost in action in Korea by one Private Carl Wallace," Wiley said pointedly.

Carl looked sheepish again. "Oh, hell," he said, handing it back, "lots of guys did that. Wanted a souvenir. I kept mine."

"Did you bring it with you to the Seaway Project?"

"Yes. Thought it might not be a bad idea, with all the strangers around. Things can get rough sometimes in work camps like that."

"Your brother was killed by a shot to the head from a Colt .45—just like this one. We can assume this is the murder weapon. Dupuis, we don't know yet." Strauss looked Wallace in the eye. "When was the last time you saw this gun?"

Wallace looked right back, for which Strauss had to give him credit. "Sometime before I left to go home. I don't know exactly when it disappeared, but one day, I checked and it was gone."

"Was this before or after your brother left?" Wiley had his note-book out.

"I'm not sure . . . I think before. I remember thinking I should ask him if he took it."

"Who knew you had such a piece with you?"

"Just Sam. I kept it in the bottom of my duffle bag."

"But anyone could have gotten to it?"

"No. It was in my footlocker. Only Sam knew the combina-tion."

"Tell us again about the gold story. Did Sam talk about it much?"

"No. I told you. I overheard it one night when he was talking to Potts outside the boarding house, having a cigarette. Heard it through the window. Took a strip out of him later about listening to such fairy tales. That Potts was playing him for some reason."

This time Strauss brought out the package. He opened a small envelope and put the gold doubloon on the table.

"Maybe not, Mr. Wallace. Any chance they could have found the stuff?"

Carl picked up the coin and looked at it, then at Strauss.

"You're pulling my leg. Is this for real?"

"Real enough, Mr. Wallace," said Wiley. "That coin was found with the bones of Vivienne Dupuis, near those of one of her hands. We think she was holding it when she was killed."

"Mr. Wallace," Strauss abruptly changed topic, "where were you yesterday afternoon? Farran Mackenzie said she dropped by to see you on her way to Iroquois and you were out."

"Went for a drive. Had to get out for a bit. Why?"

"Dr. Mackenzie said Millie told her you left her a note that said you had something you had to do. What was that?"

Carl smiled down at the table, then shot a glance at the door to the kitchen.

"I really just needed to get out and have some space for a spell," he explained, lowering his voice. "Keeps is a good lady, but she fusses you up a lot."

"Did you meet up with anyone while you were out?"

"What's this about, Inspector?" Wallace handed the coin back. "Sounds like you think I'm guilty of something."

"Julia Parmeter," Strauss explained slowly, "the tour guide at Carman House who found you after your fall, was killed yesterday."

"That nice lady? How?"

"A blow to the head. From the side. Possibly by someone she knew. The office was all messed up, but curiously, there was no sign of struggle." Strauss waited.

Carl looked from one officer to another. "You think this had something to do with me? I didn't even know the woman, except meeting her that day at the museum."

"You may not have known Julia, but you knew her sister Shelley. Shelley Piper. She worked in the Daffodil diner back in Old Iroquois." Strauss let that sink in.

"Shelley . . ." the old man said finally. "Shelley Piper. Such a nice girl. Is she . . .?"

"She's still alive and quite distraught at the moment," Strauss replied.

"She was a nice kid."

"When we told Shelley earlier that it was Sam that was found out near the water, she seemed rather upset at that," said Wiley. "Was there something there, too?"

Carl's mouth became a thin line. "Sam only had eyes for Vivienne. Shelley was a nice kid, but he didn't know she was alive."

The officers looked at one another.

"I guess that's all for now, Mr. Wallace," said Wiley rising. "We'll be in touch. Oh," he added, "and don't leave town without letting us know."

Daniel Sterling had been sitting on the back terrace with Mildred Keeps. Strauss noted as he sat down to join them that she was not wearing her pink mules this morning.

"All finished with Carl?" Daniel asked.

"For now. Mildred, when did Carl get back yesterday?"

The woman thought for a minute. "He left just after lunch and came back in time for supper. I don't usually make supper for guests," Keeps added, "but Carl is convalescing."

"He's doing well if he's out driving around all afternoon. Did he tell you where he went?"

Mildred shook her head. "Didn't really say and I don't pry." She got up to leave. "I have rooms to get ready. Did you want another tea, Inspector, before I get started?"

"No, thank you," Strauss said, then watched her leave before turning to Daniel.

"How have you been, Daniel? I should have been by earlier—"

The elderly man cut him off with a wave.

"I know how busy your job keeps you, son. It hasn't been quite a month, yet. How are you, I should ask? That barracuda giving you any more trouble?"

The "barracuda" was the Honourable Isabella Roberts, MP, Minister of Canadian Heritage. One of the many personal skeletons Jerry had had to face that spring in Sterling House. He chuckled—the first laugh he'd had in a week.

"No, no more trouble from the dragon lady, Daniel. She's had her wings clipped as far as I'm concerned."

"Good to hear it. What about the Mackenzie woman? Nice lady. Been here a couple of times to see Wallace."

"What do you think of Carl Wallace?" Strauss detoured.

Daniel gave him a look before answering. "Seems right enough. Served in Korea. Quiet fellow for a Yankee. Tough finding out about his brother, I imagine."

"It's gotten tougher," Strauss said ominously. He lowered his voice, even though all the guest rooms were on the other side of the house, and brought Daniel up to speed on the Sam Wallace case. When he was done, the older man sat back in his chair.

"So, do I think Carl Wallace is capable of murder?" he asked thoughtfully. "On the surface, no. But you and I have seen enough of life to know that people can get driven to do all kinds of things if the reason is good enough.

"You have all the 'whats' at this point, son," Daniel continued. "You need to sort out the 'whys' now. Why was it Sam and not the unloved Potts in that shallow grave for fifty years? Why was the girl there, too? Why kill the Piper sister who *didn't* work at the diner during the Seaway?

"Sergeant Wiley is right—it is a muddle. But no more than any other muddle you've had to work with as a police officer." Daniel leaned forward. "There's something else on your mind. Something personal that's bugging you. Is it about *her?*"

Strauss knew when he was cornered. Strangely enough, in this case he didn't mind. He needed someone to talk to, to look at things reasonably and without, well . . . emotional attachment.

"She's in trouble, Daniel. Big trouble, possibly. And I don't know what to do about it. No matter what I do, I'm in a bad position with this. I can't help. I can't talk to her about it. I . . ." He fell silent.

"Can you tell me about it?" Daniel asked gently.

All that had been the easier part of Strauss's week. As he continued to sit quietly in the church, watching the happy couple sign the register and be photographed, the events of the past week continued to roll through his thoughts like a documentary. . .

After taking Farran home following the coffee klatch about finding Parmeter's body, Paul Vaughn had returned to Jerry's office. Round One.

"I want to know what's happening with this Simons fella," Paul threw himself down into the chair Farran had used. "I don't like what he's suggesting."

"He's just looking into something new on the bombing. First new thing in decades. It's his job."

"You don't honestly believe that Farran could have had anything to do with that, do you?"

Strauss glared at him. "What do you think?"

"I don't know what to think. But I'll tell you this," Paul added. "I've seen his kind before. He's heading for retirement and would love to go out with a bang—a major collar like pinning the deaths of over a hundred people on Farran Mackenzie twenty-five years after the fact. Simons would be a goddamn hero back home."

"So far, he's just asking questions. If it becomes more than that, I'll be walking away from it professionally."

"What about personally?"

It was a loaded question, and they both knew it.

"I think it's best I keep that to myself, Vaughn," Strauss replied pointedly.

Paul stood up and put his hands on Strauss's desk. "We can't just leave her to the wolves, Jerry," he said in a low voice.

"I have no intention of letting that happen."

The stare-off went on for a few moments, then Vaughn turned to leave.

"Paul," said Strauss quietly.

The man stopped at the door and looked back.

"Stay close to her. Very close." Jerry kept his voice level, but the warning was there. "Don't let her out of your sight for a minute, if you can help it. You know what she's like."

Paul took in a deep breath and let it out. He nodded and then vanished.

End of Round One.

We'll take care of our girl, Ruth. A promise he intended to keep.

But Farran Mackenzie wouldn't make it easy.

Round Two had begun the next morning when Jerry had opened his front door and Lynn Holmes blew past him into the living room.

"Morning, Lynn," he said to the empty front hall. "Nice to see you."

"I don't have time for niceties." His old school friend stood with her arms crossed. "I just came from Ruth's for wedding stuff, and she told me about the Scotland Yard guy. What's up with that?"

"Sorry, Lynnie. I can't answer questions from the media."

"Media? For God's sake, Jerry, I'm family!"

"You still have professional demands, and I won't put you in a bad position. According to Simons, this is just a fact-finding mission. No investigation. I can give you his cell number."

"I don't want to talk to Simons. I want to talk to you."

"And I want to talk to you, since you're here. Sit down." Lynn remained standing. Jerry shrugged and took his favourite chair. "I want to know everything about Haley. Where are things with that?"

That took the air out of Lynn. "Haley? Farran's daughter? Why?"

"Because Ethan Chamberlain, the man I think is Haley's father, is here in the Seaway Valley and Farran isn't saying a word about it to me. What has she told you?"

Lynn slowly sank into another chair. "Not much," she admitted. "Not about the father. Apparently, Haley is here with a group of university people studying effects of water dams on the environment—or something like that. Farran was going to make contact the other day when that poor woman was found at Carman House. Needless to say, she wasn't up to it after that. She hasn't said anything about the father."

The Water People, as Farran called them. Ethan Chamberlain was part of that group, too, as was his wife, Debra Hyde. Strauss had seen the names on the report.

"She's protecting him for some reason," Strauss muttered.

"From what?"

"I'm not sure—yet. But I have a feeling she's not thinking straight. Lynn, I can't talk about anything related to Flight 39. But here's what I know about Farran. Something very bad happened years ago to a young Farran Mackenzie. It put her on the run and drove her away from her own child. Three of the players are here now, and so is Haley. Whatever evil was there in Oxford is here now—and in my experience, evil doesn't change with age."

"You're scaring me, Jerry."

He looked his old friend in the eye. "I'm scared. For Farran. If this is what I think it is, she's buried in old and deep emotions. Her good instincts may not kick in until it's too late. We have to take care of her, Lynnie. No matter what she says or does. Are you here now to stay for Ruth's wedding?"

Lynn nodded.

"Then I'll tell you what I told Vaughn this morning. Stay close to her. Don't let her out of your sight for a minute. She may do something very stupid out of old loyalties or old fear. Keep her busy and keep her in sight."

"What about Haley? Leslie told Farran last year that Haley was in trouble."

Strauss's eyebrows went up. "Leslie? Leslie Mackenzie?"

Lynn nodded again. "I know how it sounds, but I don't care. When Fan was in the hospital from the bomb that killed Alison . . . when she . . . when she *died* for a minute . . ."

Strauss got up and looked out the window. When he'd heard the Code Blue in the waiting room, he'd thought he would die, too. Then three days he waited for her to come back to him . . .

"When she was dead," Lynn continued behind him, "Farran saw her mother, and Leslie told her to find Haley. That she was in trouble."

Strauss turned back from the window. "Leave Haley to me. Is that still her name?"

"No. Her name now is Stephanie Harrison. And you'll like this one, Jerry. Stephanie is heir to the Harrison Media empire."

"*Those* Harrisons?"

"Yes. She is their only child, by adoption."

"So we have a shitload of money stirred into this, too. Do I remember correctly that her parents died during a corporate take-over last year? And all hell broke loose?"

"There is also rumour of an attempt on Stephanie's life in the last few months," Lynn added quietly.

Strauss didn't speak for some minutes. He stared unseeingly again out his front window, taking in the traffic on County Road No. 2. Lynn remained silent, knowing him enough to wait for an answer. Finally, it came.

"Lynn, you and Paul cover Farran while Ruth gets married. Let's see that done and done right. I'm going to do some digging into that cosy little group of academics hanging around Iroquois, and even Inspector Simons. He knew Farran at Oxford. I'm taking nobody at their word."

End of Round Two.

Round Three would be today, Strauss thought in the church. A quiet one, but he needed to know.

Ruth had come up the centre aisle with the air of a young girl in love. Everyone had been smiling, especially Ernie Black where he waited for his bride at the front.

Love. When Strauss had listened to the couple take their vows, he could hear Daniel's voice from the other day.

The woman you love is in trouble, son. And that's a hell of a place for you to be. Especially if she won't talk to you about it. Doesn't mean necessarily that she's protecting him. Ever think she might be protecting you from her troubles?

Strauss looked at Farran's head in the pew in front of him. He needed to know. He needed to see it in her eyes — or not.

The ceremony was over and everyone followed the happy couple out to the front steps for pictures. Lynn and Paul were both busy with cameras. Farran stood to one side, smiling. She looked over at Strauss. He started over to her.

"Hey, Jurgen! How's it going, guy?" Buck Bradshaw materialized in his path. "Lovely day for a wedding, isn't it?"

"Bradshaw." Amenities were kept to a minimum. The man was mostly harmless, but still a bloodhound. And someone who loved to lock horns with him. "Wish I could say good to see you. How are things since I last saw you? Still keeping busy with the tabloids?"

Buck grinned. "Always the joker, Jurgen. Good to see you, too. No shootouts today, right?"

"None scheduled."

By the time Strauss had disentangled himself from Buck, Farran had moved out of range. She was busy with Ruth and Caroline, helping the bride into the car to go to the reception. They all vanished together down the road.

Wedding supper done, the dance went on uninterrupted until past midnight.

Strauss stayed by the bar, nursing one drink for a long time. He did the right thing and took the bride for a waltz, both carefully not talking about anything. Lynn dragged him up on the floor, as did

Diana Wiley.

Finally, he finished his drink and walked across the room to where Farran sat with Paul.

"A dance, Ms. Mackenzie?" Strauss held out his hand. To his relief, she smiled and took it, following him out to the floor. Jerry felt Ruth's eyes on him as they passed.

They were uncharacteristically silent with each other, but she felt relaxed in his arms.

"I've missed you," he murmured in her ear.

"I've missed you, too," she whispered back.

He held her closer. Could they just keep dancing?

"We need to talk, Farran." How classic.

He felt her stiffen, yet she seemed to hold him closer.

"Not yet, Jerry," came the reply. "Not until I have some stuff sorted out. Okay?"

"Stuff like Ethan Chamberlain?"

She pulled away and looked at him. "How did you know that?"

He pulled her close again and kept dancing.

"Are you protecting him, Farran?" It came out before he could stop it.

Her eyes grew wide. "I need some air." She pulled away again and started for the door. Strauss followed her out, taking her by the arm when they reached the parking lot.

"You need to talk to me, Mackenzie."

"I can't. Not yet. It's all a mess." She covered her eyes with her hand.

Strauss grabbed Farran's other arm and made her face him.

"Why can't you trust me?" he asked. Then the question he had to ask. "Do you still love Ethan Chamberlain?"

"I do trust you, Jerry. You're my best friend, but you can't get involved personally with this. I know that."

"I don't mean the business with the airplane. I mean Haley and why you disappeared from her life, from his life." Strauss listened to his words and stopped dead. Then he looked her in the eyes. "Farran, is Ethan the reason you ran off the plane?"

"I—I can't. I have to protect—"

"Who? For God's sakes, Farran, let me help. I love you. I don't want you to get hurt."

She looked at him, then, in the glow of the hall entrance light, for a full minute, hand on his cheek. He would always remember that moment, and all that passed between them without words.

"I love you, too, Jerry Strauss," said Farran. "Remember that. No matter what."

"Do you still love Ethan?" he asked again.

She didn't reply, but neither did she turn away. Instead, Farran kissed Jerry softly on the lips. He pulled her close and crushed her mouth with his.

Then she was gone, back into the reception and the crowd.

End of Round Three.

Jerry didn't follow. He stood for some time in the growing dark, thinking.

"As on a darkling plain," he muttered, from a poem learned long ago.

Finally, Jerry flipped open his cell phone and punched in a number. When the other end picked up, he merely said, "I need to talk to you for a minute." Then slapped the phone shut and waited.

A few minutes later, Detective Sergeant Jordan Wiley came out to join him in the parking lot.

"You rang?" he asked, with a half smile.

"I rang," said Strauss. "As of this moment, I am officially removed from any further communication with Inspector Peter Simons of Scotland Yard. Personal reasons. I am handing it all over to you and am no longer available for comment. Do whatever you have to do with Simons and Flight 39."

Then it was Jerry's turn to disappear, this time toward his car and then down the road, leaving Jordan Wiley standing alone in the night.

SIXTEEN

ARENA

"Dearly beloved, we are gathered here today in the sight of God for a life celebration . . . to join this man and this woman in holy matrimony."

Ruth looked beautiful—and happy. That much was right in my life. I was taking the day and living it, putting everything else on the shelf until Ruth and Ernie had exchanged vows, posed, danced, and disappeared into their new lives. Change is the essential process of all life. Isn't that what Spock once told Kirk?

Yet watching my beloved Ruth embracing change brought it home to me so clearly that I was not. All I was doing was riding out life's demand for balance, paying more life invoices just to settle up the last thirty years of my life. And the big one had finally come in. If I could keep a handle on it, do the right thing, and possibly walk away with something real, then maybe it would be time to move forward in life and love. Could that ever happen?

I listened to the wedding vows, feeling Jerry's presence in the pew behind me like the sun on an autumn day. Then, for the first time in decades, a simple but powerful word dropped into my thoughts, sending ripples to the edges of my soul.

Want.

What did Farran Mackenzie *want*?

Not what could she get, but what did she want? I had no clue. I hadn't asked myself that question in years, and the thought of it was pretty heady stuff.

I sat there, sandwiched between my guard dogs, Lynn and Paul, in the church that Hydro had built half a century before, looking at the stained-glass window above the heads of the happy couple, thinking of the church bell outside that had come from St. John's Presbyterian in Farran's Point and all of my family history wrapped into that vanished place.

I just want to be with the people I love.

That's it. That's all.

The knowledge came to me in that holy place, profoundly and completely infusing my spirit. Life really is as simple as that, isn't it? To love and be loved. To be with those we cherish. We must pursue our selves and our dreams, but the circle is only complete when we share with our others. For the meaning of the getting lies in the giving.

You are wrong, Matthew Arnold, I told myself. There is indeed love and light in this world. I'm just not sure yet how to get there from this darkling plain.

The week leading up to the big day had been traditionally busy. Lynn had arrived the day after Julia Parmeter died, adding yet another delay to my contacting Stephanie Harrison et al. Amidst the swirl of phone calls, family arrivals, last-minute shopping and pre-wedding party, it was all I could do to figure out some careful yet casual way of setting up a meeting with just Stephanie, my daughter. I didn't want to meet with her the first time with Ethan there. It would be just too much, no matter the direction of the conversation.

I also had to call back Jennifer Farley and give her the interview she needed. I figured I was finished finding bodies for now and would have the time. She couldn't wait around forever. And something in me wanted to see her again. I didn't know if it was seeing someone who reminded me of myself from those Oxford days—those days back in my sights with a vengeance—or something else. I called and we arranged to meet for tea at my cottage.

"I appreciate your making time for me, Dr. Mackenzie." Farley was slightly breathless as she set her backpack down on the kitchen floor and took a seat at the table. "I hope you're feeling better from the other day."

"I appreciate your patience with me, Ms. Farley." I set the tea-pot down between us. "I'm sure you need to get back home at some point. Where is home?"

"Vancouver. I live right on campus at UBC. And please call me Jenn."

"Oh, that's handy." I sat down. "Is your family in Vancouver, Jenn?"

She reached down to open her backpack. "Umm . . . yes. Just me and Mom now. Ah . . . here it is." Jenn surfaced with several brown envelopes (I seemed to be haunted by them at the moment) and set them on the table, passing one to me. "That's the agreement for the interview."

I looked it over quickly and signed my name. We talked for about an hour, and it felt good to be back in academic mode.

"The story of the Lost Villages is a story of loss, grief, and recovery," I said, "a primal human cycle of survival. For the people of the Lost Villages, it was community survival in the face of expropriation of land, artefact, economic fabric, community ties, and identity. Changes to these things that might have happened over generations came overnight. Memory was the fulcrum on which this turned and is key to navigating how the process unfolded."

"How so?"

"Well, when the project first began, the promised economic boom and the mantra of progress for all were the engines that drove the ship. Nostalgia, history, memory, and legacy no longer mattered in the modern world. Those who held on were labelled as backward and standing in the way of a better life for all. At that point, memory was used as a weapon, turned against those who valued it. Many subjects of my interviews recalled not only the Seaway propaganda in general, but also many times local authority figures spoke out against memory, such as sermons in church about letting go and moving on—a direct reference to the Seaway and its losses." I offered Jenn more tea, then refilled my own. "Certainly, the local newspapers at the time reflect the influence of the project and its authors in maintaining the necessary focus on progress over past. Just take a look at the files of the Cornwall *Standard-Freeholder* at the city library. Year after year, headline after headline trumpets the accomplishments of the construction, while small pictures and mentions of historic loss are relegated to the back pages."

"So the idea was just to forget and move on?"

"Exactly. You have to understand that Hydro was very efficient in its work and outlook. They saw this as the most practical way of navigating this huge change. In my opinion, however, in the very act of marginalizing the power of memory, Ontario Hydro was making an unintentional but clear statement of its value—a value understood by the villagers."

"Did it work?" Jenn adjusted the microphone on the table.

"For a long time it did. At least on the surface. The former villagers tried to move on in their new and odd landscape. They had been raised in an economy and a society both based on the river- front, and now they found themselves planted in what amounted to a suburb without an urban base. Ingleside and Long Sault—New Towns No. 1 and 2 respectively—were built on what had been farm- ers' fields north of the new Highway 2. Not only were the villagers physically removed from their beloved St. Lawrence, most could not even see it from their homes. They were suddenly 'riverless,' adrift on the land.

"They were also adrift amongst themselves, Jenn. We sit here in the twenty-first century with our modern social realities, but this was fifty years ago. It was also an area that was still holding on to a way of life quickly vanishing for everyone else. I recently spoke to a man who came here to move the houses. He came from a city in New Jer- sey, and said it was like going back in time in many ways. Ice boxes in the kitchens, woodstoves inside the houses for heat. Using Carl's words, they weren't backward, just old-fashioned, like their homes. Honest and decent and trusting of government in a way your genera- tion could never understand.

"So, for the former villagers, putting two communities together out of six meant getting new neighbours, combining churches, and mixing social groups. Everything had to change. Collective memory had no outlet, collective ties had little reference, collective identity was not possible then. Then, for over three decades, feelings about the Seaway, the loss, the changes, the failure of the brave new world, and the economic boom that never came to the Seaway Valley. All were muffled and confined to a resounding collective silence."

"Silence? No one talked about it?"

"Basically not. And nobody talked about their feelings, the lack of closure, the continued grief for loss of real and emotional land- scape. I'm sure it was terribly hard on the older generation. Many of them didn't survive the first winter after their moves into the new communities."

Jenn stirred her tea. "Obviously, the silence was broken. I've been to the Lost Villages Museum and have a few interviews lined up with former villagers."

"Oh, yes. It couldn't last. And remember that you are talking to the children who went through the move. At the time, it was very exciting and most of them didn't understand why their parents and grandparents were so upset. Now, as parents and grandparents themselves, they get it. Many of them are now going through a renewed remembrance and grieving of what was lost so long ago.

"Memory is like a river, ironically in this case. And you can't stop a river. The project was done, the world left, and the dust settled. Then, in 1977, the Lost Villages Historical Society was formed, creating a focal point for historical preservation of village artefacts and genealogical information. I would suggest that this was not only a practical starting point for the former villagers, but also an emotionally safe place to begin recovering collective memory that had been violently eradicated."

"Violently?"

"It was a violent end to a quiet way of life," I said. "And when we are faced with violence in any form, random, or organized like the Seaway construction, we protect ourselves however we need to. There were people I interviewed who could not remember what they saw on the day of the inundation even though they knew they had gone out to watch. It was a final letting go, a final goodbye, and a deeply traumatic moment. Their minds blotted it out."

"So, the Lost Villages Historical Society was the catalyst to remembering and commemorating, like Celebration 50?"

"It was the starting point, the declaration that there was indeed something valuable to remember—even if most of it was permanently under water. And the people were still here, with their memories, their histories, and their desire for legacy, as we all have. I guess you could say that that was when construction returned to the Seaway Valley—a reconstruction of memory. One thing that has really added to the healing and discussion is the fiction and non-fiction literature being written now about the villages and the Seaway Valley. Having it in print seems to validate the experience, and reading it in a fictional framework is a natural fulcrum for passing on the stories and the discussion." I passed her a paper. "Here is a list of local work you may be interested in reading."

We wrapped it up, and I gave Jenn the phone number for Sterling House, when she asked about talking to Carl.

"He's still recovering from a nasty fall," I explained, "but I'm sure he'd be willing to answer some questions. Carl would certainly have a different perspective on the moving and how the villagers reacted."

Jenn hesitated at the door.

"I remember you had a bad accident last year. I—I saw it on the news. I'm glad you're okay."

I nodded slowly. How could I say that I would never be okay with that? I would never heal that loss of both person and friend I once knew. "It was a very bad time. Memory is a two-edged sword sometimes." I looked at her. "Jenn, have we met before? You seem familiar to me, somehow."

She hesitated, then started to reply. I heard my cell phone ring.

"I have to catch that, Jenn. This was great. Be sure to call me if you need to go over anything."

Jenn waved her thanks and headed out the door. I dove for my phone on the counter.

"Farran," I said.

"Dr. Mackenzie? Stephanie Harrison returning your call."

Moments come that act as life markers. Sometimes they are public ones, and each generation has its defining moment: the assassination of John F. Kennedy, the shooting of John Lennon, the destruction of the space shuttle *Challenger*, the death of Princess Diana. All marked a moment in time and a change in trajectory of something we valued—an ideal, an era, a way of viewing ourselves. Personal moments also have this quality of marking time, usually through loss, certainly through primal change. And the personal space of those individual markers deprives us of the sharing that the public happenings offer, leaving us sealed inside a lonely shock wave moving through our souls.

I watched myself standing in the kitchen. So much had happened in that room in the past few years. Conversations, revelations, realizations, last moments. Now a first moment. I don't know how long I stood there with the cell phone fused to my ear. The only way I can share this lonely shock wave with you is to liken it to when you finally meet a favourite star or singer, and it leaves you speechless. All the rehearsed and imagined brilliant repartee dissolves in your grey matter, leaving you functionally an idiot.

"Dr. Mackenzie?"

This was my little girl, my beautiful baby. And we were about to have our first real conversation.

"Yes," I breathed into the phone. Breathe. Remember to breathe.

"Thank you for getting back to us. I apologize for dropping in like that the other day. We certainly didn't mean to intrude."

"No problem." At least, that's what I think I said.

"I didn't realize the Chamberlains knew you. Again I apologize. They are anxious to meet with you again."

I'm sure they are, I thought.

"I'm sure we can arrange something soon, Ms. Harrison. What did you wish to see me about?"

"We're part of something called the Iroquois Project. I don't know if you've heard about it through Waterloo. There was a provincial report done in 2001 in British Columbia called River Recovery, about decommissioning river dams. The data collected was massive and very informative. A lot of the fallout in certain cases was not just environmental, but also cultural. The Iroquois Project is a spinoff of that."

"Sounds interesting. There was so much engineering going on in that post-war era, and now we're all having to deal with the costs."

"It's certainly global. The United Nations Environment Program hosts a Dams and Development initiative, and we are tapping into that."

"What can I do for you, Ms. Harrison?" Other than tell you I'm your biological mother . . .

"Can we meet in the near future? I can put the whole team together for you, or—"

"No . . . no. That's not necessary. Why don't we meet, just the two of us, and start from there. I can be in touch with the Chamberlains later. No need to work any personal chatter into your schedule. I'm sure it's tight." God. "Would sometime next week work for you? I have a family wedding to get through at the moment."

"Actually, that would be best at this end, too. We're heading for Montreal for some research and interviews there."

We set a date for the Monday following Ruth's wedding. It would give me a day after the big day to gather what few brains I had left before sitting down to talk to my daughter.

Talk to my daughter. I would have to roll that one around on my tongue for a bit before it would feel right—or real.

"We appreciate it, Dr. Mackenzie. I'm sure you have a lot of important information for us. I will see you then." The line went dead.

"I hope you do, Haley," I said to the empty kitchen. A lot of important information. Yes, my darling, like that fact that I abandoned you when you were only a day old. And it left a hole in me the Moccasin could steam through ever since.

And so, the return to normalcy for Farran Mackenzie—even if just for a few days. Each day was lived for itself, full of all the wonderful hysteria that precedes a wedding. The Hoffman-Tremblay offspring assembled and behaved themselves, the two brothers even hijacking Paul for a manly beer with them one night. Carolyn kept everything and everyone under control with her usual Darth Vader skill, making sure that her mother's day was perfect. For once we were exactly in the same spot, and I happily followed her orders as the errand girl. A brief respite from responsibility.

We had a small rehearsal party. I called Jerry to attend, but got only his voice mail—again. Ever since the appearance of Peter Simons, I had felt Jerry's absence. I understood the space considering the situation, but I missed him fiercely and tried to be a grownup about it. Not easy for me, as you know.

Lynn Holmes came down for the week and became my sidekick. We talked briefly about the visit from Scotland Yard, and after she disappeared for an afternoon, Lynn moved her things out to my house to stay with me. It was busy for everyone, but I noticed that, between Paul and Lynn, I was never alone. Admittedly, I needed a buddy system for a few days after the grisly discovery at Carman House. The shock and the inherent guilt of waiting too long to talk to Julia Parmeter weighed heavily on me. Yes, I am a guilt professional, but I couldn't shake the feeling. And there was something else still rolling around the back of my brain that had felt wrong the day of Carl's accident. Something that, for now, refused to pick a slot on the roulette wheel and come to a stop.

So I just let life take me over for the week. Ruth and Ernie looked so happy it warmed my soul. Sort of made up for a lot of things.

I watched them at the reception and marvelled at the renewing power of late love. Ernie eventually cornered me for a dance, and after accepting full responsibility for his toes, swung me out on the dance floor.

"You haven't danced with your inspector, yet, Farran." Ernie smiled conspiratorially at me, making me flush.

"He hasn't asked me."

"Maybe he's afraid," Ernie winked. "Weddings are notoriously contagious, you know."

"Ernie Black—" I started.

"I'm just saying. Just saying, you know. But there's something I do want to say to you, Farran."

"What's that?"

"Thank you. Thank you for helping me find Ruthie again after all these years."

I looked at him. "Me? All I did was upset her so much she drove her car into the river."

"It was a bad moment, to be sure," he nodded, "but it was a bad time for you, too. I know that. And I also know that if things hadn't come to a head like that with you and Ruth, I would never have seen her name in the paper when I was down here visiting. We wouldn't be here tonight if it weren't for you."

"You're a sweetheart for looking at it that way." I kissed his cheek. "You're a sweetheart anyway, and I'm so happy for you both."

"Sweetheart, nothing," he grinned. "I know what Ruth has told me and how hard it's been for you since you came here. But it's a good thing you did. I know it's made Ruthie very happy."

The music ended. I gave Ernie a hug, and as I turned to go, he whispered in my ear, "Now all you gotta do is go get your inspector fella on the dance floor . . ."

I beetled it back to my table, instead. Ernie went up to the microphone and announced a song that was the first one he and Ruth had danced to at Casselman's dance hall that night so long ago. At his cue, the sounds of Nat King Cole's "Mona Lisa" began to float across the room. Ernie led Ruth out to the dance floor and everyone clapped. Couples began to join them after a minute. I saw Jerry finish his drink at the bar and get up to head my way.

"A dance, Ms. Mackenzie?" he asked, holding out his hand.

"Do you still love Ethan Chamberlain?"

We were standing out in the parking lot, where I had gone to get air and Jerry had followed. He'd figured out who Ethan was and it rattled me.

"I do trust you, Jerry. You're my best friend. But you can't get involved personally with this. I know that."

"I don't mean the business with the airplane. I mean Haley and why you disappeared from her life, from his life." Strauss seemed to listen to his own words and stopped dead. Then he looked me in the eyes. "Farran, is Ethan the reason you ran off the plane?"

"I—I can't. I have to protect—"

"Who? For God's sakes, Farran, let me help. I love you. I don't want you to get hurt."

There it was—the "L" word between us. I looked at him, then, in the sunset's glow, for a full minute, put my hand on his cheek.

"I love you, too, Jerry Strauss," I said. "Remember that. No matter what."

"Do you still love Ethan?" he asked again.

I didn't reply, but neither did I turn away. Instead, I kissed Jerry softly on the lips. He pulled me close and crushed my mouth with his. I could feel myself letting go, moving into him.

You lying bastard . . .

I jerked back at the sound. Then I fled back into the reception and the crowd.

That was the last I saw of Inspector Jerry Strauss for almost two weeks.

Ruth and Ernie left for a week's honeymoon, wanting to be back in time for Celebration 50 at the end of the month. Monday dawned, and with it came my appointment with Stephanie Harrison, my long-lost daughter.

We had agreed to meet on neutral ground, going for a drink at the McIntosh Inn in Morrisburg. I figured it was better that way, and if there was some way to introduce the subject of our matrilineal connection, it would be somewhere that had boundaries and the safety margin of public view. Safety for whom, I didn't want to predict.

I sat in the bar at a table in the corner, watching the door. The bar was mostly empty this early in the afternoon, and I was glad of it. The blonde from the Water People came in first, followed by the redhead. They stopped at my table.

"Please sit down," I said.

"I'm Stephanie Harrison." The blonde stuck out her hand and I looked at it for a moment. It had been such a tiny baby hand, little fingers curled around my big one.

"Uh . . . yes. Good to finally meet with you, Ms. Harrison."

"This is my partner on the project, Amy Shea." The blonde—Stephanie—indicated the redhead, who also shook my hand. They sat down.

"Again, I apologize for the intrusion the other day, Dr. Mackenzie," Stephanie began. "We really just thought to stop in and see about getting an interview at a later date."

"That's all right," I replied. "I don't usually have such a congregation in my living room." I thought I was managing normal conversation quite well considering to whom I was talking. I tried to really look at her without looking like I was looking—if you get what I mean.

Both young women were quite pretty. Stephanie had that Hollywood blonde look going with long blonde hair and makeup blatantly applied, while Amy resembled more of a young Stephanie Powers with deep auburn hair cut to the chin and sharp eyes. A more classic beauty. I thought of Jenn Farley with her brunette braids and makeup-free face. Maybe the academic look had changed a lot after all.

"So, you're both academics?" What a dumb question.

The girls shot a glance at each other and Stephanie spoke up. "Amy is one of three students on the project. I'm actually more involved as a sponsor."

"And you're along for the trip?" I signalled the waitress.

"I guess you could say that. My family has always been interested in environmental causes. My parents were sponsors of the River Recovery project some years ago."

"Yes. They certainly were active in that field for a long time."

"You know who . . . Steph's parents were?" asked Amy.

I know what you cannot imagine, I thought. Prudently, I

answered, "Yes. I recognized the name from the card. I remember when your parents died. It was all over the news. I'm sorry for your loss at such a young age, Stephanie."

Stephanie shot a look at Amy, who looked down at the table. Both said nothing. The waitress saved us by coming and taking a drink order. We all had beer.

"I keep busy with things like this," Stephanie said quietly when we were alone again.

"So, tell me what 'this' is again. It sounds environmental." I took a sip of beer. "Why is Ethan Chamberlain on the team? Or Debra Hyde, if I can ask. They are both specialists in history."

"Iroquois isn't just part of the Seaway history," said Stephanie. "It's got history of its own from way back. The native people used to cross the river at Iroquois Point for generations, and that gave it its name."

"That's right."

"Dr. Chamberlain is doing ground study on the Iroquois and the Mohawk, and contributing to the cultural impact portion through follow-up with the changes in native culture here following the expropriation for the Seaway."

I nodded. "Yes, I suppose that would be right up his alley."

"Did you work with him before?"

The question came from Amy, and—caught off guard—I hedged.

"Oh . . . yes. Sort of. Long ago. Actually, I worked with Debra, his wife. She was my supervisor for my master's."

"They seemed very surprised to see you." Again from Amy. Quietly, I began to get annoyed with the Stephanie Powers lookalike.

"What can I help you with for this project?" I changed the subject. It worked. For an hour, we had beer and nachos, and talked about the Seaway. I shared what I had shared with Jenn Farley, and eventually asked the girls if they had crossed paths with her at any time. The girls shared a glance again.

"No. No. Never heard the name." Stephanie shook her head.

"Oh. She said she was from UBC, too, I think." I looked at them both.

"It's a big place." Amy looked at her watch and Stephanie took the hint.

"Yes." She began to gather her things, including the tab. "We've kept you long enough, Dr. Mackenzie."

Are you kidding me? I wanted to say. We have twenty-six years to catch up on. But I couldn't, of course. I watched her pack the notes away with Amy, and stole a real look at her face. There seemed to be little trace of me there. Why would there be? There should be the love and hopes and dreams of Frank and Amelia Harrison—those who picked up where I left off after twenty-four hours of being her mother. Then I saw Amy watching me, and had the disturbing feeling she could see right through me.

"I hope I've been of some help." I pasted a smile on my face and rose with them. "Stephanie, if there is anything else, just call. It's not an intrusion. I enjoy stepping back into the academic role now and then."

"You retired early, Dr. Mackenzie," Amy pointed out for no particular reason.

"Yes," I replied. I suddenly saw Alison standing in my kitchen, grabbing the keys and leaving the watch behind. Saving me. "Personal reasons," I added.

"He's what?"

It was Wednesday morning, and Jennifer Farley had come by right after breakfast.

"He's under arrest." Jenn was very clear. "The OPP came and took Carl Wallace away for the murder of his brother Sam. Millie told me when I stopped by."

"Why the hell did nobody tell me?"

"I . . . I'm sorry. I don't know. I guess it happened only yesterday."

"No, I'm sorry, Jenn. It's not your fault no one told me. Maybe they just haven't had a chance." I sat down on the couch. What the hell was going on?

"What are you going to do?" Jenn asked after a minute.

"I don't know," I admitted. "I don't know if there is much I *can* do. I will go and see what it's all about. He must have a lawyer by now."

Jenn sat across from me. "This is to do with the body they found out at Iroquois Point, right?"

I nodded. "And there's been a second murder, possibly connected to this."

Jenn shivered. "Maybe you shouldn't be out here alone."

"I'm not, not right now. I have a friend staying for a few more days."

"That's good." Jenn hesitated a moment, and then dug into her bag. "Dr. Mackenzie, I brought a copy of my honours thesis that is the basis for my master's now. Would you consider looking it over?" She pulled out a brown paper parcel fastened with string. "It has the prof's corrections and comments on it but . . . Dr. Mackenzie?"

I sat like stone, hands at my sides, looking at the parcel. My thesis. My mother's voice. The memory sucked me in like a black hole. I don't know how long I sat there, with Jenn probably wondering if I were having a small and quiet breakdown.

The doorbell rang and I snapped out of it.

"I'm sorry, Jenn," I said as I rose to answer. "Just remembered something." Busy morning on Ault Island, I thought. Opening the door, I found Peter Simons on my doorstep.

"Hello, Farran. Hope this isn't a bad time. We need to sort something out."

"Actually, Peter, I do have a visitor right now."

"I'm afraid this can't wait." The Scotland Yard manner set in. "I've had a talk with someone about why you left the plane that day, and I would like your spin on that." He turned to the car in the driveway and signalled with his finger to the occupant in the passenger seat.

Slowly the car door opened and out stepped Ethan Chamberlain.

It wasn't going to be a good day.

I sat with Ethan and Peter in my living room, which Jenn had just vacated to give us privacy.

"If you need me for anything, Dr. Mackenzie," she had whispered on her way out the door and I'd nodded my thanks.

As I braced myself for the Inquisition, I noticed that, in her haste, Jenn had left one of her brown envelopes on the coffee table. I scooped it up and put it with my papers on the kitchen table, returning to sit silently waiting for whatever Simons had to say.

"Ethan came to see me this morning, and I thought it prudent to come over right away."

"Should I have my lawyer here, Peter?" I asked quietly.

"Well, that's up to you," he hedged. "I'm simply here to have Ethan tell you what he told me and have your response to it. Remember, this still is not an official investigation."

I looked at Peter. When you hang around cops the way I do, you pick up protocol by osmosis.

"Okay, Peter. If you want me to hear Ethan's story, I will. But I am making no comment at this time."

Then I looked at Ethan. Really looked at him. The same handsome, boyish face I remember. Grey, now, of course. Ethan would be around the same age as Jerry. There was that same intelligence in the eyes, the same firmness of the chin, the same constant assessment of person or situation ticking away under the surface. And yet . . .

"I told Peter about us." Ethan met my eyes. "About the phone call. That I knew it was you at the time, but thought you were dead and just played stupid when the police came to see me."

I remained silent, turning back to Peter.

"Scotland Yard has the record of a call placed the afternoon of May twenty-third, 1982, at approximately the same time as the end of Flight 39," he said. "It was too short for them to trace, but it was recorded. After speaking with Ethan, I made a quick call back home. They sent it to me here." Again, the laptop. A few seconds later, my voice coming out of the past . . .

"*Scotland Yard.*"

"*I think he's going to kill her.*"

"*Ma'am?*"

"*He's going to kill her.*"

Names, address, phone number.

It ended. Peter looked at me over the computer.

"Was that you making that call, Farran?"

I didn't reply. I also studiously avoided Ethan's eyes.

"She did it to stop me from something she thought I was going to do," Ethan explained. "I had told Debra about Farran and our baby, and she went crazy. Farran must have heard the fear in my voice and imagined the worst. She was pregnant and scared—"

"Enough." I said and stood up. "I had nothing to do with the bombing of that plane. It's ridiculous to even think so. I ran off the plane for personal reasons. I will not discuss my baby with anyone at this time."

"She——" Ethan began.

"My child is obviously not involved with any or all of this." I ignored Ethan and looked directly at Peter. "So we just don't go there. Is that understood?"

Peter returned my look and didn't move. "Why would you make such an accusation against Ethan Chamberlain?"

Because I was out of my mind, I wanted to say. Because then, as now, I was trapped in an emotional waterspout that I somehow understood was only partially of my own making. Hell—because it seemed like a good idea at the time.

"Are you investigating that, too?" I shot back. "If not, then for now I have no comment. You can do what you want with Ethan's statement. I'd like you both to leave, now," I added.

Peter rose and Ethan followed suit. At the door, Ethan hesitated and asked, "Peter, old man, give us a minute alone would you?"

Peter shrugged. "Guess I can't stop you."

He left and Ethan turned to me. I put up my hand.

"I don't want to talk to you, Ethan," I said honestly. "It's all ancient history, long done and over with, right or wrong. We're all still alive. Beyond that, I haven't gone yet."

He put a hand on my arm. "Where is she, Fan?" he asked softly.

I softened. "She doesn't know me yet, Ethan. But she will. And when we talk, I will tell her who her father is. If she wants to contact you after that, that will be up to her."

He nodded slowly and squeezed my arm. "You haven't seen the last of me, Farran Mackenzie. It isn't *all* ancient history. At least not for me."

I stood in my hallway after they left looking at the closed door for what seemed like a long time. I was aware of a growing anger in me—anger with the situation, anger with the intrusion of my privacy, anger at myself for letting things get so screwed up as usual, even anger at life expecting me to pay up for the time loan I had taken out so long ago. This was not about me and yet all about me. I was the fulcrum on which this situation turned and everybody but me seemed to be calling the shots.

I picked up the phone, pulled out the card and punched in Stephanie Harrison's number.

"Stephanie? Dr. Mackenzie here. I need to speak with you today. Would you be free sometime soon?"

"Actually, Dr. Mackenzie, we're heading out to Iroquois again. Apparently the police are finished with their crime scene work and we're free to continue."

"I'll meet you out there in twenty minutes," I said abruptly and hung up.

I drove out there, Lynn's brown envelope with Haley's information on the seat beside me, with the cold and clear decision it was time to lay things on the line with Stephanie about who I really was. Not the scenario I had hoped for, but again life and my own cowardice had produced what I had to work with now. I didn't want anyone else dropping this in her lap. That would be unforgivable in my mind.

I also knew I had to speak to Debra Hyde at some point. I owed her an explanation and an apology for trespassing on her life as I had done, innocently or not. I owed her the chance to tell me to go to hell, and if chance were then offered to me, I would ask why she had stayed with Ethan after all.

As I drove past the little road to Carman House, I felt more than a twinge of guilt for Carl Wallace, who now was under arrest for his brother's murder. I didn't believe it for a minute, but obviously Jerry had something considerable up his sleeve in that regard. I noticed Jeremy Pollan back painting and something told me I had talk to that man again. In just a few days, the weekend of Celebration 50 would be underway. I felt bad for the supporters of Carman House. It would be hard to continue right now, dealing with the murder of one of their own.

I navigated the curve and continued up toward the canal road, turning in and parking just off the roadway. The area was bereft of blue uniforms and police vehicles, but the yellow tape remained. Some young boys were exploring that area, looking for more grisly finds, I guess. A few people were putting their boats out for the day and one lady was letting her two golden retrievers have a swim off the end of the old No. 2. Leaving the envelope on the car seat, I took a walk down the edge of the canal, looking for any signs of the Water People and hoping that Ethan was still hobnobbing with Peter.

Then I heard the car behind me.

I turned to see a small blue compact taking the turn onto the canal road at a dangerous speed. Making the turn against the odds, it accelerated and came straight down the road in my direction. I stood there, mesmerized, watching it as if in slow motion, until I realized it was coming right at me. At the last second, I snapped out of it and threw myself out of the way.

It was Debra Hyde at the wheel, with Stephanie sitting beside her.

I hit the dirt, knocking the wind right out of me. I heard the car swerve and waited for the feel of two tons of steel and glass driving over me. But it never came.

The car spun to the right, turning 180 degrees before disappearing over the edge of the old canal. Two seconds later, I heard it hit the water, and the horrible drowning gurgle of the motor.

Then . . . silence.

SEVENTEEN

INUNDATION

And that's when the crazies really set in.

I got to my knees and someone ran past me, diving into the canal. In my fog, I registered Amy's red hair. I struggled to my feet and stumbled toward the water.

"*Haley!*" I screamed.

Behind me, I heard another car come screeching to a halt, the car door open. Someone else ran past me, pushing me out of the way.

"Stay there!" It was Paul's voice. He went into the canal after Amy. I stood at the edge, frozen in horror, waiting for them to surface.

Amy was first, miraculously holding an unconscious Stephanie above the waterline with one arm. Paul came up on the other side and swam toward her.

"Debra's still in there!" Amy yelled. "Her window is closed. You'll have to go in from the passenger side. The doors are locked."

He disappeared again.

"Paul, be careful!" I called uselessly to the water.

By now, people were coming out of nowhere. Someone jumped in next to Amy and helped her pull Stephanie out of the water. I was on the other side of the canal with no bridge to cross — only the long way around by the road.

"Is she alive?" I called to Amy.

Thankfully, Amy nodded.

Paul surfaced, then went under again. Someone else jumped in and went under close by. After what seemed like hours, they surfaced with the limp body of Debra Hyde. We helped them bring her up and, once out, Paul immediately began artificial resuscitation. Debra's lips were blue, and there was a large gash on her forehead. I thought I was going to be sick.

Off in the distance, I could hear the sound of sirens getting louder. I ran down the road and around to the other side of the canal, where Amy sat with Stephanie.

"Hale—Stephanie?" I bent down over her.

"She's unconscious," said Amy. Tears were running down her face. "I think she hit her head when they hit the water. She has to be okay. Just has to. This is all my fault."

I touched Stephanie on the face. She was breathing and white, but very much alive. God had just given me a second chance.

Amy rode with Stephanie in the ambulance to the Winchester hospital, and I followed in my car. The brown envelope still sat within reach on the front seat, unopened. Paul had stayed with Debra in the ambulance that took her to Winchester also. After some minutes, Amy joined me in the Emergency waiting room, and we sat in silent partnership waiting for any news.

About an hour later, Paul came in looking grim. He sat down to take my hand, and looked over at Amy.

"We lost Debra," he said simply. "They couldn't revive her."

"Debra is dead?" I echoed stupidly.

"Yes. Amy, I'm sorry."

Amy's stone face melted and the tears began again. "She was really nice. Like a mother to us. All my fault," she added in a whisper.

"Why would—" I started, then heard Ethan's voice coming through the door.

Paul rose to face him.

"Dr. Chamberlain."

"What's happened? Amy . . . are you all right? You said there'd been an accident. Where are Stephanie and Debra?"

"Debra's car went into the canal this morning," Amy said woodenly. "Stephanie was with her. She's still being looked at."

"Debra's car?" Ethan looked at Paul. "Where is my wife?"

Paul glanced at me and then back at Ethan.

"I'm sorry, Dr. Chamberlain. She . . . she didn't make it. They did everything they could."

Ethan opened his mouth and then closed it again. He shook his head, looked over at Amy, and then slowly sat down. She went over to him.

Paul turned to me, silently taking me by the hand and guiding me over to a spot in the corner.

"They need some time," he said. "I need some answers."

"So do I," I replied. "What the hell were you doing out there? I didn't see you."

"I followed you."

"You *what?*"

He motioned for me to be quiet. "I followed you. Just keeping an eye on you with all these people around from your checkered past."

I opened my mouth to fire back, but he cut me off.

"First question: Why did Debra Hyde try to run you down? Still angry about Ethan?"

"She didn't—"

"I was right behind you. She went past me at full bore and headed straight for you. There was no one else on the road."

I closed my eyes. The image of Debra behind the wheel with Stephanie beside her loomed up.

"Talk to me, Mackenzie." The tone in his voice was unmistakable. "People are dying here."

I opened my eyes and looked at Paul.

I just couldn't do it anymore.

"Debra Hyde wanted me and my baby dead twenty-six years ago. She tried to kill me today and take my baby with her."

"Is this what you've been running from all these years?"

Paul stood with my face in his hands. When I nodded, he took me in his arms and held me tight. He was my cousin and my friend. I finally let go, then hung on to him with all my strength. But I didn't cry. The anger from earlier in the day returned. Debra had tried to hurt my baby.

My baby. My daughter. Mother love kicked in.

"I need to see Haley." I pulled away from him. "I need to keep her safe."

"She's still unconscious, right? I'll wait with you. Does Chamberlain know who she is?"

"Apparently not."

"Another question, then. Don't you think it's all just a little bizarre that these people were together and right here where you are? And they walked right into your house?"

I believe introductions aren't necessary.

Stephanie's words suddenly came back into my head from that day in my house.

Oh, my God. Had Stephanie found us and arranged all this to get us together for her? As strange as it was, it was certainly possible with the resources she had. She would have had no idea of the time bomb she would be setting off.

I stayed the night, with Amy. Ethan had gone to deal with the hospital and Debra. Stephanie was unconscious, but not critical, so my revelation to Ethan would wait until he was more up to it. We took turns sleeping on the so-called lounge seats until about 4:00 a.m., when I gave it up and got some brown liquid they labelled "coffee" out of the machine. Desperate times call for desperate measures.

I didn't call Jerry. Paul called Lynn at my house, and she had come with supper, although we barely ate. She said she had left a message on Jerry's cell phone. I finally shooed both Paul and Lynn out, telling them to get some sleep and that I would check in with them in the morning.

There is not much else to do in a hospital Emergency waiting room except think, and I didn't want to. I felt as though I were drowning in the past, that the dam I had built twenty-six years ago had finally burst and I couldn't hold off the deluge. But it threatened to swamp my daughter, too. All those years of staying away from her had been for nothing.

Almost. The danger was dead—and Fate had decided to keep us both alive and in view of each other until I had the courage to tell Stephanie who I was.

Keep the child safe, lass.

"I did," I told the room.

"Did what?"

I turned at the voice and saw that Amy was sitting up, also having given up on sleep.

You lying bastard . . .

"What?"

"I said, did what?" She stretched and stood up.

"Amy," I shot at her while she was still groggy, "what did Stephanie mean when you were all in my living room and she said she thought no introductions were necessary."

That stopped her in her tracks.

"I don't know what you mean," she hedged.

I stood up to face her.

"When Ethan and Debra walked into my living room behind you and saw me for the first time, there was dead silence except for Stephanie. She said she felt introductions weren't necessary. Why?"

"I . . . I don't really know. You'd have to ask Steph."

We looked at each other and both knew it was a lie. Maybe Amy had the disturbing capability to look into me, but I also had the same ability for her. Must still have the touch from dealing with the odd dog-ate-my-paper stories from my students.

"I will. Second question," I echoed Paul. "Why did you say this was all your fault?"

That took some of the wind out of her. Amy slowly sat down.

"I was supposed to keep this from happening."

"The accident?"

"Any accidents. There have been a few suspicious accidents in the life of Stephanie Harrison over the past few months."

"You're her bodyguard?"

"That's one way of putting it, yes."

I sat down with her. "Why weren't you in the car with Debra and Stephanie?"

She looked away. "We thought it best if I followed in our own car. That one was Debra and Ethan's. Ethan was gone and had left a note he would meet us out there."

"I can guarantee you it wasn't your fault."

At my words, Amy turned and looked at me. "What do you mean?"

"I'm not entirely sure yet what really happened out there yesterday," I sighed, "but it looks like it was a blast from my past. Not something you could foresee. If anything, Stephanie is in this hospital because of me."

"Is Debra dead because of you?"

I decided not to answer that. "You know, my mother was a straight shooter, too. Right from the hip. Deadly for me during the high school years. But I learned well how to parry and thrust." I smiled and held up my paper cup. "Coffee is awful. Out of the machine until the cafeteria opens. But it's something. Can I get you one?"

Amy shook her head. At the sound of footsteps, we both looked up.

A nurse was standing there.

"For Stephanie Harrison?" she asked. We both nodded.

"She's awake," the nurse continued. "They'll move her into Observation around 6:00 a.m. You can see her then, just for a few minutes."

"Hey, s — " Stephanie tried to smile when we walked in, but Amy put her finger to her lips.

"Rest," she said.

I came up from behind. "I agree. You've been through a very bad experience."

"Dr. Mackenzie." Stephanie put out her hand. "You're okay. I remember being afraid for you."

I took her hand, but didn't look her in the eyes. "Couldn't" would be the more accurate term. I wanted so much to say everything, and then be there for her if she wanted me. But she looked so tired and white from her brush with death. Once again, life was keeping us just that far apart.

Ethan floated through my mind, followed by a twinge of guilt for not telling him yet, but one thing at a time.

I sensed Amy's eyes on me again and looked up. If I hadn't known better, I would have seen concern in them for me. Like I said, the crazies.

"Excuse me." An OPP officer I didn't recognize stood at the door. "Ms. Harrison? I'm Constable Flagg. If you're up to it, I'd like to get a statement from you about the accident yesterday."

A small but formidable nurse materialized in the doorway behind him.

"I'm sorry, officer. You'll have to come back," she said firmly. "You two as well. Maybe this afternoon. Our patient needs to eat a little and rest for a bit. We also need to run some tests when the doctor gets in. Everybody out," she added.

I reluctantly let go of Stephanie's hand and followed orders. Constable Flagg followed me. Amy lingered alone with Stephanie for a minute and then joined us in the hall.

We gave our names to the officer and sat down with him to give our own statements. Amy's was as she had told me. She'd been behind Debra's car and saw it go into the canal. She'd jumped out to help, diving in to rescue Stephanie. Thankfully, the passenger window had been open and she'd been able to get her friend out.

"The car came right at you?" Flagg asked me when it was my turn.

"Well, it . . . it seemed that way. I was in the road, and it came down at top speed. Debra was at the wheel."

"The deceased."

"Yes."

"Did she see you?"

"I don't know. I threw myself out of the way and then the car skidded over the side of the canal."

"It swerved," said Amy.

"Swerved what way?" Flagg asked. "Toward Dr. Mackenzie or away?"

Amy rubbed her eyes. "I'm not sure. Kind of both."

Flagg looked at me. I shook my head.

"Kind of both," I agreed.

Flagg stayed at the hospital, so Amy and I both decided to head out until later that day when Stephanie was feeling better.

"What do we do about Dr. Chamberlain?" she asked me. "What's he going to do?"

"I don't know," I admitted, "on both accounts. He's a long way from home, isn't he? Are they both—were they both still at Oxford?"

"Yes. On loan to UBC. Well, he is. Debra came along on sabbatical, I understand."

Amy looked as tired as I felt, and she was half my age.

"Listen," I put a hand on her arm. "Where are you staying?"

"In Cornwall. It's all we could find with Celebration 50 this weekend."

"That's a long drive for nothing. I have a guest room. Why don't you ride back with me to my place, sack out on the extra bed for a few hours, we'll eat, then come back here together? Then we can find out after that what's happening with Dr. Chamberlain."

She was tough, but exhausted. Amy agreed, and an hour later was sound asleep in my guest room under a blanket I put over her. I was too wound up to try my own bed, so I opted for the couch.

Crazy was heading for surreal.

I had almost lost my daughter, then got her back, now spoken with her and had held her hand.

Debra Hyde was dead. To all appearances, she'd tried to kill me. Why? What had set her off?

Ethan was here and deserved to know his daughter was right in front of him, and had been for some time. I needed to ask Amy who had lined up the Chamberlains for this project. Had it been Stephanie?

My daughter's face looking white in the white bed came to me. I pulled Lynn's envelope out from under my purse where I had brought it in from the car and opened it, emptying the contents onto the coffee table.

What came out was not the report and the picture of my little girl in braids.

It was a larger photograph, black and white, of three girls sitting around a table with a cake in the middle. It was a birthday cake, and the girls were smiling as one of them held a knife over it.

It was my birthday cake. The one Mom made for my twelfth birthday. It was our table in the kitchen of my old house in Preston.

The girls were me, Alison, and Jeanie Ross.

I opened the door and she stood there, brown hair still in braids, ever-present backpack.

"I'm so glad you called, Dr. Mackenzie," said Jenn as she moved into my hallway. "I heard the news report this morning and was wondering if you were okay. How is Stephanie Harrison? I didn't know she was in the area."

"You know her?" I asked, walking carefully behind her as she headed into the living room.

"Yes, we worked on—" Jenn stopped dead in the middle of the room. On the coffee table, propped up, was the black and white photograph of Jeanie, Alison, and me.

I stood right behind her, waiting without a word. Finally, Jenn turned to face me.

"You found it," she said simply.

"Yes. It is yours, then?"

Jenn nodded. "I wanted to show you, but never found the right moment. You had things going on, and I didn't want to add to it then. So I left it and waited for you to call me about it."

"Where did you get that picture?" I could feel my voice rising, and I glanced at the closed door to the guest room where Amy was still sleeping.

"Can we sit down?"

It was all finally getting to me—really getting to me. I grabbed Jenn by the arms and shook her.

"*Where did you get that picture?*" I demanded again, not worrying about my volume. "Who are you? What do you want from me?"

"There were only three copies of that picture in existence," I babbled on. "I had one. and I gave one to Alison and one—"

"Is everything all right?" The voice came from the direction of the doorway. I looked past Jenn to see Amy standing there, looking sleepy and dishevelled from her nap.

Jenn turned around to see the speaker, and then smiled.

"Hey, Steph. I heard you were here. Wow," she added, "the new hair is amazing. When did you go red?"

Ever been in a fun house?

That Carl Jung thing was happening. I stood there between two people who were not who they were supposed to be, wondering who I was at that moment. The mirrors were warped and the floors slanted. What was it Jung said about mirrors? "The mirror does not flatter, it faithfully shows whatever looks into it; namely, the face we never show to the world because we cover it with the persona, the mask of the actor. But the mirror lies behind the mask and shows the true face."

The true face. That was the only way out of this fun house my life had become. Only the truth, the real thing, would guide me to the new place, the new life I had to create, negotiate, fight for. It was game over for Farran Mackenzie, and no holds barred from here on in.

"Steph?" I echoed. Amy looked at the floor. I looked at Jenn. "Jenn, who is this woman?"

Jenn looked at me, quizzically. "Stephanie Harrison. Why?"

I turned back to Amy and let out a long breath. "*You're* Stephanie Harrison?" I asked quietly.

Jenn seemed to suddenly understand the weight of the space between Amy and me. "Maybe I should come back later . . ." she began, moving toward the door.

"You haven't answered my question," I directed at Amy. "Move," I added, pointing at Jenn, without taking my eyes off Amy, "and I'll take you out at the knees."

Jenn obediently sat down.

"Are you Stephanie Harrison?" I asked Amy again.

Finally, Amy looked back at me. I knew the answer before it came. I knew why she could look right through me. Away from the distraction of the other Stephanie, from Ethan's presence, from the old fears, from even the unexpected red hair, I looked into those eyes. My eyes. My father's eyes. Oh, Mom. She's beautiful.

My eyes filled.

"Yes," Amy said simply.

"Why?" was all I could manage at that moment.

"It was Amy's idea. Switch places and stay close." Still she met my eyes. She had my mother's grit.

I knew that Jenn sat there, but had only the strength for one important question.

"Stephanie," I whispered, "*do you know who I am?*"

From across the years, the emptiness, the fear, the answer came. "Yes."

I saw one tear form and travel down her cheek. Then I saw nothing. My own vision blurred with the emotions I had tried to shut away in the hospital twenty-six years ago, as I heard her cries go down the hall and out of my life. I covered my hands with my face and stood shaking, then quickly moved my hands away—afraid that if I took my eyes off Stephanie she would disappear again. I felt Jenn come and put her arm around me, and I left it there. It seemed the natural thing. Why, I did not yet know.

Wiping my eyes, I found my voice.

"You have been in my heart and my mind every day since the day you were born."

What does a woman say to her found child? What would possibly ever be good enough? But it was what was in my heart and what I needed her to hear and know. What she needed from me—if anything—I would wait for her to tell me.

"Then why give me up?" Of course. The Question.

"I can't answer that, yet," I said honestly. "I know why, but there is still something even now that has to be . . . be understood. Cleared up. Once I have that, I'll gladly answer all your questions." We fell silent for a moment.

"Do you know who your father is?" I asked.

She nodded slowly. "It was on the birth certificate."

"Are you the reason Ethan and Debra walked into my living room a few days ago? Did you plan that?"

Stephanie didn't reply at first. Finally, she sighed. "Yes. The big reason I got Ethan on the project was to get him here, get to know him before I said anything. Same for you. That's why we're here."

At that point I had to sit down. Jenn moved me over to the sofa.

"Have you told him—or Debra—who you really are?" As I looked up at Stephanie, I felt the old fear again.

"Not yet," she said. "I suppose I should soon. Unless you . . ."

I took a deep breath. "I haven't told Ethan, either, and right now wouldn't be the best time. But, as you say, soon. I'll help you, if you like. How long is the team supposed to be here?"

"We were scheduled to stay until after Celebration 50. The guys stayed in Montreal and will head home from there. As for the rest of us, I don't know now, with Debra's death, what we'll do." Stephanie sat down across from Jenn and me.

I nodded. "It'll be basically over next Wednesday. I should call him tonight and see what is happening with Debra, see if I can help. And we need to get back to Stephanie Two. Is that really Amy?"

"Yes."

Jenn spoke up. "I'm sorry if I blew the whistle on you, Steph. Didn't know."

Stephanie grinned. "Of course not, Jenn. And it's good to see you. What are you doing here? Research?"

"Ah, yes," I turned to Jenn. "What *are* you doing here? For real?" I picked up the photograph and passed it to Stephanie. "I'm the one with the knife. It's my twelfth birthday party.

"Like I said, Jenn," I added. "There were only three copies of that in existence. I have the original, and the two copies went to Alison Perry and—"

"Jeanie Ross," Jenn finished. "I know. That's where I got this one."

I put my hand on her arm.

"You know where Jeanie is?"

Jenn smiled and I started, suddenly glancing down at the young Jeanie in the picture.

"Yes. I've known my whole life. Jeanie Ross is my mother."

I struggle now with trying to organize it all, do what I have done professionally for decades—sift through the details, the conflicting memories, the emotions to pin down exactly what happened when.

Celebration 50 began the next day, and Land of the Lost Villages saw a tremendous homecoming. Friday was the wine and cheese, and registrations. Saturday hosted a parade and the dance, while R.H. Saunders Generating Station put on an open house they still talk about. None of these I attended. Ruth called each time to see if she could change my mind, and Lynn—who had reappeared as my roommate—tried to put me in a headlock on her way out with Buck, but I prevailed in my stubborn need to be alone.

I had taken Amy (who was really Stephanie) back to Winchester to be with Stephanie Two (who was really Amy) and had a brief chat about what had transpired that day in the car. According to Stephanie Two, Debra had seemed to lose control of the car as they had approached the canal road and tried to brake to avoid me. But the car hadn't responded and Stephanie/Amy had yanked the wheel at the last moment, sending the car into the canal. It was all very vague and unsatisfying.

As I left the hospital, I turned to the real Stephanie standing in the hall.

"I will wait to hear from you," I said. "Did you want to tell your father who you are . . . or have me . . . or . . .?"

She looked at the floor. "I don't know, yet. I had a hundred scenes worked out in my head, but not with this. Not with Debra—" She fell silent.

I, the perennial coward, did the bravest thing I have ever done. It was instinct, really. Instinct and need.

I reached out and held my daughter's hand. My throat closed up for a minute so I couldn't speak, and we stood there, in the busy hallway, totally alone with each other. I braved a look at the fingers, so changed since the last time I had felt their touch.

"I am here for you," I said. "Whatever way you want me to help. Even if you want me to stay away. You decide. I have no intention of laying my own feelings on you with this. But I'm here, and we will get through this . . . all of it. I promise you that."

She did not pull her hand away, and I took that fact with me to help get through the next few days. And maybe the rest of my life.

I had hugged Jenn and shook my head in disbelief.

"Jeanie? How is she? Where is she?"

Jenn had laughed, and I saw her mother's mischievous streak in her face. God, it felt so good to be near that again! Life was certainly amazing in its system of checks and balances. I never saw this coming back to me and here it was.

"We saw you on TV when Alison Perry died," she said, sobering. "It really shook my mom. There you were, injured. You'd almost died, too. Mom felt it was time to make contact again."

"But why like this?"

"It's a long story, and she should tell you herself."

I shot a glance at Stephanie. "Is she here, Jenn?"

Jenn shook her head. "No. She's back home in BC. But I need to explain things to you before putting you both in contact. I know I've been privy to your personal lives today, but I can't share this with anyone else but you, Dr. Mackenzie. No offence, Steph. I promised my mom. I'm sorry to be so mysterious," she added, "but you'll understand when you hear it."

"Okay. Fair enough," I said. "I have to get back to the hospital, and then I have to track Ethan Chamberlain down. Can we sit down in the next couple days? And you must call her tonight and tell her how happy I am about this."

Jenn had booked interviews over the weekend with people in for Celebration 50. I passed on meeting up on the Monday. It would be the anniversary of my father's murder, and I didn't know what shape I'd be in. With the day following being Canada Day, Jenn and I were set to have dinner that Wednesday.

I had left messages with Jerry on his cell and at the detachment, asking about Carl Wallace. No replies. I finally called Jordan Wiley and touched bases on the Debra Hyde incident—successfully only because I'd been involved. Nothing new. The car was being examined for tampering, and Debra's body was with the coroner's office for autopsy. I hadn't even had a chance to really say hello to my old mentor, let alone goodbye.

When I broached the Carl Wallace arrest, Wiley clammed up. Just said Carl was the prime suspect for now, due to the discovery of his gun. Still nothing on the death of Julia Parmeter.

"Is Peter Simons from Scotland Yard still around?" I asked, not really expecting an answer. "I haven't seen or heard from him in a while."

"He hasn't been here," Jordan said, "and I haven't had any contact either."

"Maybe Jerry—" I started.

"Farran," Jordan lowered his voice, "Jerry took his name off that case the day of Ruth Hoffman's wedding. Walked clean away from it. I'm liaison officer now."

He let that sink in, and so did I. Jerry had walked away from the accusation that I was responsible for the death of 150 innocent people. And I had not heard from or seen him since Ruth's wedding. Did he think I was guilty? Or had he walked away from me as a person after our talk in the parking lot that night?

Sunday dawned. The Memorial Service was slated for 2:30 p.m., at the St. Lawrence Valley Cemetery. Since almost all of my family is buried there, I thought I should go. With cemeteries and services on the brain, I decided to try calling Ethan. It had been a few days, and it wouldn't seem as invasive now. I had not heard from my daughter since our last talk in the hospital hallway. I also figured the coroner's office would release Debra's body soon, and maybe I could help him with whatever he was going to do after that.

At least it sounded practical to me.

I got Ethan's voice mail. I was getting used to that response from the men in my life. The modern version of a conversation. Phone tag. Or, as with Jerry these past couple of weeks, hide and seek.

"Ethan," I told the phone, "I'm calling to see how you are. How things are. I haven't wanted to intrude, but if you need help with anything while you're here, please call me. I'm here until around two. Then I'm heading for the St. Lawrence Cemetery for the Celebration memorial service. I'll probably be home after supper, then."

St. Lawrence Valley Cemetery was packed for this special service. Rain threatened again, so everyone huddled under the large tent or in umbrella clusters. I rode over with Lynn, and we were uncharacteristically quiet for the short ride there. We were both thinking of Meredith and haunted by Gordon. I told myself I was going for my parents and grandfathers.

I saw a lot of faces I knew. Under the tent, the heat built despite the rain. It was hard to sit with the memories, but for once I didn't feel alone with the burden. I was surrounded by a community for whom tremendous loss was a defining truth in their lives.

When the service was over, Lynn went to schmooze at the refreshment table. I walked across the lawn, over to my parents' tombstone. As I stood there for a few minutes, I wondered if I would have the chance to bring Stephanie here, to tell her who they were.

"Was Hal Leonard your father, Fan?"

The voice came softly from behind. I turned to see Ethan standing there. He had aged since that horrid day in the hospital, and I suddenly wanted to take care of him.

"Ethan." I glanced back at the tombstone. "Yes, Hal Leonard was my father. I found out just a few years ago."

"The young man in the locket?"

"I told you about my mother's bracelet?"

He nodded. "Not knowing who he was had left such a hole in you, I remember."

I walked up to him. "How are you, Ethan? I'm so sorry about Debra."

"I'm . . ." he faltered, "I'm just glad that you and Stephanie are all right. I had no idea . . ."

"Idea about what?"

Ethan didn't reply. Then he said, "Thank you for your offer to help. You've very generous, as usual, Fan. I can't imagine what it's been like to have us all marching back into your life the way we did."

I saw Lynn come up from behind Ethan and look at me questioningly.

"Oh . . . Lynn. This is Ethan Chamberlain, an old friend from my Oxford days."

The name seemed to mean something to her, although I had never really talked about the father of my baby. She held out her hand, and Ethan shook it.

"I'm Lynn Holmes, friend of the family. Fan, it's wrapped up here. Did you want to stay longer or head home?"

I was ready to go home. "Ethan, would you like to come out for a coffee?"

He hesitated, then smiled. "If I'm not intruding. That would be lovely, Fan."

We sat out on the back deck, watching the St. Lawrence. Lynn joined us for the first bit to be sociable, but then went into the cottage to give us some privacy. She'd asked me in the car on the way back about Ethan, and I'd told her who he was.

"Be careful, Fan," she said with her usual street sense. "Don't forget that your relationship with that man in Oxford put you on the run for twenty-six years. I won't."

But Debra is dead, I wanted to say. But didn't.

So there I sat with the man I'd loved enough to risk my career for, chatting as though it were just another visit. The crazies again. We covered the "safe" details—Peter Simons (disappeared), the police report on Debra (pending), arrangements for Debra's body (waiting for release from the coroner's office), Ethan's research here (on hold).

Then, tentatively, we began to fill in the gaps. That he was still a professor at Oxford but now ready to retire, and still living in the big house I remembered from my one visit. That I had attained my own doctorate, and ended up at University of Waterloo. No marriage and family.

A silence set in after that, one I chose to break with both feet by jumping in.

"So, you and Debra worked things out in the end?" I asked, eyes on the river.

For a minute, there was no reply.

"When we th—when I thought you were dead," Ethan answered slowly, "I didn't care about anything for a long time. Something in me died with you. It's all a bit of a haze. I guess we just went on as usual, neither of us knowing what else to do. The years went by and here we are . . . were," he added grimly.

I had nothing to say to that, not being in any position to judge.

Except for one small thing.

"You said that Debra would hurt me and the baby, and that she'd rather see you dead."

"You called Scotland Yard and told them I was going to kill my wife," he shot back.

"You sounded desperate to me, Ethan. Everything was crazy and upside down. And I was very young. Too young," I added.

"And a long way from home," Ethan stated.

We fell silent again.

"How did you find your father?" he changed the subject. "You said he'd died before you were born."

I told him the basics, about the discovery of my father's remains, my mother's death, my uncle. The personal stuff—like Jerry Strauss—I left out.

"My God, Fanny. What a hell to go through. But you've retired here. Seem to have a good life, friends. Payback, I guess."

"Somewhat," I said noncommittally.

"And now you've found Haley."

Stephanie must have spoken to him, I thought. I refrained from pursuing it.

"When the coroner's office releases Debra's body, Ethan, let me know if I can help with anything."

He understood the cue to leave. I couldn't be alone with him any longer. There was too much pain still woven in, too much loss. And tomorrow was not going to be easy to get through.

You lying bastard . . .

I shut my eyes, and opened them when I heard Ethan get out of his chair.

"Thank you for the coffee, Fan. And for the visit. You've been very generous."

I stood to face him, and followed him to the door.

"Keep me posted about Debra," I said. "Let me know if you need a hand."

Ethan started to walk out the front door, then turned back for a moment.

"I need to say something, Farran. I don't know if it is appropriate now or ever. But I need to tell you what I didn't get a chance to that May." He looked straight into my eyes. "Fate tore us apart. But if it hadn't, we would be married today. I was very sure of how I felt about you back then."

Wordlessly, I watched him go, then quietly shut the door.

Keep the child safe, lass . . .

The dawn came slowly the next morning. June 30. Fifty years since my father died at the age of eighteen, protecting my mother and me.

I lay in bed, thinking it might be a good place to spend the day. Still no word from Jerry, no more visits and questions from Peter Simons, and nothing from Stephanie. It felt quiet inside me, quiet but empty, as though the past few weeks had drained all the feelings I had. It wasn't that I didn't care anymore. I guess I was numb. The crazies were gone, I thought.

It would turn out to be the lull before the storm.

You lying bastard . . .

I put the pillow over my head.

Run, child. Run. Danger.

I turned my back on the words, not easy to do to a whisper in your head. Curling up in my covers, I told the room, "I'm off today. Go away."

The phone rang. It was Ruth, checking in.

"I'm having everyone for lunch, unless you're taking the Lost Villages bus tour this afternoon. It starts at noon."

"No, I hadn't planned to. What time do you want me for lunch, Mrs. Black?"

She giggled, as only Ruth can do for a woman her age.

"Let's make it eleven," she said. "Bring Lynn with you."

After I'd hung up, I took a shower. A long one. Does life get any easier? Does it ever start to make sense? Or was it just me, still stumbling through at almost fifty years of age. Why did I still feel so lost? So unsettled? I wiped the fog off the mirror and took a look at Farran Mackenzie. Still on the run, old girl. Just a different race track.

The mirror does not flatter, it faithfully shows whatever looks into it; namely, the face we never show to the world because we cover it with the persona, the mask of the actor. But the mirror lies behind the mask and shows the true face.

"Shut up, Jung," I told the mirror. "I'm off from you, too, today."

The mirror.

Fenton's dying words about the gold.

I suddenly knew where Ira Fenton had hidden the gold. And if I were right, more than likely it was still there. Then Potts hadn't taken it back with him, which is why he hadn't paid his debts and they'd killed him. But why the deaths now? I still didn't believe that Carl Wallace had killed anybody, but I had no proof and nothing better to offer.

In fact, none of it right now made sense unless . . .

But the mirror lies behind the mask and shows the true face.

I went out to the kitchen and called the Long Sault detachment, asking for Sergeant Wiley. Fortunately, I got him.

"Jordan, what's happening with Carl Wallace?"

"Farran, I can't really discuss it."

"Is he still under arrest, yes or no?"

"Well, yes, at this time."

"I want you to send me something." I told him what it was. "Do you have that on file?"

"It's not very good quality, but, yes, we do. Why?"

"Let's just say I want to apply some Jungian psychology to Sam Wallace's murder."

"I don't think I can send that out, Farran."

"Jordan Wiley," I snapped, "for God's sake, it's me. Your inspector invited me into this case some weeks ago, and I cleared up the Massena story for you. If you don't send that along right now," I added, "I'll track down Jerry Strauss from his personal hiding place to ask him. I know he's off the radar right now and that he doesn't want to be disturbed. But I'll find him. My father, from all accounts, was one hell of a fisherman. It's up to you."

There was a pause, then, "I'll send that over this morning, Dr. Mackenzie."

I smiled at the "Dr.", thanked him, and hung up.

The true face.

You lying bastard . . .

"I said I'm off today, whoever you are."

Wickedness, it was.

Meredith. Not you, too?

But Meredith had been a good lady. I felt the first twinge of real fear.

Perimenopausal anxiety.

"Did you make coffee?" Lynn joined me in the kitchen a short time later, her curls in a greater tumble than usual from sleep.

"Absolutely. And I'm wondering if I should add a shot of brandy this morning," I answered grimly.

My old friend shot me a look.

"Because of the date today? Or the absence of the man you love? Or the presence of the man you may still love? Or—"

"All of the above." I cut her off with a look of my own.

"Where do things stand with you and Stephanie at this point?"

"In limbo, until she calls me."

Lynn poured herself a coffee and sat down in front of me. "Fan, I want to ask you something. Twenty-six years ago, you were afraid of Debra Hyde's possessiveness over her husband and the threat to you and your baby. Yet you ran off that plane and called Scotland Yard to save *her* life—you thought. Then the tragedy happened that gave you a way out at the time. But for all these years, you've still been in emotional and, to a certain extent, physical hiding. Why? There's something you're not saying here, isn't there?"

I stared into my empty mug, thinking that Lynn hadn't made a name for herself as a journalist on a fluke. She could read people with a disturbing insight.

It was on my tongue, still so small, yet weighing a thousand pounds. But there it stayed.

You lying bastard . . .

I got up suddenly from the table and walked over to the patio doors.

"I've never asked you, Lynn. Do you ever hear the voices from the Lost Villages?"

I heard her sigh behind me. "No, at least I don't think so. I guess I don't have the gift."

"I don't think it's a gift," I said, looking out at the river. "My mother had the gift of insight, but I never did. Regardless, I've heard these voices since my first days here, when I was in danger out in the sanctuary. I once told Diana that you need to be willing to listen. But for the past few weeks, I've been getting a mix of them. Different ones." I turned to look at Lynn. "Even Meredith," I added quietly.

Lynn didn't bat an eye. "What does she tell you?"

"I keep hearing her voice from that day years ago when she came here to talk about my family. That day, she called it wickedness, but wouldn't tell me what she meant."

"And that's what you hear now? That it's wickedness?"

I nodded. "And I hear someone, I think it's my grandfather Harper, telling me to keep the child safe."

"That must mean Stephanie."

I kept the "lying bastard" one to myself.

"What do you think it all means?" Lynn asked. "That Stephanie's still in danger?"

"I don't know." I sat down at the table again. "But the voice lines are really humming this morning. I have a very bad feeling about today."

A phone call later that morning should have eased my nerves. It was Stephanie (the real Stephanie) calling to see if she could drop by after supper.

"Say about seven?" she asked. "I'd . . . I'd like to talk, if that's okay with you."

"Of course it is, Stephanie." My heart started to pound. "Have you . . . have you spoken with your father?"

"I don't think it's the right time just yet."

I understood that, and told her I was looking forward to her visit. I hoped that would prove to be the case.

As we drove over to Ruth's for lunch, my mind was full of my mother and where she had been fifty years ago today. I didn't know physically, but I did emotionally. She hadn't wanted my father to come home to fix things. She'd felt the danger, but probably couldn't tell him her horrible insight into his own brother, maybe not wanting to think that Gordon would cross the line into murder. It had cost them both his life, their life together before it had really begun, my life with my father. Was this what I was feeling?

Why had I sensed others up till now and not my mother?

It felt good to be at Ruth's having lunch. Normalcy. Tradition. Routine. Jerry wasn't there, but I knew Ruth would have invited him. I fought the urge for a time and then caved.

"Where is Inspector Strauss?" I asked her when we had a moment alone in the kitchen.

"I never heard back from him," Ruth said, shaking her head. That disturbed me. Ignoring me was almost policy with him from time to time, but Jerry would never ignore Ruth.

I buried my growing anxiety in the wonderful lunch Ruth and Ernie laid out for us. The newlyweds were embarrassingly happy, and it gave me a kernel of hope to watch love renew life at their age. Paul winked at me from across the table and I smiled back. Family has its upside, too. It's not only fratricide, dark secrets, and lost children.

I fell asleep on the couch that afternoon. It was a natural nap, not brandy-induced. My anxiety was of the type that alcohol only intensifies. It was buried deep, and I think in those cases, the calming effect of a small drink only lowers one's guard.

I couldn't do that.

There's something you're not saying here, isn't there?

In my sleep, I dreamed short dreams. Faces. Moments. All linked together like pearls on a necklace. Yet I could not place one of them as anything concrete from my real world.

Except one.

I was standing in front of my father's house, still in Aultsville, but surrounded by the post-Seaway mud and vegetation. Someone put a hand on my shoulder. I turned and it was Alison, looking as she did the day she died.

"The knowing isn't always better than the not knowing, is it Fan?" she said. "But then, *you've always known, haven't you?*"

Suddenly, behind her in the trees appeared what seemed like a hundred people, all standing silently, as though waiting for something.

I woke up sitting up, shaking. *Now* I needed a drink.

The rain had started again, just enough to make everything damp. I waited for Stephanie in the kitchen. The deck was off limits, being wet, and the living room had the couch with its residue of nightmare. Seven o'clock came and went, as did seven-thirty. When eight chimed in the living room, I called Stephanie's cell phone, but no answer. I tried Amy's with the same result. Okay, nerves booting up again.

You lying bastard . . .

Now my phone rang and I jumped.

"Stephanie?" I answered.

"I was hoping she was with you," came Ethan's voice.

"Ethan? She's . . . she's supposed to be, but she hasn't showed." The living room suddenly seemed to darken with the clouds outside. "I've tried both her and Amy on their cells, but no answer."

"The girls went on the bus tour today with me. I wasn't really up to it, but they suggested I go anyway. Valuable tour, and it would keep my mind off things."

"Where are they now, Ethan?"

"I don't know. That's why I'm calling you. We were supposed to meet up at 7:30 for a beer and to compare notes from the day. Stephanie said she was going to go out for a bit first. Something about looking for foundations. Taking a walk into her own family history. Any idea what that would mean?"

I had said nothing to Stephanie about my father and his death. But Stephanie Harrison was heir to the Harrison media empire. If she had taken a bead on who I was from the birth certificate, it would not have been impossible to do follow up from the media reports on Gordon's death and the discovery of my father's remains. In fact, it would be precisely what I would do in her shoes. A thorough background search. Especially anything out of the ordinary. A fifty-year-old murder and its deadly solving by me would definitely qualify. The Lost Villages bus tour would take her to the outskirts of where

Aultsville once stood. She would do what I did long ago—park on the remains of Aultsville Road and walk in to hear the voices from the past.

Keep the child safe, lass.

"I'll call you when I find her," I said quickly and hung up.

This had to be the quietest place on earth.

The only sound I could hear was that of my feet on the bike path that led to what was left of Aultsville. There was no sign of Stephanie's car, but I went ahead anyway. Memories washed over me from my first visit to see where my father had died . . .

To my left was more sanctuary and bush. To my right was the eastern tip of Ault Island, dominated by Gordon's house. Well, straight ahead to the river. I poked around in the bushes and found a small piece of the old road leading into the water. This was the road they had used to get to the murder scene. Taking a deep breath and forcing all thoughts of skeletons and rotting hands out of my mind, I pushed my way through into a corridor of weedy trees and bushes.

It was surreal to think I was walking the same road my father had, probably many times on his way to the lumberyard. But my excitement was short-lived. After only fifty feet, the road vanished into the river. The mud and slime on the road under the water made it impossible for me to continue even a couple of yards. It looked like primal ooze, and the end of the world. I was cut off.

Then I remembered the dream that had told me unconsciously I knew the truth long before consciously facing it . . .

I hesitantly began to move forward, feeling my way along the road in the water. I seemed to hear no sound now except my heart pounding in my ears like a water crank. The water stayed only up to my ankles, and I tried to see down into it. I could just make out the form of something large and square and deep not far from the edge of the road.

And then a rotted hand grabbed me by the ankle . . .

It was Gordon.

It was June thirtieth, fifty years to the day before they blew the cofferdam and covered the roots of generations all down the St. Lawrence River Valley. The day my father died to keep my mother and the unborn me safe.

You lying bastard . . .

I heard it clearly. The whispers of others were starting, but I felt them more than heard them.

You lying bastard . . .

The evening heat was filling in the space between the sky and the sanctuary. I called Stephanie's name, but received no reply. The odd buzz of an insect passing through came and went, but for a place filled with wildlife, there was a tremendous silence.

In that, I heard him. It was his voice, and had been all along.

You lying bastard . . . How could you do that to me? To Dad?

"Dad?" I called.

It was happening again, through some crazy time loop. It was June thirtieth, 1958. I had to stop it, save him, save me.

"Dad!" I tore it out of my throat and started to run. "Dad!" Louder. "Run!"

Run, child, run. Danger . . .

The words travelled up my spine.

I reached the intersection of the two paths and plunged into the bushes. Between the undergrowth and the slippery mud, I don't know how I stayed on my feet. The old Aultsville Road came up out of the ooze and steadied me. I ran through the hallway it cut through the weedy trees and came out on the mud flat. The setting sun lit up the windows of the houses on Ault Island, but no one was home.

I veered to the left to follow the road back into the brush along the river, passing the foundation of what had been Leonard's General Store. I was not far from the site of my father's house.

You lying bastard . . .

It has to be this way, Hal . . . Where's Leslie?

"Gordon!" I shrieked "Don't!"

Bushes and small trees tore at me. I was cut and bleeding all down my arms and legs. The road continued, wheeling back around toward the river on its way to the site of the old government wharf.

She left me . . . I haven't seen her in months . . .

You're lying, Hal . . .

I'm not the one who lies . . .

In the dying light I saw footprints in the mud ahead, and I followed them off the road before making it to the open water. A sidewalk. I was somewhere near the site.

What's the sleeping bag for?

The sleeping bag. Wylie's words to me on that day a lifetime ago . . .

"*. . . we figure the corpse was covered with dirt back then, plus the water . . . It was wrapped up in what we believe to have been a nylon bag of some sort, like a sleeping bag . . . There were rocks in it to weigh the body down.*"

Planned. Calculated. Cold-blooded.

"Daddy!" I tried to see them through the growth, but tears filled my eyes. Breathing hurt. "Daddy, run! He's going to kill y—"

Suddenly there was no ground beneath me, and I fell into the old foundation, partly on something soft. Soft or not, it still knocked the wind out of me for a minute. Then I heard a groan and reached out to touch someone lying in the mud.

"Daddy?" I whispered. "It's Farran." I carefully turned him over. "We have to get you out of here before the water comes."

He was still warm.

He was bleeding from the chest.

He was Jerry Strauss.

"Jerry?" I whispered incredulously.

I put my trembling hand on his face. This was all a nightmare. It had to be. The voices had stopped, as had the rain. I remembered what had brought me there.

"Stephanie?" I called out. "Are you here?" More silence. Jerry's face was white and his breathing barely discernable.

"Jerry," I whispered. "Can you hear me? It's Farran. Who did this to you?" Feeling helpless, I moved my hand down to his chest and he moaned again. My hand came up covered with blood.

Absolute panic hit.

My God. Out here. He was dying. How the hell could I get help? My hand felt uselessly for my cell. I had left it in the car.

"*Help us!*" I screamed. "Somebody please help us!"

And then a miracle happened. I heard someone moving in the bushes, and Ethan Chamberlain stepped out at the edge of the foundation.

"Ethan!" I called to him, for a crazy moment letting relief wash over me. "Thank God you're here."

He stopped dead, looking at Jerry and me.

"My God, Fanny," he whispered. "What have you done?"

I stared back at him. "What do you mean, what have I done? Help me get Jerry out of here. He needs medical help right now or he'll bleed to death."

But the face I saw was not Ethan Chamberlain. It was the true face. The face with eyes that were black and soulless. The killer I had loved. The truth I had run from for a quarter of a century.

I felt Jerry move. Out of the corner of my eye I saw his hand move away from his side as though he were looking for something. Instinctively, I put my hand on his.

"Ethan," I whispered. "Why?"

"He had to die, Fanny." The old smile I loved appeared on his face — but not in his eyes.

It was my turn to ask. "Where is she, Ethan? Where is Stephanie?"

"She and Amy are sleeping. A little something I put in their drinks at dinnertime. They won't wake up until it's all over."

"Until what's all over?"

"This," he gestured at us. "Your killing your lover to hide your tracks and then yourself in remorse."

"And Haley, too?" I said softly. Haley, our baby. Not once, but twice. "They'll find out about the car. That it was tampered with."

"I'm afraid that will be your fault, Fanny. It will all fall on your shoulders once you're dead."

"All — including Flight 39, right, Ethan?"

It was said. That small thing on the tip of my tongue was now words.

"I never wanted children, Fan." A shrug. *A shrug* . . . "And I couldn't let you destroy my comfortable life with Debra's trust fund or my career. For a baby? Debra would have wanted to do the right thing. But she never knew. At least, not for sure." His face took on a look that sent shivers down my spine. "Then you had to almost ruin everything with your damned phone call. What the hell was that?"

"What the hell was Flight 39, Ethan?" I could feel tears streaming down my face. "*A hundred and fifteen innocent lives.* Just to kill me and our baby?"

"I wondered if you had known, figured it out. When I heard you were still alive, I had to find out." Still the smile. The only part of him I had left.

"There's been enough killing, Ethan," I said, looking down at Jerry. I saw his eyes open just a crack and look at me. "We're going to save him," I added shortly. "Jerry's still alive. We can change this."

"I'm sorry, Fan." Ethan stopped smiling. "I'm sorry it has to end this way. Don't worry. I'll tell Haley you loved her."

I felt the chill of the evening breeze bring goose bumps to my flesh. Haley.

"Don't hurt our baby, Ethan. Please." I begged.

"Oh, I won't. Right now she's far more valuable alive than dead." He shook his head. "Do you know what she's worth? Staggering. But in time, maybe once her will includes dear old dad . . ."

Keep the child safe, lass.

The wind died.

You lying bastard . . .

"You lying bastard," I echoed.

Ethan shrugged again. I felt a strange calm come over me and wondered for an instant if this was my acceptance of coming death.

Then three things happened simultaneously that I will live again and forever all of a piece:

The sight of Ethan smiling, pulling a small handgun out of his pocket as he moved toward me.

The feel of Jerry putting something cold and hard like steel quietly into my hand.

The sound of Jerry's tortured whisper to me.

One word.

"*Fire.*"

EIGHTEEN

REVELATION

I did.

PART FOUR

I'm too numb to feel the pain
I feel like Joe Lewis standing in the rain
Bind my hands and make it all right
Heal my heart so baby I can fight

There's nothing left but the rain
My heart is aching but I can't say goodbye
I think that the world is ending
I think that the messages we're sending
are going down in flames.

I see rockets
I see rockets
I see rockets

Every time I see your face

—Marc Jordan
"Rockets"

NINETEEN

YESTERDAY

Pain.

He floated without physical reality, except for the pain. It was his centre, deep and throbbing, and his mind wrapped around it like an anchor.

Jurgen . . .

The voice was also pain, an old pain.

Jurgen . . . you must try . . .

Poppa?

You must tell them what happened . . .

"Poppa," he murmured, "I will."

"Jerry?"

"Poppa," he mumbled. The pain moved toward him, and he backed away into the floating again.

"Jerry?" This time the voice was more demanding. "Wake up."

"Pain." He opened his eyes for a second and saw a face above him.

"Are you in pain?" asked the face.

He nodded and closed his eyes. There was movement around him and more floating, and then the pain seemed also to float, free of him, moving away.

"Jerry," said the voice, "you need to wake up now."

With tremendous effort, he opened his eyes again and kept them open. The face was still above him, and gradually it came into focus.

"Jordan?" he whispered.

Jordan smiled at him. "Glad to have you back, Inspector. It was touch and go there for a bit. While you're incapacitated, and it's safe for me to do so, I'll suggest you leave the more rugged field work to the younger officers . . . sir."

Field work. Forest and mud. Someone yelling, "Officer down!" Uniforms and faces. A flash of Jordan prying a handgun out of a sobbing Farran's hands. A new pain cut across his chest.

"Farran." He looked at Jordan.

The smiled lessened a bit, but stayed. "She's fine, Jerry. She's been here since we brought you in, waiting for you to wake up. She's lying down in another room here."

"What . . . day?"

"It's Canada Day. We brought you in about eighteen hours ago and you immediately went into surgery."

More flashes. Gunfire and pain from Ethan Chamberlain.

"Chamberlain?"

"Dead, sir."

"How did you find us?"

"Farran called Ruth before she went out there. Ruth called us when she couldn't get you. When you didn't respond to your pager, we tagged you with the GPS."

A doctor walked into the room. "So you're up, Inspector? How do you feel?"

"Tired . . . very tired."

The doctor worked with the nurse to check Jerry's vitals and the bandaged area on his chest. She seemed happy with everything and turned back to the man on the bed.

"Considering the close call you just had, everything looks good. And it was a very close call, Mr. Strauss. When you were shot, the bullet entered your chest and lodged right beside your heart. Thankfully, it didn't pierce the outer wall. But you've lost a lot of blood, and the fatigue from that and the surgery will stay with you for a few days. You'll be staying with us until you are feeling stronger."

When Jerry was alone with Jordan, he asked, "Farran?"

"I'll wake her up and bring her to see you. But," Jordan hesitated, "we have a man dead under unclear circumstances. I can't give you any time alone together until I have your statement. I hope you understand."

When Wiley moved to get up, Jerry put out a hand.

"Stephanie Harrison? All right?"

"Yes," said Wiley. "We found both Stephanie and her friend Amy fast asleep in their hotel room. Drugged, but just fine."

Strauss nodded.

When Jordan returned, Farran came in behind him and hesitated at the door. Jerry held out his hand and she moved in to take it, holding it in her own against her face. They sat in silence for a long time, Farran's head on his covers, his hand now stroking her hair until he fell back asleep.

The ICU had no windows, but it felt as though some hours had passed when Jerry woke up again. Farran was gone, and Jordan dozed in the lounge chair beside the bed.

"Jordan? Jordan?"

The younger officer opened his eyes and sat up. "You're up. I'll tell the nurse."

A small tray of simple foods appeared, and Strauss actually felt hungry. When Jerry was done, Jordan moved the tray away and helped rearrange the pillows.

"Where's Farran?" Jerry asked him.

"I sent her home," came the reply. "Not an easy thing to do, but Lynn and Paul helped escort her out under my orders. She needed sleep." Then Jordan looked at Jerry.

"Do you remember what happened?" he asked quietly.

So many flashes then. All coming together. Jerry closed his eyes and nodded.

"Are you up to making a statement now, or do you want to do this tomorrow?"

"Now is fine," he answered.

Half an hour later, Constable Margaret Taylor joined them, taking notes.

"Good to see you up, Inspector," she said briefly when entering the room. "It's too damn quiet at the detachment without you."

"I promise to fix that when I return," Jerry said with a weak smile.

They all fell silent , then Jordan spoke.

"Jerry," he said leaning forward in his chair, "what the hell happened out there?"

So much he needed to say. So much never to say. And what he wanted to tell Farran if he could ever have the courage. He'd put her in a terrible position, made her do the unthinkable to save them both. Had she known before she got there, or had it all been a horrific shock? He needed to hold her, ask forgiveness, listen to her voice tell him what he did not know and could only guess at. To put all the pieces together and make sense of the tragedy.

And what had he done to her relationship with her daughter? Farran had just killed the girl's biological father. Self-defence notwithstanding, what will they do with each other now?

"I got the report on the car," he began slowly, "the car Debra Hyde was driving when she died. The brakes were tampered with. So was the gas pedal. It was murder." He rested for a minute, and let Jordan help him take a sip of water. "Maybe half an hour later, switchboard gets a call for me from Ethan Chamberlain. He tells me that Farran has gone to Aultsville to find her daughter who is missing, and he is afraid for them both. I tell him I will go and take a look.

"When I get there, there is no car in the little parking place on the old Aultsville Road. I head out by foot and go in the direction of the river, following a set of footprints into the bush. By now, I'm at the old foundation where we found Hal Leonard's remains some years ago. I call out, but see no one around in the bush. Then Chamberlain steps out from the bushes with a gun trained on me. He makes me throw mine in the foundation. He apologizes, and then shoots me without warning.

"I think I fell into the foundation. After that, things are hazy. I probably fell unconscious for a bit. I vaguely remember Chamberlain moving around and muttering to himself. When he checked me, I played dead. In the deep grass, I could see my gun not far away. Then, I could hear Farran's voice calling out. I tried to call out to warn her, but couldn't. The pain in my chest was pretty bad by then. Chamberlain thought I was dead, so that was my only advantage, and I lay very still.

"Then Farran came running up and fell into the foundation on me. She rolled me over and started to cry out for help. I heard Chamberlain's voice talking to her, asking her why she had shot me. Then he went on about going to shoot her to make it look like she had killed me and Debra to hide her guilt. That's when—"

Jerry stopped. The younger officers looked at him expectantly.

"That's when I saw Chamberlain take his gun out of his pocket to kill Farran," Jerry continued slowly. "That's when I found my gun, secretly put it in Farran's hands, and then told her to shoot him."

He closed his eyes. "Farran Mackenzie shot Ethan Chamberlain in self-defence with my gun because I told her to. She saved both our lives."

He remained with his eyes closed. Finally, Jordan said, "Do you remember anything else?"

"Nothing substantial after that. Bits and pieces. I fell unconscious again and woke up here."

"Is that your full statement, sir?" This from Margaret Taylor.

He opened his eyes and looked into hers. "Yes. I have nothing else to tell you about that day."

Sleep came again with little help necessary from the medication they gave him. The morphine for the pain kept the edge off, and he took the time to rest. Once again, he felt old, tired, used up. Once again, early retirement rolled around in his head. And once again, he'd had what should have been enough pieces in front of him, yet failed to prevent a death. In fact, he'd almost let Ethan Chamberlain kill Farran.

Dreams came. His father stood outside the little house in Aultsville, watching him throw a softball with Hal in the field across the road. Then fire and smoke. A single tear rolled down his cheek. "Poppa . . ." he murmured.

His mother came, young and beautiful again.

Jerry . . . it's time to come home now.

Ma.

Then her face in the glow of the lumberyard fire.

He's working on the books . . .

"No . . ." Jerry struggled to wake up.

Farran's face came to him.

Jerry, can you hear me? It's Farran. Who did this to you?

"Farran," he mumbled. "Farran . . . watch out . . . he's crazy . . ."

Ethan Chamberlain loomed up behind her and put a hand on her shoulder. She turned and began to walk away with him.

"Farran . . . no . . . *no* . . ."

His eyes flew open. The room was semi-dark and quiet, except for the digital monitor making soft beeps—so concrete and indisputable that it was comforting—and he finally slipped back into the shadows of sleep before dawn.

"My sister Ruth is here?" Jerry asked as the nurse took the breakfast tray away. He almost started to say he had no sister, but caught himself.

"Yes. After we get you cleaned up for the day, we'll let her in for a quick visit."

Ruth came in a bit later and kissed him on the head, then held him for a minute. When she sat down beside him, her eyes were wet.

"I'm fine, Ruth," Jerry began.

"Shut up," she said unexpectedly, sounding very much like her mother, Alice. "I'm not here to listen. I'm here to talk. They won't let me sit with you for very long, so I'll get to the point."

"Somehow, I get the feeling this is going to hurt more than the surgery," he shot back. Ruth glared at him and he shut up.

"First of all," she said, putting a trembling hand on his, "thank God, you're alive. We couldn't stand to lose you, Jerry. I hope you know that.

"Second, you promised you would take care of our girl—and you did. She's safe."

"I—I can't—"

"Like I said, shut up and listen. I don't know everything that went on, but I know the basics. If you hadn't given her the gun, told her—" Her voice broke.

"It should never have gotten that far, Ruth. And don't tell me to shut up," Jerry cut her off. "The truth is, I put her life at risk. I should have done a lot of things differently. But I was caught up personally, and I didn't get help with that.

"Ruth," he squeezed her hand, "Farran had to shoot her daughter's father to save her life. They've just found each other. What happens between them now?"

Ruth squeezed his hand back, and tears welled up again.

"They will work it out. They have a lifetime ahead of them now to have some kind of relationship. They need each other, and it will all be all right. You'll see. The important thing is that it's finally over.

"After twenty-six years, Jerry, Farran's nightmare is over."

She didn't come back to see him until that night.

They sat together wordlessly at first, holding hands.

Finally, Jerry tried to start.

"Farran—"

She shook her head.

"I don't want to talk about it. Not yet. Not until you are fully healed. Physically." She rubbed his hand softly. "It's just too much right now. There's going to be an investigation going on for a while, as you know. It's not going anywhere, and neither are we. I can't take any more of this, and you don't need it right now, either. But we will talk," she added, smiling at him. "I will answer any questions, Jerry, when you are feeling stronger. So let's wait until then, okay?"

He opened his mouth to reply and then closed it again.

"I'm just so grateful I didn't lose you," she whispered and began to cry.

Carefully putting his arm around her, Jerry whispered back, "And I you. Lying there on the ground, seeing that bastard pulling a gun on you . . . I couldn't bear it, Farran."

"I'm sorry. I should have told you everything—"

Jerry put a finger to her lips. "Remember, we aren't going to talk about it now, right?"

She nodded, and quietly laid her head on his shoulder. "What will we talk about? I've never been good at small talk."

He stroked her hair again.

"We've never done small talk, and I'm not about to start now. What about Fenton's fool's gold? Did you ever settle that one?"

Farran jerked her head up.

"You arrested Carl Wallace, that poor man. How could you?"

"His gun was found with his brother's body. It's the right calibre for the murder weapon."

She sat up and looked at him thoughtfully. "Why don't I think you believe it any more than I do?"

He shrugged and winced. "Not much motive. But someone shot Sam Wallace in the head . . ." He stopped.

"What?" Farran asked.

"I'm not sure." He thought a minute. "Well, that's definitely something to look into."

"Jerry . . ."

"Something I heard that I just remembered. Should have gotten on that right away." He brushed her cheek with his hand. "I was distracted."

Farran's eyes narrowed. "Are you going to tell me, or am I going to send you back in for more surgery?"

He smiled. "Someone said to me that Ricky Potts deserved to be shot in the head, but not Sam Wallace." He told her a name. "Someone who shouldn't have known that, right?"

Farran chewed her lip, then looked sideways at Jerry.

"They're going to kick me out in a minute. Would you like a bedtime story?"

The next morning found them in Jerry's new room in Observation. Jordan Wiley leaned back in the lounge chair, looking from Jerry to Farran.

"I admit, it sounds rather wild, but if the Inspector says to go ahead with it, we will. If it were anyone but you, Dr. Mackenzie," he added pointedly, "the answer would be no."

Farran smiled at him. "I appreciate your faith in me." She outlined her idea. "We need a surprise attack. Even if I'm right, without a confession, we've got nothing."

The men looked at each other.

"I agree," said Jerry.

Farran took a deep breath and let it out.

"Okay, then. We'll set it up for Saturday. Give us enough time to stir things up." She smiled at Jordan.

"C'mon, Sergeant Wiley. Let's go catch us a big rat."

Three days later, the headline in Strauss's newspaper was big and black:

IROQUOIS MUSEUM CLOSED
FOR TREASURE HUNT

CARMAN HOUSE SITE OF LOST GOLD
FROM WAR OF 1812

(South Dundas: Iroquois) Almost two centuries after vanishing during the days of the War of 1812, a shipment of Spanish gold doubloons has been found under the floor of the Iroquois museum known as Carman House.

According to local legend, the gold belonged to the property's first owner, Ira Fenton, who was paid with the gold coins for work building part of a fort on Iroquois Point for wartime defence. At the time of the Battle of Crysler's Farm in November of 1813, Fenton was killed and his house burnt to the ground. The gold vanished but never surfaced across the border.

"It never surfaced because it never left the property," says retired history professor Dr. Farran Mackenzie. "Fenton buried it in his cellar. When the Carman family bought the property after Fenton's death, they built a new house but on the old foundation. It's been here all along."

The only clue to the whereabouts of the gold was Fenton's dying words. He told the soldier who found him that he could "see the gold in his own face."

"He couldn't have meant a mirror," says Mackenzie. "Not permanent enough. So the other option was water, and somewhere safe. We dug into the basement cistern and there it was."

In recent years, the basement of Carman House was given a new cement floor to help maintain the cellar. Fortunately for the museum, the cistern was untouched.

"I don't think Carman House will have to worry about funding for a while," Mackenzie smiles.

* * *

The darkness in the old basement was almost palpable.

Jordan Wiley stood in the cellar of Carman House behind the new furnace in the middle of the floor, out of sight of the cistern. He pressed the digital glow button on his watch for just a second. Only an hour had passed. He hoped for Farran's sake the wait wasn't for nothing.

Was that a sound? His radio beeped.

"10-14, Sergeant. We have a visitor," came Taylor's voice.

"10-4," said Wiley. "Assuming blackout. All hands to battle stations," he added in a whisper to the room.

He heard a door close upstairs, followed by stealthy footsteps across the dining room floor. The door to the office above the stairs slowly opened, and Wiley held his breath, gun ready. The footsteps hesitated at the top of the stairs, and the glow of a flashlight appeared. The person holding the flashlight slowly came down the cellar stairs, face hidden behind the light. The legs turned at the bottom of the stairs and headed toward the cistern covered in a tarp in the corner of the cellar. The light stopped on the floor, where something sparkled in the glow.

The intruder stooped to pick it up.

"My gold . . ." came the mutter. "*My* gold. Not theirs." Then the sound of the tarp being pulled off. "I've waited all these years—"

Suddenly, the cellar light came on in a blinding glare. Wiley remained behind the furnace, listening. The intruder whirled around.

Farran stood on the stairs.

"Hello, Mr. Pollan," she said quietly.

"*You,*" Pollan said accusingly, moving toward the stairs. "What are you doing here?"

"I could ask the same of you," she said evenly, "but then I already know."

"I work here. The museum is closed. You have no right to be here."

"You tried to kill me." Carl Wallace appeared from behind the stairs. He moved toward Pollan, pointing a finger at him. "I remember now. I didn't fall. I went into the office looking for a bathroom, and when I turned around, you stabbed me and pushed me down the stairs. What the hell did I ever do to you?"

"It wasn't what you did but what you could do," said Farran. "You could recognize him. And you did, you just couldn't remember. You were delirious when I found you, but you told me who he was."

Carl looked from Farran to Jeremy Pollan. He walked up to Pollan and stood, their faces inches apart. After a few seconds, his eyes cleared.

"Yes . . . yes. My God. You old weasel. They said you were dead, you son of a bitch. You're old now, like me, and the beard hides your face . . . but the eyes. I'd know those weasel eyes anywhere."

"You're old and crazy." Pollan moved toward the stairs. Another person came up from the shadows and blocked his way.

"Ricky Potts," said Shelley Piper Frost. It came out almost a whisper. "I don't believe it. What are you doing here?"

"Tell them, Rick," said Farran. "Tell them why you killed a man and took his place in Iroquois, working on the Point and then the international lock to stay in the area. Tell them why you've stayed here for fifty years, while your wife had a breakdown because she thought she witnessed your death." Farran came down the stairs and stopped in front of him. "Tell them why two people spent those same years buried under the shoreline of this village."

Pollan's face became ugly.

"You're all crazy. Even if you prove I'm Potts, you can't pin anything on me."

"You killed Carl's brother Sam and Vivienne Dupuis so you wouldn't have to share the gold."

"I . . ." Shelley began, "I heard you talking to Vivienne at the diner about not sharing the gold. I tried to find Sam that night to warn him, but I couldn't. Then he disappeared and Vivienne never came back to work. I was so scared but I didn't know for sure . . ."

"You spread the rumour that they had run off together," Farran continued, "and then you left town. Went back to Massena."

Pollan put his face in hers.

"If I did all that to keep the gold, then why is it still here? I never found it, and I never killed anyone."

"Yes, you did. Killed, that is. But you didn't find the gold. You found a chest full of silver dollars, which was a big disappointment, but you felt the gold was nearby. You had to leave to take the heat off, but you planned to come back later that fall.

"And then the real Jeremy Pollan followed you to Massena. He heard you talking about the gold at work, saw you find something, and wanted some for himself. When he tracked you down at work and you argued, Jeremy fell into the cement and died. It was a golden opportunity for you to take his place and disappear from your own life and the shady people you owed money to, for good. Did you know that Charlotte saw it happen?" she added.

Pollan glared at her for a minute, then dropped his eyes.

"Yep," he said. "Seemed a good idea to have her think it was me that died, so she could spread the word."

"But Charlotte didn't spread the word," Farran replied grimly. "She went into shock at the loss of a husband she loved, despite how he disappointed her, and witnessing what seemed to be his gruesome end caused a mental breakdown from which she never recovered. Charlotte was the real treasure in your life," Farran added, "but you were too busy taking short cuts, playing games with people, and chasing lost gold to understand that."

"She had a breakdown?" he whispered.

"Did you kill Julia?" Shelley moved closer. "She never hurt anyone, and she really liked you, Mr. Pollan . . . Rick. Why? Why would you kill my sister?"

Something passed over the man's face.

"Julia Parmeter knew that you had been involved with Carl's 'accident'," Farran offered, "and she was covering for you, right, Rick?" Pollan looked away, and Farran continued. "She told me when I arrived looking for Carl that you hadn't shown up that morning, even though you said you would. At that point, she thought she was telling the truth. But you had been there, and panicked when you saw Carl Wallace drive up in a car."

"Julia told the truth," Pollan cut in. "I never did show up that day. Wallace is hallucinating again."

"No, he isn't," said Farran. "When I left the museum to follow the ambulance, your ladder and paint cans were out. An experienced workman like you would never leave his tools and materials out overnight, particularly at a public place like a museum. You had indeed shown up to work and then attacked Carl when he was alone in the house, turning off the basement stair light to hide what you thought was the body and then hiding in the office while trying to figure out what to do next. I came and left. Then you went to Julia and told her there had been an accident, that you were afraid the man had tripped over some tools you'd left out. She promised not to tell you had been there that day, and you left using the kitchen door away from the parking lot. That's when Julia came out to find me.

"When it came out that Carl had been stabbed before falling down the stairs," Farran continued, "Julia started to wonder what had really happened that day. She faced you with it in the office later and you killed her."

"You have no proof," Pollan began to back toward the cistern.

"Yes, we do," said Wiley, coming out from behind the furnace. "We tested all the tools in your kit and found traces of blood on one of the hammers."

"A hammer?" whispered Shelley.

Pollan looked wildly from one face to another, then grabbed Farran and pushed her into Wiley. He started up the stairs with unexpected agility at full speed, and then came to a full halt halfway to the top.

"I wouldn't suggest it," said a voice from above. Constable Taylor looked down at them from the top stair, gun pointed at Pollan. "From this distance, Mr. Potts, I can't miss."

That, as Wiley later told Strauss, took the last of the wind out of Ricky Potts.

"Rick Potts, a.k.a. Jeremy Pollan," he'd said as he snapped the handcuffs on Potts, "you're under arrest for the murders of Samuel Wallace, Vivienne Dupuis, Jeremy Pollan, and Julia Parmeter. Anything you say can and will be used against you in a court of law. You will be given the opportunity to retain the services of a lawyer . . ."

"My gold," muttered Potts. "It was *my* gold. My great-great-great grandfather found it and didn't live to go back for it. It's mine by rights. I've looked for it for fifty years—"

"That gold belonged to Ira Fenton," Farran cut in. "It cost Fenton his life, and it's possible that Henry Potts was the one who killed him for it. Potts found only the silver where Ira said it would be. Is that what you found with the map in the diary?"

Potts nodded without speaking.

"But no gold," she finished.

"I looked for fifty years . . . *fifty years.*" Potts looked at his hands in the cuffs. "We found the box that summer and couldn't bring it up for a couple of weeks, as the guys were too close with the machines. I told Sam when we could do it and then went for it early. Get it and get away without splitting it with him. Vivienne must have let it slip, and there he was, demanding his share. It was my gold." His face went dark. "I wasn't sharing it with anybody."

"So you shot him," said Wiley. "How did you get Carl's gun?"

"The kid had it on him," came the reply. "Threatened me with it. We fought, and I took it from him. Buried him with the dozer and dug up the chest."

"But no gold," Farran repeated.

Potts looked away. "No. Just a chest full of silver dollars with a few gold ones mixed in. Then Vivienne comes up out of the dark and starts digging in and laughing. She grabs a gold coin and says we're going to split it fifty-fifty. I say not on her life; it's mine. And she says on Sam's life it's half hers. She saw everything. So I got rid of the witness and buried her, too." His one hand opened, and he looked at the gold doubloon still in it. "How much do they think is there?" he asked Farran.

"We don't know," she said. "We haven't found it yet, either. That news story was just a bluff to flush the killer out into the open." When Potts looked at her uncomprehendingly, she took the doubloon out of his hand. "This," she said, holding it up, "is courtesy of Vivienne Dupuis."

Taylor took Potts away in the squad car. Carl and Shelley stood silently, watching from the old kitchen. Farran came up to them with Wiley.

"It's over, Carl," she said softly.

He did not reply, and Shelley took his hand.

"A lot of blood spilled over the years because of that gold," she said to him.

The elderly man squeezed her hand. "Yes," he said simply. "I'm sorry, Shell," Carl added, "for the loss of your sister. I feel responsible somehow."

"No," she whispered. "Rick Potts did that. To someone who had always been good to him. Like Sam. A friend he used and then killed when Sam got in his way. Sam was a nice boy, Carl."

Carl let go of her hand and pulled Shelley into a hug. Then he turned to Farran.

"How did you guess it was really Rick Potts?"

"The first problem I had with Potts was that he was supposedly killed in Massena, shortly after he left here," said Farran. "Charlotte said he came back and was 'flush' with money. If he was because he'd found the gold, then why did the loan sharks kill him, as we thought? He could pay his debt—and then some.

"Next problem was you, Shelley, telling the inspector you thought you saw Potts back in the area once a few weeks after he, Sam, and Vivienne had disappeared. How was that possible, if he died the night Charlotte saw the accident? And did Carl see him back in Old Iroquois, too? Is that what he meant in his delirium about Potts coming back?

"Finally, the attacks," she continued. "There was absolutely no reason for the attack on you, Carl, or Julia's murder," Farran answered, "if Potts were dead and the gold found years ago, as it seemed. I wondered at one point, Shelley, if you had killed Sam because he wanted Vivienne and not you." Shelley flushed, and Farran smiled. "But if so, why attack Carl? And why would you suddenly kill your sister after all this time?

"The other tipoff was the remark Pollan made to Inspector Strauss about Potts deserving to be shot, not Sam. He said 'shot in the head' and the inspector hadn't told him that. Neither had I. He must have known, but why would Jeremy Pollan kill Sam Wallace?

"So what if Potts' death wasn't true? Once I turned everything around and began to look at it backward, Carl, your talking to Potts when you were wounded and delirious was the clincher. All Charlotte saw that night at the Robert Moses Generating Station were two figures fighting in the dark. When Rick didn't come home from work, she assumed he was the one that went into the cement and thought her brother had killed him. But Charley had spent the last fifty years thinking the same thing about Charlotte. There was no tangible proof, in the end, that Rick Potts had died. That's when I asked Sergeant Wiley if he had an old picture of Rick Potts. Beard and age aside, the young Potts looked very similar to Jeremy Pollan. But I had to let you see him to know for sure."

"All those lives and still no gold, Dr. Mackenzie. Do you think they'll ever find it?"

Farran smiled at them, and winked at Wiley. "Since my hunches are paying off at the moment," she said, "I'll tell you where I think the gold really is.

"Ira Fenton was worried about the safety of his money, but kept the silver in a chest where he could get at it if he needed it. The gold, less valuable than the silver, but much more of it to hide, had to go somewhere not easy to get to or to find—but where he could get to it with little problem after the war was over. Somewhere no one else would see it, if they weren't looking for it.

"Fenton told Henry Potts that you could see the gold in your own face. In other words, a reflection. Water. But not the cistern. The well. He probably lowered the gold in chests into his well and hid the ropes so the chests could be pulled up again whenever things settled down. If the Americans took over the area, they would camp where the fort was. This would keep the gold right at home with Fenton and right under their noses.

Farran held up the doubloon. "I'm willing to bet this that if the museum locates the original well for this house and digs down to the water level, they really won't have to worry about funding for a while."

TWENTY

TODAY

For Carl Wallace, it was over. For Farran Mackenzie, well, I wasn't so sure.

Ruth said the nightmare in my life had ended, and now I could move on and heal. There were many loose ends, however, twisting in the gentle breeze that follows a tornado. I felt as numb and disoriented in my life as someone who has lost everything to a natural disaster. For that was what my life seemed when I looked up in the settling dust to see where I stood and what was left.

The Water People disappeared as quietly as they had arrived in Iroquois. There was nothing to hold them once the statements had been taken. Stephanie and Amy had been found drugged but alive in their hotel rooms. Beyond ascertaining that, I had made no move toward my daughter—having just shot and killed her biological father in self-defence. Stephanie Harrison vanished in a puff of smoke, and I almost wondered if she had ever been real. All I could do was wait to hear from her. If I ever did.

Peter Simons returned from where he had disappeared to for the last week or so. Naturally, we had another coffee klatch with the OPP and my lawyer, this time with Wiley and Taylor taking Jerry's place in the "discussion," and the addition of one Superintendent Holland. I had no fight left in me, and no reason to hide anything. Lenore agreed that full disclosure was the best way to go, and I spoke of things I had thought of but never said in over a quarter of a century.

"Ethan Chamberlain was a charming man and an excellent professor," I began. "He always seemed to be someone out of a movie, and when you are young, you think this is magical. Looking at it as a much older woman, I think I felt even back then that it also meant you were dealing with a performance. Not a person.

"But I was lonely so far from home, and it seemed impossible to make any friends. The university was so full of cliques and people trying to scale the social ladder. I had none of that and didn't want it, so I stayed on the fringe. When Ethan became my friend, it was a lifesaver for me.

"But some things never added up. Once I found out Ethan was married to Debra, questions started that I tried to ignore. Debra Hyde was a pretty, intelligent, and impressive person. Why would Ethan Chamberlain wander and risk all that? And with a student? My ego kept me busy, telling me I was the only one. But it's been my experience that people who cheat do so as a matter of policy. So I guess I was to be the flavour of the season. Then I got pregnant.

"Ethan must have panicked, although his theatrical flair helped him put on a stellar performance for me. What if I spoke to Debra about it to come clean? So he started this thing about fearing for his life and mine, and then our baby's. He sounded so sincere that I didn't argue, but my guts were saying no. Debra Hyde was too even-tempered, too normal for anything like that. The business about Debra not wanting children didn't jive with me, either. Yes, she was dedicated to her work, but no more than anyone else. I just kept going along with it until that last day when he phoned before I left for the airport and said he would take care of everything. In my heart, I still didn't believe that Debra was the threat he said, but it seemed he did. It worried me how desperate he sounded. Yet when I had picked up my thesis, Debra had been more quiet than usual, but still herself. No emotional displays whatsoever.

"I sat on the plane that day and tried to just disappear back to Canada. But I couldn't. What if Ethan really tried to do something to Debra? I couldn't be responsible for that. So I ran off the plane and did what Ethan never dreamed I would do. I called Scotland Yard and warned them about the situation. And trying to save Debra's life saved mine."

I stopped and took a long drink of water. That day at the airport was as fresh in my mind as though the last twenty-six years hadn't happened. At least, it was until the point when I saw the news about Flight 39.

"What tipped you off that the bomb had been meant for you, from Ethan?" Peter asked.

"*I said it was meant for me!*" I screamed.

I closed my eyes at the other memory, too damn similar except for the body count. Then I drew in a deep breath, let it out, and opened my eyes.

"I think I knew it as soon as I saw the news on the monitor," I said slowly. The words, kept wrapped tightly for so many years, began to form sentences and be spoken. "I knew it in my guts, and I couldn't handle thinking that way about the man I loved. The man who was the father of my child. But the real horror didn't hit until I made it home two weeks later to see my mother. She had some stuff from the university they had sent—including my thesis."

I stopped and swallowed.

"Do you understand?" I continued. "*My thesis*. The same thing Debra Hyde had handed me in a box wrapped up in brown paper. It was the copy with her comments that she said was in the package. So what had been in the box I had with me in my backpack, and left on the plane?" I looked down at my hands. The silence in the room was deafening. "It was the bomb. I knew it then, too. I had carried that horrid thing past security somehow, and left it on the plane when I ran off. I left it there and all those people died."

I felt my stomach show interest in coming up, and I battled it. There would be time later for falling apart.

"So I left home and stayed out of sight, having Haley and giving her up for adoption. She needed to be safe, and she needed a better person for a mother than I was. I had terrible blood on my hands . . . ended so many lives. I had no right to spend mine taking care of hers. Then I buried the memory so deep that I lost it. Trauma. It wasn't until everyone had shown up here and a student named Jenn Farley gave me her thesis in a similar package that the horror resurfaced for me."

Tears welled up in spite of my best efforts.

Lenore made a sound in her throat.

"I think we've covered everything for now. Obviously, this is very stressful for my client, and Dr. Mackenzie is here on her own volition."

Peter put up a hand. "One more thing, please. You say that Ethan admitted responsibility for the bombing of Flight 39, the day he died. Yet it was Debra who gave you the package, and her copy that was replaced by the explosive device. Do you have any proof other than your statements that it was Ethan Chamberlain and not Debra Hyde who possibly placed a bomb in that package?"

I rubbed my eyes. "Talk to Stephanie Harrison and Amy Shea, from the environmental project team. They said that Debra was like a mother to them, and she was to me back in the Oxford days, even though there wasn't much difference in our ages. Ethan told me then that Debra couldn't have children, which he then said to me that last day was a lie. Check her medical history. If you find she didn't have infertility problems years ago, there's your answer. Not only was Ethan Chamberlain a liar, but Debra Hyde was a woman who wanted children and couldn't convince her husband to do so.

"Debra might have wanted to kill me for sleeping with her husband, but a woman like that could never have planned to kill an innocent baby — or any other children that might have been on the plane."

Peter Simon eventually headed back to England, with a folder full of details and reports. What would come of it with Scotland Yard simply would. An internal investigation into the shooting of Inspector Jerry Strauss and the death of Ethan Chamberlain was under way. Once completed, a second external inquiry might take place if there ended up more questions than answers.

The summer of light emotional entertainment was over, and I found myself buried in the winter of my own discontent.

Jenn Farley had said she would return to explain things about her mother, yet she, too, seemed to disappear from my life right then. For a week after the shooting, I heard nothing from her and wondered if my chance to reconnect with Jeanie Ross, my childhood friend, had disappeared with Jenn.

Then, one afternoon, I opened the door, brandy in hand, and there she was.

It didn't click for a minute, but when I saw Jenn standing shyly behind the woman facing me, I knew.

"Jeanie? *Jeanie!*"

Hugs, tears, laughter. All the good things when an old friend comes back into your life. Jenn stood smiling, looking at the two of us as though she were the adult and we the children.

I led them into the living room, offering coffee, food, and alcohol. Jeanie refused all but coffee, as it was early afternoon, and she made no reference to the brandy I had going. I brought the coffee for them and a refill for myself.

"Jeanie," I said, sitting down and looking at her. She had short brown hair in a cut not that unlike the one she once sported in Preston. "Here. In my house. It's been, what . . . over thirty years?"

She smiled. "Thirty-five, to be exact. I left Preston before we started Grade 10."

"You left so fast, I didn't even have a chance to say goodbye," I said, but without rebuke in my voice. "Why? Where did you go?"

Jeanie looked at Jenn, and put her hand on her daughter's. Then she looked back at me.

"My father took a job out West," she said quietly. "He'd been thinking about it for a couple of months and decided finally to take it. We left very quickly after that, so he wouldn't lose his place."

"But you left first, Jeanie. Remember?" I leaned forward. "I went to your house the first week of school to get you one day, and your mother said you were visiting relatives. A week after that, your family was gone, too."

Jeanie nodded. "It was very sudden."

I glanced at Jenn before adding carefully, "Rumour had it you were pregnant and you went away to have your baby."

Behind Farran, two girls twittered about another classmate who had not returned to school in the fall. Jeanie Ross had been a little, well, wild, and the rumours about her absence were, too.

"Pregnant, you know."

"That's no surprise, considering."

On an ordinary day, Farran would have ignored the chatter and let the teacher handle it. It was her job. But Jeanie Ross had been her friend, too, and today there was just too much sand in Farran Mackenzie's shorts.

She turned around to face the girls.

"SHUT UP," she said in a clear voice.

The chatterers stopped in mid-gape. Every head in the class turned, except Alison's. Farran slowly turned back and looked at the teacher who stood, chalk in hand. Miss Lawson looked at Farran, then the two girls behind her. But no rebuke came, only raised eyebrows before continuing the lecture.

Farran slumped down in her seat and said no more.

Jeanie slapped her knee and laughed uproariously. Catching her breath, she said, "Really? Oh, that's just too precious. I'm sure the gossip girls had a field day with that one."

"As a matter of fact, they did," I grinned. "I told them to shut up right in class."

Jeanie grew sober. "I almost wish it had been that simple. But it wasn't. Fan, my father did have a job offer out West, but my family left because of me."

I saw Jenn put her other hand on top of her mother's.

"What do you mean?" I asked slowly, not sure I wanted to hear the answer.

"Do you remember the Simser boy, the kid who was killed by one of those bombs on his way to school? A terrible case of the wrong place at the wrong time."

"I remember it well," I said, squelching the memory with a sip of brandy. "I also remember what it did to Alison's father. He blamed himself for not preventing it, for not shutting the gangs down in time."

"I saw it happen."

For a minute, the import of the words didn't sink in. I looked at Jeanie. "What?"

"I said, I saw it happen. And I saw the man who put the bomb in the car. He drove past and threw it in the window. I didn't know what it was, and then seconds later, all hell broke loose. The Simser boy was a few yards ahead of me on the sidewalk. Next minute, the car was a fireball and I couldn't see him anymore. People came running, and I ran away. I got sick behind a building and stayed there until after lunch when I went home."

"Jeanie," I said softly. "Oh, my God. You never told me this."

"I never told anyone. I told my parents I was sick and stayed home from school the next couple of days. The killing was all they talked about. I just kept throwing up, thinking about it. Finally, I spilled the whole thing. I was so scared, and afraid I would be arrested for running away. I didn't get what my father did immediately: I was an eye witness to a murder and could pin a member of that gang for it."

"He was afraid for your life."

Jeanie nodded and looked at Jenn. "He did what I would do for my child. He sent me away, took the job transfer, and immediately moved the whole family out of town. I wanted to try to find the murderer. I felt so bad for that boy, as we all did. But my father made me swear to never speak of it again, and we started a new life somewhere else. We also cut all ties to Preston," she added. "That was the hardest part. I wanted to call you, or write. But I gave my word I wouldn't. Then we heard about Alison's dad and Dave Carlson." She shook her head. "Those were dark days, even for us so far away."

We sat in silence for a minute, each of us dealing with memories and feelings we had struggled with as teenagers, let alone now as adults.

Jeanie let Jenn's hands go and reached over for mine.

"When I saw the news about Alison's death and your near miss, I had to find you. The news about the possible mistake in John Perry's shooting spun me around, as you can imagine. I thought I might finally have to step forward, and I didn't want to put my own children in danger. So I waited, then I wished I hadn't. I wish I had come before Alison died."

I could feel my throat closing up as I battled the tears.

"She said she missed you, Jeanie," I whispered, "and asked if I knew where you were. I hadn't seen her in years. She left Preston, too, not long after her father was killed."

"It must have been awful for you, Fan," Jeanie said quietly, her eyes shining with tears of her own. "To find her again and then lose her that way."

For the children, Fan.

I closed my eyes.

I said it was meant for me!

I put my face in my hands.

"Fan . . ." Jeanie's hand squeezed my arm.

"Jeanie," I managed, "you have no idea."

The falling apart time had come. Life in its inexplicable way had given me a great gift—the presence of someone who had known me in the Before Time, someone I had had no contact with for three decades, yet someone I knew was completely trustworthy. My old friend. The love was still there between us.

For the children, Fan. Remember.

Yes, Alison. I will remember.

And for the rest of that day, and all that night, I told my old friend everything of my life, my losses, my pain, my truths—holding nothing back, and feeling for the first time in years a tremendous weight come off my shoulders. Jeanie would help me carry it, and remember, too.

"How long do inquiries take?" I asked Paul one night as he braved my dinner table. The beautiful flowers he'd brought me made the meal seem almost fancy. Once Jerry had been moved to Observation and I started living at home again, flowers had come daily from Paul, but no visit until he called. Then he showed up for dinner, wisely bringing takeout with him.

"I want to make sure you're eating," he'd said over my objections. So now we sat with wonderful tubs and boxes laid out around the flowers.

"Inquiries can take as long as several months, sometimes years," Paul replied, spooning some high-fat heaven onto his plate. "But this situation doesn't involve a whole bunch of people, so it should move along fairly quickly. If they get to it right away—and they will with the Mounties breathing down their necks in response to Scotland Yard's presence—it should be wrapped up by summer's end." He shot a look at me. "Unless there are any surprises still waiting?"

I shook my head and held my hands up in mock surrender.

"I'm out of ammunition, I swear," I said a little too brightly. "I have nothing left. I'm . . . I'm . . . empty." My voice trembled.

Paul put his fork down. "Are you okay, Farran?" he asked softly. "I remember the first time I had to shoot a man on duty. Took me months to get my head back to normal. Are you talking to anyone about it?"

I played with my food. "I told everything to Jeanie, an old friend who's in town. We talked for hours, actually. It helped a lot."

"You need to see someone professional. I'll suggest that right now. It's bad enough when you end the life of someone you don't know, a criminal that has to be stopped from killing someone else or you; but you had to shoot someone you knew and were involved with. The father of your daughter. It's going to take a long time to work all this through. I'd like to know you're having help with this, and I know Mother would agree with me here."

All I could do was nod. I didn't trust my voice. Paul got up and came around the table, pulling me into his arms. I didn't fight it. His strength felt good again, and I leaned on him for a bit.

"Almost lost you again," he whispered huskily.

"I'm sorry."

"Can this be it now with the brushes with death?" he asked. "Are there any more dark secrets from your past that could blow through and put you in danger, or is it going to be the normal life from now on?"

I smiled, my head on his chest. "I'm not sure what normal is, Paul, but no more dark secrets. Promise."

He pulled away and held me at arm's length. "So it's time for Farran Mackenzie to start planning her new life. Retired from teaching, no aging homicidal maniacs left to run to ground, no more secret relatives to uncover. Is it time for a life with someone special in it?"

I knew what he was asking.

"I . . . I don't know," I said honestly. "I've been a loner for twenty-six years. I don't know if I can, if anyone would be crazy enough to try that with me."

"I know one man who would."

I looked at his kind eyes, touched his beautiful face, and said nothing.

He sighed. "But you don't love me—not that way. You love him, right?"

I nodded slowly. Paul kissed me on the forehead and let me go.

"Well, at least I have the comfort of knowing my rival is a good man," he said. "I came here early because of him. He asked Mother to get me here, to tell me he needed my presence, because you might be in a lot of trouble he couldn't help you with. I respect him for that. And," he added, "it tells me he takes care of you. Might be the only man on earth who can totally handle that."

I squeezed Paul's hand. "You're very special to me, do you know that?"

He squeezed back. "Absolutely. Now, let's eat."

We sat back down to it, and fell silent for a bit.

Finally, Paul sat back in his chair and looked at me.

"I have to ask—what happened with Stephanie?"

I pushed my plate away. No seconds. A first for me.

"Nothing," I said simply. "I stayed with Jerry in the hospital those first couple of days. Jordan told me she was fine, that they had gone on my instructions that horrid afternoon to check on Stephanie and Amy. They found them drugged as Ethan had said, but all right.

"I left messages on Stephanie's cell phone, but she never returned them. Apparently, once the OPP had their statements, they were free to go. And they did. I assume she's gone back to BC. Probably doesn't want to see me again after what happened."

"I wouldn't be too sure about that," he replied. "It's a hell of a mess, but you acted in self-defence. You also acted to save Jerry's life. Basically, you had no choice, and Chamberlain was obviously off his bird. You probably ultimately saved Stephanie's life, too, from what you said Ethan told you that day."

I looked at Paul.

"What if she never comes back?" I whispered.

He leaned forward and took one of my hands in his.

"She'll be back, Fan," he said firmly. "I can guarantee it. No matter what, you are her mother and the only family she has left. Other than me," he added with a grin. "But, seriously, as an adopted child, I can tell you for certain—she will come back."

The days just after were the roller-coaster type, good and bad. Jerry was alive and would recover. Stephanie was gone, but now real and within reach. Ethan and Debra were dead, with both the psychological unreality and the emotional release that brought. The remembering of my realization years ago about the package and my associative guilt brought both nightmares and an unexpected sense of relief in equal shares. It also brought back the anger.

This time what I felt inside was now self-directed. I cursed myself for time wasted, time lost, time spent running and letting others run over me. This was a valid observation for a time, but not—I had to remind myself—an essential life analysis. For if there is one lesson I have learned in the last few years here in the Seaway Valley, it is that we truly have no idea where we will be even five years from now.

Some lessons, however, need to be learned more than once.

Lynn returned to my house when Jeanie and Jenn had gone.

"The inspector told Paul and me not to leave you alone for a minute," she grinned, standing in my kitchen one morning, "and that order has not been rescinded."

"Order?" I set the coffee pot down. "What order?"

Her smiled faded, and she gave my arm a squeeze.

"Jerry knew you were surrounded by people from the past, and probably in over your head because of all the old emotions. He didn't trust anyone and told us to think the same way. Said the evil that had been there in Oxford was here now, and we had to stay very close to you. Keep you safe."

"Jerry . . ." I said softly. "I should have told him everything I knew, when I remembered it all. It's my fault he went out there, Lynn. He could have died . . ."

Lynn gave me a gentle shake. "But he *didn't,* Fan. Jerry is fine. And Ruth is right," she added. "It's over. It's time for you to move on."

I dropped my eyes, and she dropped her arms with a sigh.

"Fan—"

"I killed a man, Lynn," I said in a low voice. "I aimed the gun and pulled the trigger and Ethan died."

Lynn crossed her arms. "You had no choice," she returned.

We stood at an impasse.

"You saved Jerry's life," Lynn added.

I turned back to the coffee and poured two. Putting them on the table, I asked, "Have you had breakfast?"

"Fan," she said, sitting down at the table, "I remember sitting here with you just a few years ago after everything had played out the first summer you arrived. Part of that was my losing Meredith. Her murder was an act that was callous, selfish, and evil. You blamed yourself for it, remember?"

I sat down with Lynn and put two lumps in my mug. "I remember," I said.

Wickedness, it was.

Lynn looked around at the kitchen, then smiled at me. "Yes, wickedness. It was that. And it had little to do with you. You were simply there when it was done."

"I set it off."

"You came here to ask questions you had every right to ask."

I looked at her. "Jerry almost died," I said again.

"Well," said Lynn, pulling something out of her pocket, "I brought you something." She placed a small white business card on the table in front of me. "We've always spoken the same language, been very much alike in our lives. I figure you could hear this from me."

I picked the card up. It was the name and address of an Ottawa psychologist, specializing in grief counselling.

"I went to see her myself after Meredith died," Lynn said quietly. "Not at first. The following winter. I tried and tried to sort things out and move on, but for some reason I couldn't. These sessions really helped.

"I thought about suggesting this after Alison died," she continued. "It seemed too many, one after another. But we were looking for Haley and focusing on that, so I let it slide. You seemed to be coping all right. But this is too much," Lynn added. "I think you need to talk to someone to help you work it through, especially everything that just happened."

"Have you been talking to Paul?" I asked suspiciously.

"Why?"

"When he was here last, he told me the same thing. To get some professional help with this. Especially with what happened with Ethan. Paul said it took him months to get past having to shoot a man in the line of duty."

Lynn put her head on one side and looked at me. "I think, then, that the man knows what he's talking about. If you don't want to listen to me, at least listen to him."

Wickedness, it was. Yes, Meredith. It was.

I looked at the card again, and then took her hand to squeeze it.

"Thank you, Lynnie," I said gruffly, tears starting.

"Will you promise to call for an appointment this week?" she asked. When I nodded, Lynn added, "Good. I'd hate to see a good person—and a good friend—destroy herself because others tried to do just that, and failed."

Speaking of good friends, Ruth had been the usual rock through all of this. What I would ever do without her solid and guiding presence in my life now, I do not know. The one intelligent thing I did as my life began to unravel was call Ruth before heading out to find Stephanie at the Aultsville mud flats. If I hadn't, both Jerry and I might now be dead, and Ethan would be consoling Stephanie—with secret plans for her and her money. It's a thought I cannot bear to entertain.

I ended up at Ruth's on a glorious afternoon. Summer had finally arrived after many rainy days, and we took advantage of the sun to investigate her gardens. I'm as hopeless with gardening as I am with cooking, but my love for beautiful flowers is rivalled only by my love for food. Go figure.

There were wonderful things blooming everywhere, and green stuff coming up in other places. The smell of the earth was intoxicating. It made me wish once again that I could do some kind of a garden.

"Your gardens are lovely, Ruth," I said wistfully. "I wish I could have some gardens out at the cottage, but I'm hopeless."

Ruth smiled at me and handed me some gardening gloves. "Lesson Number One: Weeding."

I laughed and put the gloves on, then started to help with the thankless task.

"You have old beds around that place," Ruth continued as we searched and pulled. "It would be easy to bring them up to speed again and plant some things."

"Isn't it too late?" I asked. "Spring is over."

"It's never too late to plant," said Ruth, "depending on what you're working with. Perennials or anything you buy already flowering are still fine to put in during the summer. It takes time, but you have to start somewhere. If you want, I can come out this weekend to help you get the earth ready. We'll need to get someone strong to turn the soil, but after that, it's pretty simple."

I stopped weeding and looked around. "Some of the former villagers I've talked to said how hard it was for their mothers to give up gardens they had put their lives into. One lady went out to tend hers right until they blew the cofferdam. She said that until the water came, those gardens still belonged to her. Did Alice have a hard time with that, too?"

"Mother didn't talk much about her feelings, as you can imagine." Ruth gave a strong tug and something gave way. "But when we lost the cherry tree, she was quite upset. Hydro would come around and cut things down on your property to get it ready once you had signed off. They wouldn't ask or give you any warning. We had a young cherry tree outside our kitchen window that my dad said could be moved to the new town with us. Then one day it was gone. Cut down. One of the few times I actually saw my mother cry."

I thought about that for a minute, then changed the subject. "How long did it take you to get these gardens like this?"

Ruth stood up to stretch her legs. "Well, these were Mother's beds for a long time, of course. I've had them for the past few years, since I came back here. They were still good, but she had let them start to grow over because she was getting older, and the work was becoming too much, I guess. I took some things out, cut others back to let new growth come in, and planted some new things that I like.

"The trick, Fan, is to go at it with love and patience. Don't ever do it just because you want some decoration around the house. That's a waste of time. You can tell the gardens that are planted for effect and those that are planted with love. So just move into it, enjoy it, experiment, learn. Some things work and some things don't. Some things take, but don't turn out the way you expect them to. It's a lot like life, but that's what's so great about it. So reaffirming."

I gently touched a budding head of something yellow. "'The Big Good Thing,'" I quoted softly.

"The Big Good Thing?" Ruth asked.

I looked up and smiled. "Dickon's mother Susan in *The Secret Garden*. She called it the Big Good Thing—the power of life and renewal. She tells the children that the Big Good Thing doesn't care what we call it. It just goes on making worlds by the millions, and we should never stop believing in it."

"*The Secret Garden*," Ruth remembered. "It was always one of my favourites when I was young."

"Mom's, too," I said. "She read it to me so many times when I was little. I loved it."

A breeze came through the yard, making all the flowers dance. I suddenly knew she was there, with me, with us. I could feel the love, the goodness, the peace. My eyes blurred, and when I looked up at Ruth, she was smiling through tears of her own.

"'Thy own mother's in this 'ere very garden, I do believe,'" Ruth quoted back to me, nodding. She took my hand. "'She couldna' keep out of it.'"

Celebration 50 finished up as success, with both regional and national media coverage that included discussion about the decisions made fifty years ago on behalf of two nations—decisions that forever changed the lives of almost 9,000 people on both sides of this great river.

And she is still a great river. The St. Lawrence River valley is home to over six million people, the birthplace of Canada, the cradle of Upper Canada, and a major part of the greatest inland fresh water system in the world.

I know what you're wondering, and at that point (to be honest) I was wondering, too. Where did all this leave Jerry and me? As usual, we were in an odd place. I guess it fits so often because we are an odd couple, although over most of the last few years we've avoided the couple thing and concentrated on the odd.

This time, we had both said some pretty serious things, including the "L" word. I had admitted my feelings for Jerry, not just to him but openly to others and there was no turning back. The dance was over. Now what?

Once Jerry was fully ambulatory, he eased back into work and subsequently disappeared on me again. It seems to be his characteristic reaction to intimacy, and with my personal history, there is no room for pointing fingers. I did what I have always done at this stage: I wait. I know that, sooner or later, my cop will return. That's also his way.

This time, however, I was still wrestling with the burden of having put Jerry in such danger that it almost cost him his life. Sure, I know. It's his job. But since I had popped up on the radar a few years ago, it seemed his danger quotient had doubled. Certainly the body count left in my wake was substantial. I guess I wondered how much more excitement Jurgen Strauss could tolerate in our relationship.

Paul's time estimate for the inquiry into the shooting of Ethan Chamberlain and wounding of Inspector Jerry Strauss was bang-on. Suits from the Special Investigations Unit arrived a week after the incident and made a final report near the end of August. Peter Simons officially reopened the case of Flight 39 upon his return to England, and all the evidence from the SIU report was sent to the hearing. There was no contest to the statements given by me, Jerry, Stephanie, and Amy. Later that fall, the ruling would come down as finding the late Ethan Chamberlain guilty of 114 counts of murder in the bombing of Flight 39 on May twenty-third, 1982. I hoped it would finally bring some closure and peace to the families who suffered because I loved the wrong man.

For the summer, I was a homebody, having a home for the first time in years. Green things had come up in the old beds around my cottage/house that I had ignored until now. Ruth came and told me what they were. Being somewhat at a loss for able-bodied men, I finally called Jordan Wiley to come out one Saturday to turn the earth. The Wileys came out en masse with tools, and we dug up the old beds, created a few new ones, and put fertilizer in both. Michelle brought a rose bush, and we put it near the windows of my bedroom, planning for fragrant evening breezes someday.

"What will you call this place, Farran?" Diana asked, as they were getting ready to leave after supper (I bought pizza instead of trying to cook. They are my friends, after all.).

"Call it? Should I call it something?"

"Yes. You know, like they do in England."

England. Oxford. No, go to another England—one of growth and renewal, second chances, faith, and love conquering all.

"Misselthwaite," I said, without hesitation.

"Misselthwaite?" Michelle came up and put her arm around her daughter. "Where have I heard that before?"

"That's the name of the English estate that Mary Lennox goes to in the book *The Secret Garden*," I explained. "It's where the secret garden is found."

"It's where the magic happens," said Diana. "I remember that story."

"That story is almost a century old," I thought aloud. "It came out in serial form in 1910, and then in book form a year later. But it just never gets old."

"Some things are always true," Michelle smiled, "even if it doesn't seem that way from time to time."

Some things work and some things don't, Ruth had wisely said. Some things take, but don't turn out the way you expect them to. I had arrived here several years ago, confused, scared, grieving, and thinking that all I had to do was find out who had killed my father to move on. It had worked. I thought to quietly dig around and then disappear back to Cambridge with my truth, I guess. That hadn't worked. I had tried to find out what these villages had been, who my parents' people had been and still were, and that had not turned out as I expected. I found the history and the people I had been missing in my life, but I also found something I didn't think I was looking for. I found Farran Mackenzie, still there, waiting where I had left her so long ago.

Does love still conquer all?

My cop came back sporadically through the summer, as we dealt with the inquiry. We did dinner out, some Shakespeare in Prescott, the Playhouse in Morrisburg. It was always brief, on the spur of the moment, and wrapped around doing something. It was about spending some time together without being really alone. I had told Jerry I would answer all his questions when he was fully healed, and I knew he would eventually take me up on that. The day the report came back from Toronto, he called.

"Superintendent Holland dropped by this morning," Jerry told me. "Toronto is done."

"And?" I asked.

"It's over. They're happy with all the evidence and the report is being sent on to Simons in London." There was a pause. "I think Holland was a little disappointed," he added, with a smile in his voice.

"Do you think I'll have to go to London myself with this?"

"Depends on what Simons recommends with the evidence. You may not hear anything for months."

We both fell silent. The thought flittered through my mind that maybe, having met during a crisis and basically one of us always having something critical to deal with, we were now in unfamiliar territory: peace and quiet. The ordinary life. What if we couldn't function in a relationship now that the seasons of crisis were over?

As though he were reading my thoughts, Jerry said suddenly,

"Farran, we have to talk."

Startled, I shot back, "I thought we were."

"Do you have plans tonight?"

"Uh . . . not really."

"Meet me at Farran Park, in the southwest corner by the river. Make it seven o'clock." He hung up.

Having a cop for a significant other certainly puts a level of security into your life. On the other hand, having a thick skin becomes a necessary condition.

Farran Park lies directly south of the village of Ingleside across County Road 2. Although owned by the St. Lawrence Parks Commission, it has been run by the Township of South Stormont for many years. A beautiful campground, boating and beach facility, it is also all that is left of my mother's childhood home of Farran's Point.

I waited by the river that evening, remembering another conversation Jerry and I had shared by the St. Lawrence when he came out to my then rented cottage on Ault Island, the night before I went back home to Cambridge after my first visit here. We had talked about time and change, about the prodigal nature of the geese, about the river and its people. I had said I would come back, that the prodigal always returns. And here I was.

Jerry asking me to meet him here, instead of his just dropping by or having me stop in at his place meant something. It also didn't elude me that we would both be here with our own wheels—therefore, both would be free to leave independently if either wanted. Paranoid? Sometimes, contrary to what Shad says, paranoid is not a good thing to be. But I knew whom I was dealing with, and all this told me that something was up.

He came about fifteen minutes behind me. I waited for him by the trees, and when he caught up to me we walked to the river's edge. It was a beautiful August evening, but the first feel of autumn was in the air. The Canada geese knew it, too.

"Can you hear that?" I said, breaking the ice. "That's a migrating cry. They're already starting to get ready to leave."

Jerry nodded. "Fall seems to start earlier every year, or maybe that's my age talking." He looked at me. "So, it's all over—at least on this side of the Pond. And I'd be surprised if there were any serious questions at Scotland Yard after getting the SIU's final report. Toronto is very thorough."

"Jerry, I said when you were well again, I would talk about everything. Answer any questions you have. I never meant to keep things from you," I explained. "It just blew in so fast, and Stephanie was there in the middle of it—"

He shook his head. "You don't need to explain, Farran. I do, or at least apologize."

I looked at him, slightly confused. "You?"

"Yes. I didn't handle things correctly. I should have started putting things together faster, but I was emotionally involved. I didn't hand it over to Wiley until I'd already wasted precious time. I should have gotten Chamberlain before he got me—and almost you." Jerry looked away.

"Just like your father," he said unexpectedly.

"What do you mean?"

Jerry turned back to me. "One reason your father left Aultsville to work on the canal boats was that he thought I believed the rumours of his guilt about my father's death. He told my mother before he left that our faith in him was what he couldn't stand to lose." Jerry pointed past me to a hedge that ran down to the river. "One night in November 1956, about fifty yards beyond that hedge at Lock 22, your father got on the *Lake Emerald* and left his life behind him. There would be almost nothing left by the time he came back. I should have stopped him, stopped the chain of events that lead to his death."

"Jerry," I protested, "you were a *boy*. Just a boy. Christ, my father was a boy then, too. Seventeen when he left and eighteen when he died. And you were both dealing with an evil you hadn't put a name to." I looked at him. "Where are you going with this? I'm the screw-up, not you. I owe you an apology for the way I handled things this summer, not you, if you think about it."

"I've thought of nothing else for the past two months," he replied quietly.

I waited. I could see that Jerry had something to say that was going to very difficult, and for once I had the sense to shut up. Deep inside me, a small flicker of pain appeared. Pain . . . and fear.

He stuck his hands in his pockets.

"I remember the day I walked into my office to find you sitting where Wiley had left you. Meredith had just died, and we hadn't located Gordon yet to tell him." Jerry looked at the river and then into my eyes. "I remember feeling immediately that I had known you my whole life, just hadn't met you yet. Even before you began to tell me who you were—and who you *really* were. That has never happened to me in my entire life, except with you." He took a deep breath and let it out.

Still, I waited. Still, I stayed silent. Still, the knot of worry grew in my guts. I longed to tell him how I had felt the first time I'd looked into those grey eyes, that it was an understanding beyond words, the recognition of a part of me I hadn't known I needed to find.

"I changed when I met you," Jerry continued. "Things suddenly weren't so black and white. I didn't like it," he admitted. "Then things kept happening. Gordon. Alison. Vaughn. And now this past summer.

"You said you would answer any questions I have. I have one. But I need to explain something first."

"Okay," I whispered. My throat suddenly felt tight, and my stomach seemed instantly unsure of itself.

He took another deep breath. I realized I was holding mine and let it go.

"The problem isn't you, it's me," Jerry started, looking somewhere past me. "This . . . this relationship thing. Dating. I . . . I can't do it. I'm just no good at it. God almighty, Farran, I'm sixty years old. I wasn't much good at it thirty years ago, either."

My throat closed off completely. *But I love you,* I wanted to say. *Don't leave me, too.*

"I have to be honest," Jerry said. "I hope you understand when I say I can't continue like this."

Something in me started to die. I was turning back into the pillar of salt I'd been for twenty-six years, and I wanted to go there. Be anywhere except where I could feel.

"Farran," said Jerry softly, pulling one hand out of his pocket to take one of mine. "Fan." It was the first time he had ever called me by my nickname, and the sound of it on his lips brought the tears I had been losing the fight to. "Please do this old war horse a big favour and put him out of his misery."

The other hand came out of his pocket, and I felt him place something in mine. Something small, hard, and square. Through my blurred vision, I saw a tiny, black box.

Jerry's hand moved up to touch my face.

"Farran," he said again softly. "Farran Leslie Mackenzie Leonard.

"Will you marry me?"

The phone call came at 6:17 p.m. on September ninth. The voice was so crisp and professional that I almost didn't recognize it.

"Dr. Mackenzie?"

"Stephanie?" I answered slowly, rising from my chair, phone glued to my ear. "Is that you?"

There was a pause.

"Yes."

I didn't know what to say next, afraid to scare her off again.

"Where are you?" I said finally. "Are you all right?"

"Yes . . . yes, I'm fine. I'm calling because . . . because I'm . . . I'm here."

"Here? You mean South Stormont?"

"Yes."

My heart took a leap.

"How long have you been here?" (I could have bitten my tongue. It sounded so *grasping*.)

"About an hour," came the reply. "I just flew in to Ottawa this afternoon and drove down."

There was another pause. Then, "We need to talk."

"Yes," I said quickly. "Yes, we do. Would you like to come here? Have you had supper?"

"No." The reply was also quick. "No. I'd much rather you came here. I need to talk to you here. Can you come now?"

Of course I could come right then. I would have left dinner with Bloom Boy to see Stephanie again, even though it was possible that all she came to do was tell me she never wanted to see me again.

"Of course," I said. "Where is 'here'?"

I remember hearing her voice tell me where she was waiting, and thinking how like me she was. Of course, I thought to myself again as I hung up. I grabbed my coat, put on sneakers, and headed out to the only place on Earth where my daughter and I could have the conversation we both needed to survive.

It was still the quietest place on earth.

I stood on the remains of the old No. 2 Highway where it rose out of the water, covered with mud. Stephanie stood in the bush, at the edge of the old foundation, her back to me. That ring of antique stone once held the house my father Hal Leonard was born in. It ultimately became his unmarked grave for over forty years, until the ebbing of the river revealed the secret.

The river was low again this year, even lower now than when I had found Jerry and Ethan in the same place. The road went on past me, curving around the old shoreline on its way to the former site of the Aultsville wharf. Sidewalks were bare, other foundations and front steps seeing the light of day for the first time again in years. This must have been what it was like here when Shad and her friend unexpectedly found my father's remains.

I had eyes only for Stephanie, thinking how vulnerable she seemed to me. She wasn't much older than I had been when I gave birth to her, and it struck me then how young and vulnerable I had been at that time. The perfect target. Yet, things had not turned out as planned for Ethan. He had controlled and manipulated me, but I had made the final decisions, including the one that saved my life. I had that much to hang on to.

"Stephanie?" I called hesitantly.

She turned and came out of the bush. I saw the red hair was gone, and my daughter had straight, blonde hair not unlike mine.

"Oh," I said. "I like your hair. Is this your natural colour?"

Stephanie nodded, then pointed into the bush. "Was this where it all happened?" she asked bluntly.

I could see we weren't going to mince words, or waste time with fluff. Okay. I had thought about this moment all summer, wondering not only how I would handle it, but even if I would ever get the chance. Here we were. This was one moment of my life I just could not screw up.

"Yes," I shot back. "Everything. It's where some of my ancestors came to build new lives when they lost everything in the American War of Independence. Where my father's family lived until their village was torn out by the roots and moved to a new town. It's where my father was murdered at the age of eighteen by his older brother the night before the great inundation, and left to be covered forever by the new Lake St. Lawrence. Where I came looking for answers and almost died at the hands of my father's killer. Where I came with my friend Alison to show her some of what I had lost before I even knew it was mine, and before she died in my driveway. And where I came looking for you, scared you were in trouble, and found your father, Ethan Chamberlain, thinking he'd killed my friend Jerry Strauss and was planning to kill me, too. It's where I shot him to save Jerry and save me."

We looked at each other in the silence that followed my rapid return fire. There it was, out on the table right off.

"I know about your father, Hal Leonard," Stephanie replied quietly. "Once I found the report on your friend's death, I went back for anything else I could find. That's how I found this place. I read up on Aultsville, the Seaway, the Lost Villages. I did a full background on you, even your mother, Leslie."

"Your grandmother," I pointed out.

"I read all the news reports about the shooting," she continued evenly. "I know Ethan Chamberlain has been found responsible for the bombing of that plane, as well as Debra's death."

"I had to keep you safe from him," I said softly, "and from me. Knowingly or not, I helped Ethan kill all those passengers. I carried the parcel on to the plane and left it there when I ran off."

The sun was starting to get low in the sky, and the evening breeze came to us off the river.

Keep the child safe, lass.

Stephanie looked around, startled. "What was that?"

I looked around and they came to me again, like another evening long ago.

. . . tell the neighbourhood. I'm not here to stay, just makin' a scheduled . . .

. . . that sign up myself in '33 . . .

Will you dance with me one more time?

Looking back at Stephanie, I smiled. "They're your people, Stephanie. The voices of the past, the voices from the Lost Villages. The legend is that the villagers so mourned the loss of their lands and farms that when they died, their souls went back."

. . . this here's a game . . . of you and me . . . table . . .
. . . Point . . . seen you . . . park . . .

"Some evenings," I continued, "when the wind is right, you can hear the voices coming across the river from the old sites."

Stephanie shot me a look. "That's impossible," she said.

"Nothing's impossible, if there's love enough," I replied.

Danger, child.

"No," I answered back. "The danger is gone. And the child is safe. It's all right now. You can be at peace."

I still think you're a brat, but sometimes . . .

The voices were getting faint. Stephanie moved closer to me, searching the trees with her eyes for a less spiritual source of the sounds, but without success. Finally, they were gone.

We stood on the old road in the growing shadows, a few feet and emotional miles apart.

"It's a big river," she said, looking past me to the St. Lawrence. "I thought the Fraser River was big, but this . . ."

"It sure is," I said. "For the past 6,000 years, the St. Lawrence has been flowing at two million gallons per second, and it will be doing that 6,000 years from now. It forms the border of two provinces and one state. Six million people—American, Canadian, and Mohawk—call it home. The Seaway made it political. The people never did."

"And a major environmental issue," Steph added. "The old river used to naturally regulate the outflows and water levels. Now the control dams try to do the same job, but it affects the river and Lake Ontario. The International Joint Commission is still using the old Plan 1958-D, and it's outdated. There's been a lot of erosion damage to the riverfront since the Power Project went through. We're long overdue on getting everyone involved and getting real about this."

"Yes," I agreed, "and the fiftieth anniversary reminded everyone of what happened here, and the debt we owe the river."

We fell silent again, having run out of things to talk about other than our personal snafu.

"I'm glad you didn't die," Stephanie said suddenly, then looked at the ground.

It was something. I glanced at the sun, now low over the horizon.

"We need to go," I said. "This is no place to try to walk through in the dark. Let's go to my place and talk."

She shook her head. "What are we supposed to do next?"

"Live our lives," I replied.

"And pretend the past never happened?"

"No, Haley Leslie Mackenzie. No, never that. But the past is a framework. Our lives are all about the present day. Right now. Who we are and where we want to go." I held out my hand. "Come with me, Stephanie?"

Stephanie started to reach out, but stopped and crossed her arms.

"I don't even know what to call you. 'Mom' is taken," she added.

I put my arm back down to my side. "It's up to you, Steph. As long as you do call me. I hope you will. I need you in my life, and I hope you need me, too." I smiled and turned to go. "If it ever feels right, maybe you can call me 'Mother' someday."

The shadows were all around us. I wanted to take her with me, to hold her, to talk all night, and begin the long process of reconnection between mother and daughter. I wanted to start learning how to be a mom. So many things I wanted, yet it wasn't my place. She had to come to me on her own time and terms.

"You know where to find me, Steph," I said. "I love you. I always have. Know that."

She didn't reply, but watched me start to make my way carefully on the mud-topped road out of Aultsville's remains, out of the past, out toward the lights of the new towns, toward home.

My back was to her, and I quietly started to cry.

Then, in the fading light, I heard it.

The sound of moving feet coming toward me,

a hand on my arm,

and a breathless voice.

One word.

"*Mother . . .*"

Then I turned, and she was in my arms again, again, again, my Haley, my baby, my soul, my love, my life, safe with me, never leaving, never parted, my own, my own, my own once more.

TWENTY-ONE

TOMORROW

There are days come to us that, once having been lived, remain in the palm of our hearts forever.

This day is one such day.

The little white church at the Lost Villages Museum, this brilliant autumn afternoon, is almost full, so there is room for me only near the door. The plus side to this is no one notices my arrival—or my hesitation about which side of the church to sit on. You see, I am related to both the bride and the groom. Directly related. You could say that much of who they are and where they've been comes from me.

I look over the crowd of family and friends, quietly chatting, waiting for the service to start. There are others here that my people have loved and lost. I sense Alice Hoffman's staid approval, Meredith Murphy's inquisitive gaze, Eric Leonard's warm concern, Harper Mackenzie's quiet strength. Do the others see them, too? I would like to think so. In this church, it feels like love.

The groom, I see, looks nervous, and I realize that I have never seen Jerry Strauss nervous. Or in a tux, for that matter. Both are entertaining, and I say that with affection. I still view the man as the thorn in my side because he didn't follow orders. Then, to be fair, he's never followed orders in his life.

Jordan Wiley stands beside him, as he has done since they met over the remains of Farran's father in Aultsville. So many conversations shared since then, both spoken and unspoken. Two men who so often worked as one. Jerry helped Jordan grow in his career. Now Jordan has to help Jerry survive his own wedding.

Ruth Hoffman Black rises suddenly from the front pew and hustles down the aisle. I turn and see Diana Wiley—a vision in yellow—motioning to her from the door. The bride must be here. The energy in the room rises, and as everyone turns to see the procession, I take a last look at the faces I call family.

Paul Vaughn sits in the front where his mother, Ruth, just vacated, with his half-sister Carolyn and another woman. I look closer. It's

Debbie, the waitress that has served Paul breakfast for years back in St. John's, always saying no to his jesting marriage proposals. Maybe she finally said yes. Across from them in the other pew behind the groom sit Daniel Sterling and Mildred Keeps. I wonder if Daniel senses Emme Strauss sitting beside him, with Jerry's father, Bill. She is smiling. I feel she knows that Daniel's return to Jerry's life will fill the hole in her son she had once hoped their friendship would so long ago.

Behind Paul and Carolyn sit Lynn Holmes, Brad Buckshaw, and Ernie Black. They are in earnest conversation—about what I can only imagine. Farther back sits Leah (Shad) Shadbourne with her family, and Jenn Farley with her mother Jeanie. There are a small number of OPP officers and spouses on the other side, including Margaret Taylor with her mother, Peg, and . . . yes . . . Superintendent Holland. (Wonder how *that* happened.)

Ruth returns to her seat in the front pew, with a quick nod to the organist. The opening notes of "Amazing Grace" fill the little church, and we all rise to our feet. I remember this is the song played at Harper Mackenzie's funeral, and understand Farran's choice, to give it renewal in meaning. The soloist, a woman from the choir at St. Matthew's, begins to sing the familiar words, and Diana Wiley steps into the church.

It is right then that it hits me Diana is no longer a girl, but a young woman. I do not need to look at the faces of her parents to know they are sharing my thoughts. They must be very proud at this moment of their intelligent and beautiful young lady. I am.

Behind her comes Stephanie Harrison, the former Haley Leslie Mackenzie. She, too, is a vision in yellow, smiling hesitantly at her new family and friends. I had hoped she would be here, for Farran. As maid of honour, she is standing with her mother in the wedding as she will do from now on in her life.

As my eyes follow Stephanie, they come to rest on Jerry's face turned toward the door. The stress is gone, replaced by something it takes me a few seconds to identify: contentment. I follow his gaze to see the bride entering the church.

Farran Leslie Mackenzie Leonard walks softly on the arm of Bick, her father's old friend from his shipping days. She is wearing a simple, elegant white gown with yellow roses in her hair, carrying a cascade of the same flower in her hand. I watch her walk past and understand it is only now that I can let Farran go. She is ready to be happy. I have often joked with my readers that what was to be one novel became a series for the most part because Farran Mackenzie had so many issues it would take me four books to sort her out. I was only half joking, really, and often wondered if we would ever get here. I watch Bick hand her to Jerry, and I silently give thanks that we have finally arrived.

The service is traditional, and I sense I am not alone in holding my breath when the minister asks if anyone knows why these two should not be joined in holy matrimony. Then we all breathe and go on to the vows. As Farran said in Aultsville to the voices from the Lost Villages, the danger that was here is gone.

One brief moment of panic sets in when Jerry turns to Jordan for the ring, and the sergeant cannot find it. Michelle saves the day when she produces it from her purse, and everyone has a good chuckle. The bride and groom exchange rings and vows, becoming husband and wife. When the minister tells Jerry to kiss the bride, it is the one order he follows without question. The entire church breaks out in applause.

Looking at them standing there, I realize that these two lost souls somehow found themselves in each other. And that is how love should be.

The bridal party rushes past to the outdoors where an OPP honour guard is waiting. Then come what seem like thousands of photos, laughter and tears, and embraces. I stand to one side crying, too; mother I am to both.

For I am the one who is leaving. Our lives flow like the great river, and we make stops now and then on the shore, as I have done here. It is time for me to return to the flow and see where it takes me next. I will say goodbye and leave them safe in their happiness and community. I will leave them where I wish they could be forever.

I know a few things that will happen. Today, on the table of the wedding dinner will be Evian Mackenzie's white tea set with the blue forget-me-nots. All that is materially left of the matrilineal line, but it is enough. It is the heritage of the soul that counts, because it can never be expropriated.

I also know that Stephanie and the other Water People will help search for Fenton's lost gold, finding it exactly where Farran said it would be. Carman House will bloom, thanks to the foresight of its original owner during a time of danger and conflict between two great nations.

"We've met before, haven't we?"

I find myself face to face with Inspector Jerry Strauss, newlywed. I smile and extend my hand.

"Many times, Inspector. I'm a friend of the family. Congratulations on your special day."

He is too well brought up to ask me my name outright, and is forced to shake hands without really being sure who I am. Serves him right for not doing what I had planned for him when I wrote *A Violent End*.

I head for the car, not wanting to crash the dinner, too. It's then that I see them, also on the sidelines, also watching the people they love.

"Hal?" I whisper. "Leslie?"

There is a hand on my shoulder and I jump. It is the bride, momentarily free of family, friends and photographers.

"Are they here?" she asks me.

"Yes. Right behind me. Like Ruth says," I add, smiling, "they couldna' keep out of this garden."

We look to see them—Hal with his lopsided grin, Leslie young again with her long dark hair standing beside him, holding his hand. They are smiling, they are together, they are gone.

Farran and I stand together in a shared moment of silence, then she turns to me.

"Will you ever be back?" comes the simple question.

"I don't know," I answer honestly. "But like you, I am a prodigal daughter. And as you once said yourself, the prodigal always returns."

It is all we can do. Farran Mackenzie gives me a quick hug and is also gone, into her new life, her hard-won family and friends, and the light of a new day. It is where she deserves to be.

Change will continue to come here, as it has always done. The Seaway bridge in Cornwall, built for an all-Canadian seaway that never happened, will come down and be replaced by something contemporary. The townships along the Seaway Valley will take a new name—Upper Canada Region—to encompass the deeper histories that were temporarily buried beneath the Power Project. Here, in the land of the Lost Villages, we will continue to grow on our heritage farmlands and the new riverfront as families come to find what we were not encouraged to value half a century ago: green space, neighbours, and communities forged by friendship and support. These are the values that allowed the people of the St. Lawrence River Valley to carve out their nations here, creating and enduring constant transformation for generations beside the great river that never changes.

This is the human truth that T.S. Eliot put best:

We shall not cease from exploration, and the end of all our exploring will be to arrive where we started and know the place for the first time.

With love,

Maggie Wheeler

Maggie Wheeler

APPENDIX 1

MY FATHER'S DETACHMENT

My father, Sergeant Harold Wheeler, on the steps of
the Long Sault OPP Detachment, circa 1968.

In August of 1967, I got my first glimpse of Long Sault—or New
Town No. 2 as it was called during the Power Project—the Seaway
village I was to call home for the next ten years. My clearest memory
is of our tour of the large, new OPP detachment building where my
father would work as a newly promoted sergeant. It included the
two small jail cells in the basement (very cool), the radio room on the
main floor, the large and sunny reception at the front, and my father's
new office right behind that.

Built for the new community of Long Sault, the detachment sits
at the front of the village. It was originally an attractive, terra cotta

brick building; an imposing sight to any budding local criminal. Every Halloween, the station was open for the trick-or-treaters. My father also had every window ablaze with light for the evening, sending a signal to older tricksters that their every move was being watched. I don't remember much mayhem on Halloween in those days.

The Long Sault detachment is now the mothership for the OPP in SD&G. It is home away from home for Inspector Jerry Strauss, Detective Sergeant Jordan Wiley, and Constable Margaret Taylor. It is also slated for demolition after the new facility is built. A long-awaited expansion for the OPP is underway, providing room not only for administration, but also a police unit, an emergency response, a K-9 unit, and Victims' Services and staffed by sixty-eight officers, who will provide these services to 75,000 people.

A new 16,000-square-foot building is under construction to house the OPP and the new municipal offices for the Township of South Stormont. Behind the old building will be a new forensic storage facility. When these are completed, the old detachment will come down.

All this is certainly good news for our community and the officers who serve it. But I need to pay tribute to the original OPP administration building in Long Sault, where my father proudly served from 1967 till his death in 1980. There is a large part of my dad still there, and I will mourn this loss when the building is gone.

APPENDIX 2

THE HARTSHORNE HOUSE-MOVERS

The men from New Jersey: (top left) Bill Davis, (top right) Bobby Parks, (on ground, left to right) unidentified Hydro official, William Hartshorne, Clarence Hartshorne, Bill Kensler, Raymond Moore, Jack Calhoun, Pat Patterson, Henry Harris.
Photo supplied by Pat Patterson; used by permission.

By early 1955, Ontario Hydro could see they needed another option for the villagers affected by the massive expropriation for the Seaway and Power Project. Most were deeply unhappy with having to leave their beloved houses. Many refused to be forced into taking out a mortgage to finance building a new house to replace the mortgage-free property they were losing. Enter the Hartshorne Brothers House-Moving Company from Moorestown, New Jersey.

The team arrived later that year, with two massive machines on rail cars. They started the process in Old Iroquois of transporting houses that could be moved—on average a house every two days, 24/7, even through our Canadian winters. Three-and-a-half years and more than 500 buildings later, the men from New Jersey went home, leaving behind new communities planted along the new front of the St. Lawrence.

Several years ago, I had the pleasure of interviewing Pat Patterson from Moorestown. The last surviving member of the original Hartshorne moving team was a tall, smiling man in his late seventies with a New Jersey accent and a booming laugh. The interview was a delight. Pat was back visiting family; he had met and married his wife Shirley in Old Iroquois during the Project. "She served me at the Daffodil Restaurant," Pat told me, "and she had a nice smile. So I married her."

Whatever happened to those two great machines that could lift a house without damaging a piece of china? To all reports, they no longer exist. However, in this land of myth and legend, story has it that one still resides in a farmer's field near Moorestown, broken down with a tree growing through its middle. I would love to search for it someday soon. If it exists, I know that those who may see it from a country highway will never know the amazing history it once carried—literally—on its shoulders.

APPENDIX 3

CARMAN HOUSE MUSEUM

Carman House Museum, Iroquois, Ontario.
Photo by Murray Richer; used by permission.

If you take the Carman Road turnoff for Iroquois on the 401 and follow it south across County Road 2, into the village of Iroquois (and don't take the deep turn to the west), you will roll right into the little parking lot beside Carman House Museum. The charming Georgian cottage-style house is one of only four buildings not moved in Iroquois during the Seaway construction.

Built of limestone blocks, the heritage building has a chimney on either end, twelve-pane windows, and a half-storey above the main floor—all indicative of the Carman family's middle-class status. The Carmans owned farmland on the Old Point, including where the museum now stands. They built the house sometime between 1803 and 1825, but the exact date is unknown. The museum operates as though from 1815.

Ira Fenton and his gold are a figment of my imagination. The fort he was contracted to build during the War of 1812 was actually a job given to Michael Carman. The locals called it "Fort Needless," as the British were also building the first Fort Wellington in nearby Prescott. The fort in Iroquois was never completed, but Carman was paid in chests of silver—all silver, as far as we know.

There are no Carmans left in Iroquois today, but Carman House still stands. However, rumours of any real murders in the museum office are greatly exaggerated.

APPENDIX 4

THE WAR OF 1812 AND
THE BATTLE OF CRYSLER'S FARM

Dennis Carter-Edwards
Historian, Parks Canada

The War of 1812 was part of a global conflict fought in Europe, on the oceans and across North America. However, for the communities settled along the shores of the St. Lawrence River and Great Lakes the realities of this conflict were more immediate—invading armies, destroyed homes and farms and the loss of life. The devastation along the Detroit frontier, the Niagara Peninsula, the provincial capital at York, and the communities along the St. Lawrence River can be measured in the hundreds of claims filed by citizens at the end of War. The Commission set up by the British Government to compensate residents for losses suffered contain heard woeful tales of homes destroyed, livestock stolen, farm equipment lost and personal effects either damaged or looted. More poignant are the muster rolls for the incorporated and regular county militia units with the list of killed and wounded from battles, privation and disease. This enormous sacrifice in lives and property preserved British North America from American territorial ambitions.

The War of 1812 left a legacy that is imprinted on the very fabric of the nation. This legacy has its tangible evidence at places such as Crysler's Farm. The battlefield monument, first unveiled in 1895 by grateful citizens, honours the bravery and determination of the British regulars, local militia and First Nations warriors who beat back the invading American army that chill day in November 1813.

The events of that fateful day on the fields of John Crysler's farm have recently been replayed in battle re-enactments by a dedicated core of volunteers who kit themselves in appropriate period costumes, shoulder reproduction Brown Bess muskets and perform manoeuvres as they might have been done nearly two hundred years ago. All this to keep the memory alive, to inform and entertain the audience, and no doubt to enjoy that esprit de corps of comrades in arms.

The Bicentennial of the War of 1812 in 2012 will offer a unique opportunity to present the story of that conflict at the many historic forts and battlefields that have been preserved and interpreted by various public and private agencies. Of special interest are the surviving battlefields—the sacred ground where men fought and died for deeply held principles. Many of these battlefields are in need of modest development and presentation so that the stories of the participants can be told and honoured.

More than this, as a nation we need to reflect on the significance of this critical event in our country's history. The War of 1812 was a "nation building" experience that played a major role in defining the Canadian identity. When threatened with armed invasion in 1812, a diverse population of newly arrived immigrants (many from the United States), long established French Canadians and First Nations fought together to protect their families, homes and a way of life. The experience of shared hardships and sacrifice through three years of fighting contributed to our collective sense of distinctiveness from the United States and the American identity.

Although the Treaty of Ghent, signed in December 1814, ended the War, it did not remove the mutual distrust between Canada and the United States. A defended border remained as a safeguard to Canadian sovereignty through periods of conflict in the 1830s and again in the 1860s. The War, however, did lay the basis for a new relationship between Canada and the United States based on negotiation and mutual co-operation in areas of common interest. Its legacy is the joint efforts of both nations in war and peace—such as World War II, NORAD and, most recently, the NAFTA trade agreement.

A nation's history can be thought of as a collective biography of the people, both the mighty and the humble, who through their daily lives and especially at moments of crisis have contributed to its development. The citizen soldiers, British regulars and First Nations warriors who fought that fateful day at Crysler's farm and the many other battlefields across the land have a story that needs telling, remembering and appreciating.

RESOURCES

Brior, John. *Taming of the Sault*. Watertown, N.Y.: Hungerford-Holdbrook, 1960.

Caro, Robert. *The Power Broker: A Biography of Robert Moses*. New York: Random House, 1974.

Doheny-Farina, Stephen. *The Grid and the Village: Losing Electricity, Finding Community, Surviving Disaster*. Harrisonburg, Virginia: Yale University, 2001.

Fader, Joyce et al. *Iroquois History: Year of Celebrations 1857–1997*. Souvenir book. Iroquois: Henderson Printing, 1997. (Gift from the Matilda–Iroquois Lions Club. Thank you).

Graves, Donald E. *Field of Glory: The Battle of Crysler's Farm, 1813*. Toronto: Robin Bass Studio, 1999.

Harkness, John Graham. *Stormont, Dundas and Glengarry: A History*. Ottawa: Mutual Press. 1946.

Kennicott, Philip. "For Better or Worse: How Robert Moses Shaped Modern New York." *Watertown Daily Times*, Watertown, N.Y. Courtesy of the *Washington Post*. Sunday, March 18, 2007.

Marin, Clive and Frances. *Stormont, Dundas and Glengarry: 1945–1978*. Belleville: Mika Publishing Company, 1982.

Marin, Clive and Frances. *Stormont, Dundas and Glengarry: 1975–2007*. Maxville: Optimum Publishing International, 2008.

McCullough, A.B. *Money and Exchange in Canada to 1900*. Toronto: Dundurn Press with Parks Canada, 1984.

O'Flaherty, Rosemary. "Damming the Remains: Big Beau and Big Mo." Unpublished PhD thesis proposal made to Concordia University, Montreal. January 14, 2008.

Parnham, Clair Puccia. *From Great Wilderness to Seaway Towns: A Comparative History of Cornwall, Ontario, and Massena, New York*. Albany: State University of New York Press, 2004.

Parnham, Clair Puccia. *The St. Lawrence Seaway and Power Project: An Oral History of the Greatest Construction Show on Earth*. Syracuse: Syracuse University Press, 2009.

Rutley, Rosemary. *Voices From the Lost Villages*. Ingleside: Old Crone Publishing, 1998.

Snider, Thomas J. *Power Dam Politics*. Ohio: BookMasters, Inc., 2003.

Wheeler, Maggie. "Turning the Ship Around: Memory as Both Weapon and Tool in Navigating the Cultural Impact of the St. Lawrence Seaway Project." Paper presented to the 3rd Annual Conference of the Communication Graduate Caucus, School of Journalism and Communication, Carleton University, Ottawa. 2008

The author would also like to acknowledge the generous use of the files, archives, and research of Dalton and Nancy Foster, Wilson Hill Island, N.Y., members of the International Water Levels Coalition.

ABOUT THE AUTHOR

Born in Simcoe, Ontario, Maggie Wheeler moved with her family several times before settling in Long Sault—one of two new towns created to accommodate villagers relocated by the St. Lawrence Seaway and Power Project. Now a resident of Ingleside, formerly New Town Site No. 1, she lives in Misselthwaite Cottage, a "moved" farmhouse from the Lost Village of Dickinson's Landing.

Maggie is a corporate writer by trade, a recent graduate of the University of Ottawa's Faculty of Education, and a student in the master's program with the English department at Carleton University. Her focus is the interactive process with literature, history, and culture.

Maggie's first novel, *A Violent End*, placed her on the best-seller list for eastern Ontario. The Lost Villages mystery series has been used for the past eight years to teach English and history, from the intermediate classroom to post-secondary institutions, keeping Maggie on the public-speaking circuit throughout eastern Ontario and Upper New York State.

Maggie shares Misselthwaite Cottage with her family and Bagel the beagle.

TO ORDER MORE COPIES, CONTACT:

General Store Publishing House

499 O'Brien Road, Box 415
Renfrew, Ontario, Canada K7V 4A6
Tel 1.800.465.6072 • Fax 1.613.432.7184
www.gsph.com